Seaside Dreams on the Scottish Isle

Lilac Mills lives on a Welsh mountain with her very patient husband and incredibly sweet dog, where she grows veggies (if the slugs don't get them), bakes (badly) and loves making things out of glitter and glue (a mess, usually). She's been an avid reader ever since she got her hands on a copy of *Noddy Goes to Toytown* when she was five, and she once tried to read everything in her local library starting with A and working her way through the alphabet. She loves long, hot summer days and cold winter ones snuggled in front of the fire, but whatever the weather she's usually writing or thinking about writing, with heartwarming romance and happy-ever-afters always on her mind.

Also by Lilac Mills

Love in the City by the Sea
The Cosy Travelling Christmas Shop

Tanglewood Village series

The Tanglewood Tea Shop
The Tanglewood Flower Shop
The Tanglewood Wedding Shop
The Tanglewood Bookshop

Island Romance

Sunrise on the Coast
Holiday in the Hills
Sunset on the Square

Applewell Village

Waste Not, Want Not in Applewell
Make Do and Mend in Applewell
A Stitch in Time in Applewell

Foxmore Village

The Corner Shop on Foxmore Green
The Christmas Fayre on Holly Field
The Allotment on Willow Tree Lane

Coorie Castle Crafts

Surprises on the Scottish Isle
Summer Escapes on the Scottish Isle
Seaside Dreams on the Scottish Isle

LILAC MILLS

Seaside Dreams ON THE Scottish Isle

CANELO

First published in the United Kingdom in 2026 by

Canelo, an imprint of
Canelo Digital Publishing Limited,
20 Vauxhall Bridge Road,
London SW1V 2SA
United Kingdom

A Penguin Random House Company
The authorised representative in the EEA is Dorling Kindersley Verlag GmbH.
Arnulfstr. 124, 80636 Munich, Germany

Copyright © Lilac Mills 2026

The moral right of Lilac Mills to be identified as the creator of this work has been asserted in accordance with the Copyright, Designs and Patents Act, 1988.
All rights reserved. No part of this publication may be reproduced or transmitted in any form or by any means, electronic or mechanical, including photocopy, recording, or any information storage and retrieval system, without permission in writing from the publisher.
No part of this book may be used or reproduced in any manner for the purpose of training artificial intelligence technologies or systems. In accordance with Article 4(3) of the DSM Directive 2019/790, Canelo expressly reserves this work from the text and data mining exception.

A CIP catalogue record for this book is available from the British Library.

Print ISBN 978 1 80032 892 1
Ebook ISBN 978 1 80032 891 4

This book is a work of fiction. Names, characters, businesses, organizations, places and events are either the product of the author's imagination or are used fictitiously. Any resemblance to actual persons, living or dead, events or locales is entirely coincidental.

Printed and bound in Great Britain by Clays Ltd, Elcograf S.p.A.

Look for more great books at
www.canelo.co | www.dk.com

Prologue

Contrary to popular belief, Giselle was brave. But it was a quiet, understated bravery, which was why it went largely unnoticed, sometimes even by her own sister. In some ways it wasn't surprising, since they were total opposites in personality (although not in looks, as they both had silvery blonde hair and pale skin, despite being non-identical twins), which was why Giselle had left Izzy and her friends in Milan and was currently on the train to Venice this morning.

It was late September, so the fierce heat of the summer had diminished somewhat. Apparently.

It still felt roasting to Giselle, who was more used to Scottish summers where anything above twenty degrees Celsius was considered a heatwave. Despite the light-weight floaty dress and her long hair tied up off her neck, she was roasting, and when she got off the train at Stazione di Venezia Santa Lucia, a wall of heat hit her. Since it wasn't quite ten a.m., she feared it was going to be another hot day.

Hitching her bag higher onto her shoulder, she consulted her map. It was a paper one, because although she was brave, she wasn't daft. She looked like a tourist, she behaved like a tourist and she was alone in a strange city, but that didn't mean she intended to be a target for pickpockets or mobile phone snatchers. Which was why she kept her euros and her bank card in her bra. Her phone was in her bag, buried beneath a hat, a spare pair of knickers, a tiny wash bag containing some toiletries, a T-shirt, a pair of shorts and the all-important factor 30. Oh, and a bottle of water and some sandwiches that she'd made before she'd crept out of the hostel early this morning. Hopefully they would sustain her until this evening, when she intended to treat herself to an evening meal with a view of something impressive, like the Grand Canal, for instance.

Giselle wanted to save her money for more important things, and there was so much to see that she didn't think she'd manage everything in a day (or even a week), so she might have to stay overnight – assuming she could find somewhere that a) had vacancies and b) didn't break the bank. Izzy wouldn't mind, and she wouldn't miss her either.

Giselle had hardly seen her twin or the others since they'd arrived in Milan, and the reason for that was Fashion Week. Unlike Giselle, they were doing a fashion degree and would start their second year at university shortly, so unless stick-thin people wearing weird clothes were involved, they weren't interested. Giselle, on the other hand, was desperate for the romance, history and culture of Venice, and she was perfectly happy to explore the city on her own. It would have been nice to have had her twin with her, but they were two very different people, interested in different things, so she was used to going solo. But that didn't mean there wasn't a strong bond between them, because there was. So strong that when Giselle had fallen while climbing over the garden fence when she was seven and had broken her arm, Izzy had been the one crying with pain!

Having spent several weeks planning this trip, Giselle had a list of must-sees, and a secondary list of like-to-sees. She was pretty sure she'd not make it halfway through the first one. Never mind; she fully intended to come back again one day when she'd saved up enough money and had decided what she wanted to do with her life – because, unlike Izzy, Giselle didn't have a clue.

She did have one thing in common with her sister, though – they were both creative. But whereas Izzy had settled on fashion, Giselle flitted from one pursuit to another. She had yet to find her niche, because she was currently a jack of all trades but a master of none. Painting, sewing, embroidery, decoupage, weaving… she'd tried loads and really enjoyed them, but she wished she had an interest as consuming as Izzy's. And if she could combine that with nature and wild places, she'd be in her element. It was a big ask!

Giselle breathed deeply, inhaling sun-warmed air, redolent with the scent of brine, coffee and perfume, along with a waft of mouthwatering pastry. There was also a scent she recognised as damp stone. After visiting numerous old castles in her homeland, it was an aroma she was familiar with, and she happily set off to explore the city.

By mid-afternoon, Giselle was hot, tired, thirsty, hungry and kind of lost. She'd bought a St Mark's Square Museums ticket which had allowed her to visit the Doge's Palace, the Museo Correr and a couple of others, and by the time she'd emerged, blinking, into the bright sunlight, she'd felt an urge to see some of the less popular areas of the city.

After wandering along narrow streets that opened into surprising squares and bridges arching over canals, it hadn't taken long before she'd become hopelessly lost. But she felt as though she was beginning to discover the real Venice, since there were fewer tourists around.

The tall narrow streets were like deep ravines with high canyon walls, gated doorways, shuttered windows, smooth-worn cobbles, tiny shops and white, cloth-draped tables outside aromatic restaurants.

Giselle halted and stared upwards at the sliver of cerulean sky visible between the tall buildings. A woman leaning over a Juliet balcony caught her eye, and she wondered what it might be like to live in an apartment here.

Engrossed in her thoughts, she stepped back, still gazing upwards, and promptly banged into a table, sending it and its contents flying.

'Oh, gosh, sorry, so sorry!' she cried, frantically trying to think what 'sorry' was in Italian, closely followed by *Oh, my God he's hot*, when she spied the man who'd been sitting at the table she'd upended.

She hurried to right the table, but the guy beat her to it, just as a waiter emerged from the restaurant, tutting.

'I'm so sorry,' she repeated, surveying the damage with dismay. Broken glass was strewn over the cobbles, along with several pieces of cutlery and a menu.

'No worries.' The guy had an English accent, she noticed with relief.

'Sorry, sorry,' she said to the waiter, who crossly shooed away her attempts to clear up the mess she'd made.

Giselle straightened and turned to the man whose drink she'd annihilated. 'What were you drinking? Can I get you another? And I'll need to pay for the damage.'

He shrugged. 'No need. It was only water.'

Water wasn't free. It wouldn't have been the stuff out of the tap. 'I insist,' she said, reaching down the front of her sundress for a ten-euro note. Hopefully that would cover it, but this was Venice, so... 'Will this be enough, do you think?'

'You're going to need another one of those,' he said, and with a resigned sigh she withdrew another note and held it out.

'Maybe one more?'

Her mouth dropped open. '*Thirty euros* for a glass of water? You've got to be kidding me!'

'I am. I just wanted to see you rooting around down the front of your dress.'

'*Oh!*'

He was laughing at her, but in a nice way, and he was *hot*. Like, the centre of the sun hot. Dark, almost-black, curling hair, tousled and sexy as hell; grey eyes, a deeper shade than her own; square jaw, patrician nose and a hint of a beard. He wore beads around his wrist, a silver chain around his neck which disappeared beneath a scruffy, tie-dye T-shirt in shades of grey and black, a loose linen-type jacket and black jeans.

Could he be a model? An actor? He looked like one. He had a little dip at the base of his throat, and she could see his collarbones under the T-shirt, along with a hint of muscled shoulders and chest.

If she hadn't heard his English accent, she would have assumed him to be Italian. He still could be. A bilingual one. A hot, sexy bilingual Italian, who was staring at her with appreciation in his gorgeous eyes.

Giselle wasn't often moved by male beauty, but she was earth-quaked by this specimen.

While she'd been drooling, the waiter had whisked the fallen cutlery away and was now sweeping up the glass shards using a pan and a long-handled brush.

Abruptly, she realised she was still holding the euro notes, and she closed her fist, crumpling them in her hand.

'Do you usually keep your money down there?' the guy asked.

Giselle's already warm face flamed. 'Sometimes.'

'Join me for a drink.' It wasn't an invitation; it was more of a command.

'Why?' Her tone was suspicious.

'Because you look hot and bothered.'

Nuh-uh, *he* was the hot one. 'I've got a drink, thanks,' she said. Letting her long hair fall forward to cover her face, she rooted in her bag and brought out the bottle of water with a flourish. There was only a mere thimbleful left in the bottom.

Feeling even more embarrassed, she peered at him through a veil of silver strands, wondering just how red her face was.

The guy pulled out a chair and lifted an eyebrow.

Giselle melted. Oh crumbs, he could do the one-eyebrow thing. There was no hope for her. She was lost.

She sank onto the seat.

He smiled, a slow curve of his lips, and signalled to the waiter, who had reappeared with fresh cutlery and glasses.

'Wine? My name's Rocco, by the way.'

'Giselle. Er, just water please.'

'Make that two.'

The waiter nodded and handed them a menu each. Giselle only took a quick glance at it, but it was enough to tell her she could barely afford the water. Anyway, she still had half a sandwich left, although it had lost its appeal a couple of hours ago.

'Hungry?' Rocco asked.

Rocco... Was that an Italian name? 'Not really.'

'Do you mind if I order some food?'

'This is your table, not mine.' She was acutely aware she was gate-crashing his meal.

He said something to the waiter. She caught one word: *bruschette*.

'Are you Italian?' she asked.

'My grandmother was. I'm only a quarter Italian.'

'Do you live here?'

'No, London. Holland Park. You're Scottish, I take it?'

'What gave it away?' she joked, beginning to relax. 'I live in East Kilbride. Near Glasgow,' she added, in case he'd never heard of the place. 'Are you here on holiday?'

'Gap year. Or should I say, a gap six months. I've got a job lined up for January.'

'Doing what?'

'Asset management.'

Giselle made a face.

'It probably is as boring as it sounds,' he said. 'What about you?'

'Holiday. I'm here with my sister and her friends from uni. Well, not *here*, exactly – they're in Milan. Fashion Week. Venice didn't appeal to them.'

'But it does to you?'

'Definitely. It's so romantic.'

'I suppose it is. So, you're in Venice on your own?'

'Yes.' She stared at him defiantly, daring him to make a comment, like *that's brave of you*.

'Me too. Kind of. I'm actually here with a mate, but he's got one hell of a hangover and refused to leave the hotel this morning, so I'm exploring the city on my own. We're only here for a couple of days and there's so much to see. I don't intend to waste it.'

The waiter reappeared, bearing an assortment of *bruschette*, the toppings held in place with toothpicks. *Gosh, Rocco has a good appetite*, Giselle thought in astonishment.

'Oops, it seems I've ordered too much,' he said.

She narrowed her eyes. There was no 'oops' about it. He'd known what he was doing, but the food looked delicious, and she was too hungry to care, even though it was eye-wateringly expensive.

'Help yourself,' he urged.

So she did, and as she lifted a piece of *bruschetta* onto her plate he said, 'Tell me about yourself.'

'Not much to tell,' she replied. Her life was boring compared to her sister's.

He tried again. 'What are you studying?'

'I'm not a student.'

His eyebrows rose. 'Oh, I thought—'

'That because my sister is at uni, I am too?'

'It's a reasonable assumption. So, what *do* you do?'

'I'm working in a bar at the moment.' If she sounded defensive, it was because she felt it.

'Not decided what you want to do when you grow up yet?' he asked.

Some of the tension seeped out of her shoulders. He wasn't judging her. 'Not yet.'

'Any leanings towards one thing or another? Not fashion, I take it?'

'Because I'm not dressed like a Venetian model?'

He opened his mouth, then closed it again, his expression adorably dismayed – until he realised she was teasing, and he raised his glass, acknowledging that he'd been had.

'Anything arty, really,' she said. 'Painting, textiles, pottery... You name it, I've tried it. But I haven't found my passion yet. Not like my sister. Isadora – Izzy – has always loved fashion.'

'Maybe you'll find it in Venice.' He smiled, and her heart did a somersault.

'Maybe.'

As they finished their meal, she found herself telling him that Izzy was her very different non-identical twin, that she loved history, nature and wild places, and she also loved romance and wanted to visit Paris at some point. But first, there was Venice.

'What have you seen so far?' he asked.

'The Doge's Palace, the Grand Canal and lots of little backstreets.'

'Fancy exploring together? It'll be more fun.'

She studied him, debating whether to refuse. But she didn't, and as the afternoon turned into music-filled evening and then hot sultry night, she was glad she hadn't because she didn't want this day to end.

When he finally took her in his arms to kiss her, and she kissed him back with a passion that matched his, she hoped it didn't have to.

Sunlight flooded into the room through the gently moving voile curtains, and the sounds of the city drifted up from the narrow street below.

Giselle stretched luxuriously and turned her head to find Rocco watching her. He was lying on his side, his sun-tanned skin dark against the white sheets. Desire flared in his eyes.

'I'm hungry,' she announced.

'So am I.' The growl in his voice did something exciting to her insides.

Last night had been magical. To experience that degree of intimacy for the first time, with such a gorgeous man and in such a beautiful city, was beyond her wildest expectations. It had been *so* romantic. The only thing lacking was love, that deep emotional connection Giselle yearned to experience someday. But not yet.

She had too much life to live, and she was also under no illusion that she would see Rocco again. They weren't soulmates. They weren't destined to be together, and she was fine with that. She wasn't in love, but she was probably in *lust*. Rocco was a very moreish kind of guy. Breakfast could wait.

Eventually, though, it was time to leave the *pensione*. Venice called, and Giselle heard the city's siren song. There was still so much more to see before she journeyed back to Milan this evening.

Still, she didn't want to leave Rocco just yet. She wasn't quite ready to say goodbye…

'What time is your train?' he asked.

'Eight thirty this evening.' It was slightly later, but she wanted to make sure she arrived at the station in plenty of time.

'I don't want to let you go,' he murmured, wrapping her in his arms.

'You have to; we need to check out soon.'

'We have all day. *If* you want.' His gaze was sombre, intense. He'd had his wicked way with her, but he wasn't going to love her and run. She appreciated that, even though she'd been fully prepared for it. Hell, she'd been considering doing that very thing herself.

'Do you have anything in particular in mind?' she asked.

'Glass blowing.'

She raised her eyebrows as he continued. 'Venice has been making glass for hundreds of years. The city is famous for it.'

'I read something about that. Isn't it made on an island?' She'd seen loads of shops selling the most exquisite glass yesterday, all of it well out of her price range.

'Murano,' he confirmed. 'There are about a hundred glass factories, apparently. My grandmother told me about them.'

'Then that's where we'll go,' Giselle stated.

A few more hours with Rocco would be wonderful. She had an image of one final passionate kiss on the station's platform. Oh yes, Giselle was definitely a romantic…

The *vaporetto*, or water bus, took around fifteen minutes from San Zaccaria near St Mark's Square to reach the island of Murano.

It was another warm day, and the breeze on the open water was welcome. But the growing heat as midday approached didn't prepare her for the furnace temperature of the glass blowing demonstration, and her dress, already limp from yesterday's wear, now clung damply to her. She was glad to slip inside the air-conditioned museum afterwards, although she did her best to avoid the shop and temptation, despite that she'd dearly love to take a physical memento home with her to go with her fabulous memories.

She thought Rocco was being careful with money too, because he suggested buying a snack for lunch and sitting on the steps of Faro di Murano, the thirty-five-metre-tall lighthouse, next to where they were to board the *vaporetto*.

Perching on the sun-baked white stones, facing out to the Adriatic, Giselle and Rocco ate their food, letting the chatter of people in the cafe behind wash over them, and listening to the waves lapping on the jumble of rocks below.

After they'd finished their picnic, Rocco stood up, wiped his hands on his black jeans and peered down at the water.

'Fish!' he cried, and Giselle leant forward to look.

They were small and lithe, darting and diving.

Rocco clambered down onto the rocks, and as she heard the crunch and skitter of pebbles under his feet, she wondered if he was allowed to be there, so near to the clear water. Feeling content and replete, she propped her back against the lighthouse and turned her face to the sun. Pink, red and orange flared across her eyelids, a rainbow of warmth.

'Look what I've found,' he said.

She opened her eyes, squinting up at him.

He was holding out a red-coloured stone in the shape of a heart.

No, not *stone*. Frosted glass? Then she realised what she was looking at – sea glass! She'd seen similar when they'd lived on Skye, before the family had moved to East Kilbride. She'd loved Skye and had been desolate to leave it. Izzy had been overjoyed.

Rocco handed the piece of sea glass to her. 'There's more,' he said, bending to sift through the pebbles, and she watched him indulgently.

He reminded her of her sister – bubbling with life and enthusiasm, a foil for her own quieter and more reserved nature.

Scattering a selection of sea glass on the hot stone step, he sank down beside her, and Giselle picked up each piece to examine it one by one.

'Beautiful,' she murmured. Each was different in shape, size and colour, and as she rearranged them, a picture began to form.

Suddenly, a flame ignited within her, and she stared at Rocco in wonder.

'Thank you,' she whispered.

'For what?'

'For today.' And possibly for the rest of her life. Because she now knew what she wanted to do. She might never see Rocco again, but as her palm closed around the little red heart, she knew she would never forget him.

Chapter 1

Ten years later

The sun had dipped below the mountains on the opposite shore of the loch, bathing the sky in apricot, sienna and dove grey. Giselle tilted her head back to scan the heavens, a deep sense of peace settling over her.

With the light fading, sunset wasn't the best time of day to scour the shoreline for sea glass, but it was her favourite. The visitors were long gone from the craft centre, and she should have left for home too, but this evening she hadn't been able to resist coming down to the water's edge. She was tired, but it was a weariness born of a productive and busy day, and she was pleasantly contented. A walk would do her good, and while she wouldn't actively be looking for sea glass, if she happened to find any little gems, she'd be happy. There were always treasures to be found after each high tide.

The air was redolent with the base-note scents of seaweed and salt, overlain by pine needles and damp earth, and if she concentrated hard, she could detect the faintest aromatic perfume of the heather flowering on the hillsides above.

Giselle wandered over to a rock and sat, her back to the shadowed castle behind, which was partially hidden by the trees, and gazed out across the water. The loch at Duncoorie was a sea water loch, sheltered from the open ocean by the mountains and a small island at its mouth. But 'sheltered' was a relative term, because in the winter, when storms raged, it became wild and rough, with white-topped waves and dark, angry water. Tonight, it was calm and quiet, a sleeping sea serpent, whose gentle breaths barely stirred the surface. When she managed to find enough of the right coloured glass, Giselle would create a picture of that mystical creature.

That's what she did, painted pictures with glass and shell, driftwood and pebbles, and she was good at it. She wouldn't have been invited to occupy a studio in the castle's craft centre if she wasn't. Mhairi Gray, the castle's elderly owner and founder of the craft centre, had high standards, and Giselle wouldn't want it any other way.

She should make a move. Dusk would soon fade to night, and Giselle had to walk home. Her bothy wasn't far – a thirty-minute walk – but the road was unlit, and although darkness didn't bother her, twisting an ankle on the uneven path would. Originally a basic farmer's hut, the bothy was now a home, and even though it was small, it was *hers*.

As the gloaming gathered, lights from the village twinkled in the distance and a glow emanated from the cottage near the boathouse. Cal, the castle's estate manager, lived there with Tara, one of the crafters. Giselle envisaged them settling down for the evening, and she looked away, not wanting to intrude on their privacy as she picked her way carefully along the shoreline.

Despite the encroaching dusk, she decided to stay out a while longer because it was such a lovely evening and she had no reason to hurry home. No one would be waiting for her – she lived alone – and she wasn't overly hungry yet, having availed herself of a decent lunch from the craft centre's rather nice cafe. She ate there most days, so she didn't have to cook. The kitchen wasn't her favourite place.

She'd wandered quite a distance when she realised the breeze had picked up, the light had almost faded from the sky and stars were putting in an appearance. The surrounding mountains were black tumps and the water glittered darkly.

The walk had grounded her, book-ending her day as she'd also strolled along the banks of the loch first thing this morning looking for sea glass, shells and interesting pebbles: the tools of her trade.

Relaxed and pleasantly tired, she made her way home.

A few more minutes won't hurt, Giselle decided, perched as usual on her favourite rock. Morning came early to Skye at this time of year, and she'd been drifting along the shoreline for the past hour or so, but there was still time enough to linger and enjoy her solitude for a while longer before heading to the studio with her bounty. She'd sort through her finds, grab a quick breakfast of poached eggs and ham on sourdough from the cafe before it opened to the public, then go see Mhairi. The old lady was in her eighties (no one knew for certain how old she was, not even Cal) but she still took a very keen interest in everything that went on in the castle and the craft centre.

As Giselle settled her canvas bag more firmly on her shoulder, her thoughts drifted to the smooth oval of black glass nestled safely inside. It was called pirate glass because it came from old rum bottles, and appeared black until a light was shone through it. When she'd held this piece up to the sun it had gleamed with a subdued yellow glow, and she'd hugged herself in delight.

Sometimes she knew precisely what she would do with her finds; other times, like this one, she would cache them, hoarding them as jealously as a dragon hoards gold, knowing that one day she'd find the perfect place for them.

Giselle made a note to take it with her when she saw Mhairi later. The old lady was always so interested in everything, and Giselle enjoyed their little chats and she had a soft spot for her landlady. Many a time Mhairi had slipped quietly into Giselle's studio to watch her work, not saying anything, before leaving again just as unobtrusively.

As Giselle picked her way along the crescent of sandy beach, she thought how fortunate she was to have found Coorie Castle and Mhairi, and how privileged she was to live in such a magical place. Born on Skye, the island was her spiritual and physical home, and she couldn't imagine living anywhere else. This was where she belonged.

Lost in thought, she made her way along the lane towards the long L-shaped building that housed the craft centre. It was old, although nowhere near as old as the castle, and had fallen into disrepair until Mhairi, due to the financial pressure of keeping the castle running, had decided to bolster the estate's income by transforming the former barns and service buildings into craft studios, a cafe and a gift shop. Giselle rented one of the smaller units, since she didn't require the same amount of floor space that the glassblower, for instance, needed.

As she strolled along the cobbled walkway running the length of the studios, she noticed that several of her fellow crafters had already arrived. One of them was Tara, who made doll's houses.

'Any good finds?' Tara asked, unlocking the door to her studio.

'A stopper, maybe from a perfume bottle,' Giselle said, 'and a piece of pirate glass.' Then she had to explain what that was when she showed her. 'And I also found this weirdly shaped pink piece that looks like a shoe,' she added. It wasn't as weathered by wave action as she would have liked, and Giselle was tempted to return it to the sea this evening to allow it to cure for a few more years so that it became more frosted. If she did, she might never see it again, but on the other hand she might be lucky enough to find it once more. She'd show it to Mhairi first though.

'Wow, that's gorgeous!' Tara exclaimed, gazing at it.

'Not as gorgeous as *that*.' Giselle pointed to an exquisite thatched cottage sitting in the centre of Tara's window. 'Every time I walk past, you have another new dolls house on display.'

Giselle was in awe of all the talented craftspeople who worked at the centre. Not only that, but they were also her found family, as dear to her as her real one. With her parents in East Kilbride and her fashion designer sister based in Milan, she saw far more of the people who lived and worked at Coorie Castle than she did her family.

When she entered the studio, Giselle took her canvas bag over to the tiny sink in the corner and removed the contents. As well as the incredibly tactile pirate glass, she'd collected some small pale green fragments, a brown one, several white ones and the pink shoe-shaped one, which had possibly come from an ornament of some kind.

Along with the glass, she'd found a conical shell, a flat pebble with striations of amber and cream running through it, and some small slivers of driftwood.

After carefully washing her finds, she placed them on a scrap of old towel to dry before sorting them into colour, size and shape. The common glass colours (green, brown and white) were stored in easily accessible trays on her workbench. These were her bread-and-butter pieces, and were the ones she most often used in her art.

The rarer finds were kept in a cabinet of slim drawers and were used far more sparingly. The more common the sea glass, the less she charged for her work. Pictures made using rarer pieces commanded a higher price. And some, the few precious ones, such as the vivid red heart, would never be used. In fact, she would never part with the heart from Venice. Even if it didn't have a substantial intrinsic value (the glass, she'd subsequently learnt, had been made with gold to give it the red colour), the value to her was enormous. That heart had set her on the path she walked today. It was because of that glorious little piece of sea glass that she'd discovered her passion.

Satisfied her studio was ready for her to start work, Giselle went in search of breakfast.

'You look happy,' Gillian observed as she took her order. Gillian was the cafe's manager. A middle-aged cheerful woman, she made the best sourdough Giselle had ever tasted. Gillian winked at her. 'Don't tell me you've got yourself a fella?'

Giselle raised her eyebrows and gave her a look.

The woman uttered a resigned sigh. 'You've found something on the beach, haven't you?'

'Yes, and it wasn't a man.'

'Sea glass?'

'Of course.'

'Will we see you in the pub tomorrow?'

Friday evenings in Duncoorie's one and only pub were a tradition. Not everyone managed every Friday, but there was usually a good turnout.

'Probably,' Giselle replied.

She had nothing else planned, but that wasn't unusual. However, she liked it that way: she wasn't exactly a social butterfly. She didn't do parties or late nights, preferring peace and early mornings. Izzy teased that she was old before her time, more sixty-nine than twenty-nine, but Giselle didn't care. She was sublimely happy with her life the way it was. And she was also used to being urged (gently, for the most part) to find herself a man and settle down.

The idea of being in a relationship didn't give her the heebie-jeebies, but neither was it a burning ambition. She simply wasn't interested. Izzy did enough dating for the both of them. Sometimes Giselle felt sorry for her parents, and her mum, especially. Mum had hinted on more than one occasion that it might be nice to be a grandma at some point, but with no fella on the horizon for Giselle, and far too many of them for Izzy, neither daughter would be producing offspring anytime soon. Both were happy as they were, even if their lives were so vastly different. Anyway, Giselle's body clock had yet to start ticking, so she had plenty of time to find someone to settle down with, *if* that's what she wanted to do.

And she wasn't entirely convinced she did.

Giselle knew that if she took her breakfast back to her studio she'd end up working as she ate, so she sat in the cafe instead, taking a table at one of the large picture windows with stunning views over the loch.

It was a view she would never tire of, and as she slowly consumed her meal, she let her gaze drift across the water to the hills on the opposite shore. Giselle had lost count of the number of times she'd recreated this scene out of sea glass and other found items, and no two pictures were ever the same, just like the ever-changing vista in front of her.

Breakfast polished off, she had an hour before she was expected at the castle, so she returned to her studio to work on her latest piece. This one was fun and light-hearted. She'd already created the sky and the sea background with a wash of blue and aqua watercolour paints. Now she arranged several bits of driftwood on the canvas to look like a rickety old fence, then placed some tiny pebbles, along with the odd shell or two, across the bottom of the picture to signify the shore. Finally, she added the seagulls using white and black glass, and used more white glass for the clouds, before drawing a pair of little legs and an eye on each bird.

The whole thing took about an hour, and when she was done, she set it aside. Once the glue was dry, she'd frame it.

Checking the time, she realised she'd better get a move on. She was late. Mhairi was one of the kindest and most generous people Giselle knew, but she was a busy woman, and she disliked tardiness. If she said eleven a.m., she meant eleven a.m., and it was already five minutes past.

Leaving her workbench in a bit of a mess, Giselle hurriedly washed her hands, picked up the more interesting morning finds then dashed out of the studio.

The castle was on the opposite side of the gravelled car park, white and luminous in the late morning sunlight. Arched windows with mullioned glass adorned each side, an impressive porch sheltered the enormous wooden front doors, and four turrets, one at each corner, reached into the sky, one of them sporting a flag.

Each time she saw Coorie, Giselle was amazed anew. The castle had been built in the thirteenth century, but there'd been a fortress on the site even before that, and everything about it screamed history, from the wide wood-panelled hall, the sweeping staircase, the coat of arms over the door, and the ancestral portraits and faded old tapestries on the walls. The smell of beeswax hung in the air, mingling with the scent of the fresh flowers on the reception desk.

One of the receptionists, Avril, was behind the desk and her friendly professional smile widened into genuine pleasure when she saw Giselle. Avril had worked at the castle for almost as long as Giselle and was her closest friend. Avril 'got' her, like few other people did. In the past, Giselle used to wish she was more like Izzy, but not now. She was happy in her own skin. Not everyone could be the life and soul of the party. The world also needed quieter people, and Giselle's preference was to let others waltz in the spotlight while she enjoyed a solitary dance in the rising sun.

'Go through,' Avril said. 'Mhairi's expecting you. I'll bring a tray of tea in a minute. I expect she could do with a cup. She hasn't rung for one this morning.'

'Lovely. Thanks.'

Avril beamed and Giselle waggled her fingers as she headed towards Mhairi's parlour. The parlour was a sitting-room-cum-office where the old lady held court and spent most of her time. The door was closed, as it usually was (Mhairi wasn't an open-door person – she liked her privacy), so Giselle tapped gently before going inside.

The room was large and sedate, stuffed full of antiques, with a huge mirror above a marble fireplace, several chairs set at right angles to it with an ornate coffee table between them and a heavy wooden desk next to a tall window.

Mhairi was seated in one of the upright wingback chairs by the unlit fireplace. A tall woman, she was slim and regal looking, with styled white hair and an English-rose complexion. She had a notepad on her lap, but she wasn't writing in it. She was taking a nap.

Oh, bless her, Giselle thought, wondering whether to creep out and let Avril know that she'd pop by and see Mhairi another time.

But just as she was about to turn around, something made her hesitate.

Mhairi was very still.

Too still.

Giselle swallowed hard. Her heart in her mouth, she said, 'Mhairi?'

No response.

Louder now, she called her name again. 'Mhairi!'

Still nothing, and even before Giselle screamed for help and began CPR, she knew Mhairi was dead.

Chapter 2

'Here, get this down you.' A chunky cut-glass tumbler half-full of amber liquid was thrust into Giselle's hand.

The tang of oak-aged whisky hit her nose before she took a sip, the liquor sliding down her throat without her tasting it, the heat warming her stomach. She wished there was something she could drink to warm her heart. She'd never felt so cold, so numb.

Someone had draped a soft woollen blanket over her shoulders (she thought it may have been Cal), but the fabric did little to dispel the chill settling into her bones.

Mhairi was dead. Giselle hadn't been able to save her.

'There's nothing you could have done, hen.'

Giselle looked around to see Cook smiling sorrowfully down at her.

Cook continued, 'She was an old lady and—'

'I was late.'

'Pardon?'

'I was late,' Giselle repeated woodenly. 'I was supposed to be here at eleven. If I'd been on time, I might have—' Her voice broke and she bit her lip, her chin trembling.

'You did your best, hen.'

Giselle wasn't convinced. Her best would have been if she'd managed to save her. Those ten minutes could have made all the difference. Mhairi had only just passed…

Tears fell at last, hot and fast, and she sobbed, her shoulders shaking. She felt an arm around her and looked into Avril's white, grief-stricken face.

Her friend's cheeks were wet. 'I should have known something was wrong. She always rang for her morning tea. *Always.*'

'She was waiting for me to join her,' Giselle said through her sobs. 'I shouldn't have been late.'

'Stop blaming yourselves.' Cook shoved a second tumbler at Avril. 'It was her time to go.' Although she said it in a matter-of-fact tone, her eyes brimmed with tears. Cook (not her real name, but her title) had worked at the castle for years, long before the craft centre had come into existence. Although the castle's kitchen was now run by a head chef and an array of kitchen staff, she was still a formidable presence and saw to Mhairi's meals personally, the way she'd done for forty years. The two women had grown old together, although Cook was over a decade younger than Mhairi.

'Did they say what it was?' Avril asked.

Giselle lifted a shoulder in a shrug and the blanket slipped down her arm. Cook hoisted it back up, then lowered herself slowly into the chair next to her after moving a book aside. They were in the library, having been ushered out of the parlour when the paramedics arrived.

'Heart attack or stroke, I expect,' Cook said. 'There'll have to be a post-mortem.' Her expression was pained and sorrowful, her face pale with shock. Mhairi's loss would hit her the hardest out of all of them.

When Cal walked into the room, everyone stared at him, falling silent as they waited for news.

He shook his head, his grief apparent in the set of his jaw and the tension around his eyes. 'They've taken her to Broadford,' he said. 'I wanted to go with her, but there wasn't any point.' He blinked hard, sank into a chair and buried his head in his hands.

'What's happened?' Jinny demanded, hurrying into the room, breathless and anxious. 'Why was the ambulance here? Who's hurt? One of the guests?' Jinny, the gift shop's manager, also had a close working relationship with Mhairi. She was going to take the news hard, too.

Giselle's face crumpled again and she pressed her hands to her face. 'It's my fault.'

Cook patted her on the arm. 'Hush, hen, it's not your fault.'

'*What's going on?*' Jinny repeated.

Cal spoke. 'It's Mhairi; she's dead. A stroke or a heart attack, they think.'

Jinny shook her head. 'No, no, that can't be right. I sent her yesterday's sales figures first thing this morning, and she... *Oh, hell.*' She began to cry.

Avril asked. 'What do we do now?'

Cal's face twisted as he fought to control his expression. 'The show must go on. We've got guests in the castle and a couple of coach tours on site. We can't simply turf them out. And I've got to tell the others – they'll have seen the ambulance, and I want them to hear the news from me. Then I'll need to inform her solicitor.' He looked drawn and grey, his tan faded by grief.

'But Cal! She's dead!' Jinny looked appalled.

'I know. I was with her when they called it.'

'Called it?' Avril asked.

'Made the decision to stop resuscitation.'

Giselle gasped. 'I thought she was dead before I…' She put a hand to her mouth.

'She was. There was nothing you could have done. The paramedics had to try, but she was already gone.'

'But we can't carry on as though nothing has happened,' Jinny protested.

'We have to,' Cal said. 'We can't simply ask the guests to leave. And if we did, how long would we shut the castle and craft centre for? The rest of the day? The weekend? Next week?' He ran a hand through his hair. 'Mhairi made her wishes clear. In the event of her death, we have to keep everything running as normal until I take instruction from her solicitor.'

Jinny subsided, her eyes brimming with tears. 'I don't think I can. And look at Avril – and Giselle. You can't expect them to just go back to work.'

Cal caught his bottom lip between his teeth. 'Avril, would you like to go home?'

Avril shook her head. 'I'd rather keep busy.'

Giselle couldn't face opening her studio today. She kept feeling Mhairi's birdlike chest under her hands as she desperately tried to pump life into her.

She wanted to go home and cry in private.

Then Cook asked the question that had been hovering in the back of Giselle's mind, and probably in everyone else's. 'She's not got any living relatives as far as I know, so who will inherit Coorie Castle?'

And although Giselle was deeply distressed over the death of the castle's owner, she too couldn't help wondering. She hoped whoever it was would keep Coorie Castle and Craft Centre just the way it was – because if they didn't, it would be her fault.

She would never forgive herself for being ten minutes late.

—

'Can I have a word?' Rocco Moore's mother caught him just as he was about to enter the finance director's office.

Rocco hesitated. 'Yeah, sure. Can it wait, though? I've got a meeting with Claire.' He was already late, having been caught up in a longer than expected conference call with a client.

'It'll only take a minute. But not here. In private.'

Uh-oh. He didn't like the sound of that. Even though the CEO happened to be his mother, Beverly Moore wanting 'a word in private' was rarely a good thing. Rocco wondered who was for the chop. It wouldn't be himself, obviously, because not even she was that ruthless, and besides, Rocco owned substantial shares in the company.

He followed her along the plush carpeted hallway and into the corner office with its views over London.

'Close the door,' Beverly instructed, as she took a seat behind her chrome-and-glass desk.

Rocco often wondered how she managed to avoid getting finger marks over its polished surface. As usual, there was very little on it, except for a glass paperweight, which was purely decorative since the company was largely paperless, and a computer screen so slim that it was barely wider than a credit card.

Rocco hovered, debating whether this unexpected meeting would be worth sitting down for.

His mother gazed pointedly at one of the leather chairs, so Rocco sat.

'Nice suit,' she began. 'Is it new?'

'I've had it a couple of months. What's this about, Beverly? You didn't bring me in here to discuss fashion.' Rocco called his mother Beverly when they were at work – it seemed more professional and less sycophantic, somehow. It also put them on a more equal footing as senior executives, and not mother and son. And now he called his mother Beverly most of the time. It was easier that way.

Beverly steepled her manicured fingers, her elbows on the glass, as she leant forward. 'Mhairi Gray is dead.'

'Who?'

'Your great grandfather's sister. She's your cousin, twice, or three times removed.' Beverly wafted a hand in the air. 'I can't remember which. Anyway, she's dead.'

He took a second to process the information. 'I thought she was already dead?' He hadn't heard her name mentioned in years.

'She was very much alive and living in Scotland – until this morning. Her solicitor has just been in touch with ours.'

Rocco nodded absently, vaguely remembering something about her, and wondered what the relevance was and why his mother had deemed it important enough to delay his meeting with Claire. They had some crucial figures to go over and it was going to take some time. He sighed, knowing that yet again he wouldn't be leaving the office until late. Then again, he wasn't a nine-to-five person, and neither was his mother. Nor Claire. It was expected that they'd stay until whatever needed to be done was done.

'Mhairi owns a castle,' Beverly was saying. 'Or she *did*. *You* own it now.'

Rocco tilted his head as he studied her. Was she joking? Rocco didn't think so. His mother wasn't one for humour.

'I own a *castle*?' he asked slowly, certain he must have misheard.

'That's right. Your great-great-grandfather, Tandy Gray, bought it at a knockdown price in the late nineteenth century when the laird who owned it ran up substantial gambling debts and was obliged to sell. It was in a sorry state and Tandy didn't have the funds to do anything with it. But Mhairi's father did.'

'Wasn't he the wealthy shipping magnate?' Rocco had heard stories from his father, but he'd assumed that's what they had been: stories. He hadn't actually believed any of them. And to be honest, he hadn't much cared, being more interested in the here and now rather than ancient family history. But his father had been dead eight years, and Rocco hadn't thought about those stories in a very long time.

'Well remembered,' Beverly said in answer to Rocco's question, then she smiled. It didn't quite reach her eyes. 'It's about money, so of course you remembered. You're so like me in that respect.'

Rocco didn't entirely take that as a compliment. His mother was savagely ruthless when it came to the business, but there was no doubting her aptitude.

'Why me?' Rocco asked, thinking, *Bloody hell – a castle!* What on earth was he supposed to do with *that*?

Beverly shrugged, daintily lifting a designer-clad shoulder. 'There isn't anyone else.'

Rocco said nothing. He waited, and sure enough his mother filled in the details.

'You're the last of the Tandy Gray line. They weren't a particularly fertile lot. He had two children – your great-grandmother and Mhairi's father, who inherited the estate. Mhairi's father only had one child, and that was Mhairi, but she never married. With her death, the next in line would have been your father; but our solicitor informs me that since he's no longer with us, the castle is yours, along with everything else she owned. If there *is* anything else.'

'A proper castle, like with turrets and a dungeon?'

'I suppose.' Beverly's tone was dismissive. She clearly had no interest in the details of this unexpected inheritance of his. Her interest would be in its value.

'Where is it?'

'The Isle of Skye, apparently.'

Rocco was none the wiser. He knew nothing of Scotland, aside from one incredibly romantic and magical encounter with one of its residents a decade ago. Every now and again, when he least expected it, an image of a girl with long, white-blond hair as pale as liquid silver, alabaster skin, and eyes that had appeared navy in some lights and purple in others, would float into his mind. Rocco shrugged it aside. Now was not the time to be daydreaming about old romantic encounters.

'What am I supposed to do with a castle?' he mused aloud. It was a complication he could do without.

'Sell it,' his mother said. 'The Americans love anything to do with Scotland – it might appeal to someone in the States.'

'Any idea what it's called?'

'Coorie Castle.' Beverly rose gracefully to her feet and Rocco knew she was done. 'Better get off to your meeting,' she instructed. 'I just thought I'd give you the heads-up. The firm handling her side of the legals will be in touch with you soon.'

For once, Rocco's mind wasn't fully focused on his job and as he entered the finance director's office, she immediately picked up on it.

'What did Beverly want?' Claire enquired, her gaze on her computer screen. 'Anything important?'

'Just some family stuff.'

Those dark brown eyes with their sweeping lashes narrowed fractionally. She hated to be excluded, especially since she would dearly like to be part of said family. And if his mother had her way, she'd marry him off to Claire like a shot. With her acute financial acumen, Claire was an asset to the company, and Rocco admired and respected her. But despite her high cheekbones, glossy brown hair and curvy figure, he wasn't attracted to her. Even if he had been, he wouldn't have muddied the business waters, so to speak. Unlike his dad, who had run Moore Asset Management with Beverly, Rocco had no ambitions to work alongside a wife.

And right now, he had no ambitions to actually have a wife at all. He didn't have time for such luxuries.

After hurrying through those aspects of the meeting that could be hurried through and uncharacteristically rescheduling those that couldn't, Rocco returned to his office. Nora, his PA, tried to intercept him, but he waved her away. 'Later, yeah? I've got something I need to deal with.'

Curiosity was eating at him. It wasn't every day one became an owner of a castle.

Coorie Castle was easy to find on the internet, although not as easy to get to in real life, assuming he would want to, although he was surprised and pleased to discover it wasn't the mouldering pile of old stones he'd been expecting. It was certainly old, as in thirteenth-century old, but it wasn't a ruin. It was in better nick than he'd thought and was currently being run as a hotel and a craft centre.

Rocco studied the castle's website with interest, examining the photos with growing excitement.

Set on a rocky outcrop above a loch, surrounded by mountains and with a village nearby, it was incredibly picturesque. Surprisingly, it was white (he'd expected bare stone), but in other respects it was a typical castle – towers, crenelations, wood panelling, old tapestries… No dungeons, as far as he could tell, more's the pity. It had extensive grounds and a variety of outbuildings, most of which had been converted into a craft centre complete with a gift shop and a cafe.

It was worth a bit, he surmised, but whether that could be translated into hard cash was another matter. Not that he'd had much experience with castles, but he suspected demand wouldn't be high. As his mother had suggested, maybe a wealthy American could be persuaded to buy it. One with Scottish heritage, deep pockets and a yearning to own a piece of history.

The nearby village of Duncoorie was small, offering little more than a church, a shop with a post office, a pub, a guest house or three, a bakery and several businesses specialising in outdoor activities. And the Isle of Skye, he read, was a magnet for tourists, so if he wanted to sell the castle as a going concern, there might be some takers interested in a business opportunity.

Of course, it would largely depend on the state of the accounts.

An incoming email caught his attention.

It was from Mhairi's solicitor in London, a firm not too far from the office, in fact. He'd ask Nora to call them and set up a meeting. Then he supposed he should go visit this castle for himself. Only by seeing it would he understand its worth and be able to decide how best to deal with it. Because the sooner he was shot of it and the money from its sale was in his bank account, the better.

Chapter 3

The dawn chorus started even before the first few rays of the rising sun began to drive the night away, as though the birds understood that daybreak was just over the horizon.

The blackbird was the first to celebrate the end of the night, followed by the melancholy falling notes of the willow warbler, then the unmistakable rippling song of the cheeky robin who often perched on the back of the wooden chair and peered into the bothy, hoping for a crumb of bread.

Giselle was seated in that very chair, wrapped in the thick woollen throw that she'd taken off her bed, her hands cupped around a mug of fragrant chamomile and lavender tea. She was staring into the distance, oblivious to the beauty around her. Her thoughts were turned inwards to her grief and to Mhairi. She doubted whether Cal had slept either, considering the funeral was today. He'd been even closer to the old lady than Giselle, and she knew what he must be going through. She'd lost her grandmother seven years ago, so she was no stranger to grief, and even though Cal and Mhairi weren't related, they'd shared a close bond.

As well as her guilt, it was the suddenness of Mhairi's passing that Giselle found hard to take. There'd been no indication the old lady was ill – or none that was common knowledge. If Mhairi had been unwell, she'd not shared it with anyone. Not even Cal.

The post-mortem stated that it had been a heart attack, so sudden that hopefully Mhairi hadn't been aware of it. And she'd died at home, in the castle, the place she'd poured her heart and soul into, and without a long lingering illness. But Giselle still couldn't get those wasted ten minutes out of her mind.

Guilt and remorse were eating her up, and the uncertainty about the castle's future wasn't helping. The happy family community feel of Coorie Castle had been replaced with sadness and worry, and everyone was tense. No matter how irrational she was being, Giselle couldn't help believing it was all her fault.

Cal had been close-mouthed about his dealings with the solicitor, skirting around the subject whenever anyone asked him about it, so speculation was rife. All he would say was that Mhairi's solicitor was handling everything, including the funeral arrangements.

Poor Cal. He looked so frazzled that Giselle's heart went out to him. He'd confided that he was under strict instructions not to change anything, and so the castle and the craft centre had carried on as normal. Apart from today, because today was Mhairi's funeral and everyone wanted to pay their respects, *including* the new owner, apparently, who'd been due to arrive last night.

With a sad sigh, Giselle got to her feet, pulling the throw tighter around her slender shoulders. Although she wasn't hungry, she knew she should have something. The day would be difficult enough as it was without her feeling faint because she hadn't eaten.

Her house was small, but it suited her needs. A stable door led straight into the one main room (aside from the bathroom), with a compact kitchen area to the right that opened up into the living–dining area with its stone walls, wood-burning stove and fantastic views over the loch. The bedroom was crammed into the eaves above the kitchen and bathroom, and was accessed by a wooden ladder.

The dress she'd borrowed hung from the ironwork balustrade around the mezzanine bedroom floor, and she gazed at it with distaste. Not because it was a horrid dress (it was actually very smart – one that Avril sometimes wore to work), but because it wasn't her. Giselle didn't do smart black dresses. Aside from a pair of old trainers, she didn't own anything black. It wasn't her colour, not suiting her pale complexion and silver hair. And why wear a non-colour when there were so many glorious hues in the world?

Still staring at it thoughtfully, Giselle wished she had the courage to wear something bright and to braid her hair with flowers. Mhairi had once told her that black was such a dreary colour and Giselle had agreed wholeheartedly. But although Giselle could be brave when it really mattered, today wasn't one of those times. Not when Mhairi's heir would be putting in an appearance. She didn't want to make a wrong first impression, so with a heavy heart she wriggled into the formal dress, disliking how constricting it felt, and slipped her feet into a pair of leather sandals. Hopefully, no one would notice how incongruous they looked, and she'd be sitting towards the back of the kirk anyway, so her feet would be hidden.

She did braid her hair, though, but left out the flowers she'd picked yesterday evening. They reminded her of Mhairi, who had always been partial to wildflowers. The tweed and pearls she'd favoured had hidden a freer soul.

Giselle guessed that was the reason the old lady used to enjoy examining her finds from the seashore.

Och, she'd miss their chats. They all would; Giselle hadn't been the only crafter invited to share her mid-morning coffee. But Giselle was the only one who'd been late…

With the thick braid hanging heavily over her left shoulder and a knitted shawl in muted dove, heather and white draped over her arm (even though it was early summer, the inside of the church might be chilly), Giselle set off with a heavy heart.

—

The bedroom was impressive: a large wooden bed that looked as though it had been in vogue a couple of centuries ago, a fireplace with an ornate mantelpiece, a polished dark-wood wardrobe, a nightstand, a chest of drawers and a table. None of the furniture matched, and every piece was as old as the hills.

Rocco knew nothing about antiques, but he knew class when he saw it, and from what he'd seen of the castle so far, it was seriously classy. Old world, old money kind of classy. Then there were the modern touches: the deep, luxurious mattress and the high-thread-count sheets and pillowcases, for instance, along with the power shower, the coffee machine and the hairdryer, amongst other things. He hoped he would be as impressed with the rest of the castle. No doubt he'd find out later.

Having flown into Inverness airport yesterday evening, he'd hired a car, then had driven the three hours plus to Duncoorie to arrive late last night. It had been dark, he'd been tired and irritable and all he'd wanted to do was to have something to eat and go to bed.

The estate manager, a man by the name of Calan Fraser, had met him at the door and shown him to his room. The chef (who was apparently referred to as Cook – or was that the woman's name?) had left a deli selection for him, which he'd eaten, then he'd had a shower and had fallen into bed, grumbling to himself that it would have been quicker and far less hassle to travel the three and a half thousand miles from London to New York than it had been to get to this bloody castle. The inconvenience factor alone was reason enough to sell the place!

He'd informed Fraser that he'd take breakfast in his room this morning. Having been out of action for a big part of yesterday, he had work to catch up on, and then there was the funeral to be got through, followed by a wake here at the castle, which he intended to avoid. He wanted to get his bearings first before being introduced to a bunch of strangers.

Anyway, he'd be better off spending that time dealing with client issues than making nice with people he didn't know and would probably never meet again. It was harsh, but true. As Beverly kept reminding him, time was money, and his time was too valuable to waste. While the locals were enjoying free food and drink at the castle's expense, he'd do some more work, then Fraser could show him around the estate. Afterwards he'd hightail it back to London to think how best to market it with a view to selling – once it had been valued, of course.

His Rolex Submariner told him it was six twenty. He'd slept well and deeply in the comfortable bed, but he needed to get up. He was usually on his way to the office (via the gym) by now, so this late start was an indulgence. Grumpily, he decided he'd better skip the idea of going for a run. He'd brought trainers and a pair of shorts with him in the hope he could fit one in, but today was out of the question. Maybe he'd go tomorrow, before the long journey back.

Naked, he padded to the window and twitched a drape aside. A single glimpse had him opening the curtains wide.

What a view!

His room looked out over the loch, and he drank it in greedily. The images he'd seen online hadn't done it justice. The water was shades of navy, grey, green and turquoise, glittering in the early morning sun, and was backdropped by low mountains.

Rocco mentally added a few more pound signs to his first impression of the castle. People would pay good money to own a view like that. He just hoped the rest of the estate was as good.

Too curious now to remain in his room, he decided to take his breakfast in the dining room, so he phoned reception to inform them of his change of plan, and when he went downstairs half an hour later, he wasn't surprised to find the estate manager hovering in the hall.

As Rocco walked over to him, arm outstretched for a perfunctory handshake, he glanced at the receptionist behind the desk, who was watching him curiously.

Calan Fraser said in his soft Scottish burr, 'She doesn't know who you are, but since you're the only guest in the hotel just now, she can probably guess.'

Rocco had asked that his name not be mentioned prior to his arrival. He'd wanted to keep things as low key as possible, but now he was here, he supposed the cat was out of the bag.

'I'm about to have breakfast. Join me,' he instructed.

Fraser shrugged in acquiescence. 'The dining room is through here.'

The room was as opulent as Rocco's bedroom. There was a touch of Claridge's or the Dorchester about it, but with greater age; however, he doubted that the tables and chairs, although of good quality, were genuine antiques. Crisp white tablecloths, silver-plated cutlery, the aroma of freshly brewed coffee in the air and another view of the loch, albeit from a different angle, made a pleasing impression.

Rocco didn't bother looking at the menu. 'Scrambled eggs, brown toast, coffee and orange juice – freshly squeezed, if you have it.'

The young man who was taking his order glanced at Fraser and was about to say something, but Fraser shook his head and said, 'Ask someone to squeeze some oranges, Simon. I'm sure they can find a couple.'

'Certainly, sir,' the young man said to Rocco, then his eyes darted from Rocco to Fraser. 'Anything for you, Cal?'

Fraser hesitated, clearly uneasy.

Rocco said, 'Have you eaten?'

'No.'

'Then you'd better do so now. It's going to be a long day.'

Fraser nodded. 'OK. Just toast and a coffee. Thanks, Simon.'

'The funeral car will be here at ten thirty, correct?' Fraser had already informed him of this via email, but Rocco wanted to check.

'That's right. The service is at eleven a.m. in the kirk. The church,' he added, seeing Rocco's blank expression.

He said, 'Ah, yes, the *church*.'

'You'll soon get used to the colloquialisms.'

Rocco highly doubted that. 'What time do you anticipate the wake ending?'

'One, one thirty?'

'One would be preferable. I want to look around the estate afterwards.'

'Of course.'

'I won't be at the wake.'

Surprise flitted across the man's face. 'Oh, er, right.' Fraser took a breath. 'The staff are already asking questions about the new owner, and when they see you at the funeral they'll be asking even more. What should I tell them?'

'Nothing. I'll introduce myself later, once I've had a chance to look around.' He glanced up as the server approached with a plate and a rack of toast, and he shook the white linen napkin open, draping it over his lap. 'After breakfast, I want to see the accounts and the rest of the paperwork relating to the estate.'

The sooner he had a grasp on what he actually owned, the better, because then he'd know exactly what it was worth and could price it accordingly when he put it up for sale.

—

The kirk gleamed white in the sun, its arched, mullioned windows reflecting the light. It was set back off the road, the grassy graveyard dotted with snaggle-toothed headstones. Most were mossy and daubed with splotches of green and pale yellow lichen, their names and dates weathered into oblivion. Some were more recent, and as Giselle made her way to the oak-doored entrance, she walked slowly, reading the ones which were legible.

Mhairi's final resting place was in the churchyard, and Giselle thought it fitting the old lady would be spending eternity with a view of the loch and the castle she'd adored.

Giselle filed in with the other mourners, unsurprised to see how many people were here to pay their last respects. The entire village had turned out. *Mhairi would have been pleased*, she thought.

Organ music played softly, low and sombre, and Giselle slipped inside to claim a place at the back. The pew was half-full already, and when she saw a space at the end furthest from the aisle, she slipped into it next to Freya. Freya didn't have a studio at the centre (she was a potter, renowned for her unusual ceramics) and Giselle didn't know her particularly well, but she knew her boyfriend, Mack. Before Mack had fallen head over heels in love with Freya, he'd hit on her a few times. And once or twice Giselle had been tempted by his Viking good looks and rugged outdoor charm. But she hadn't succumbed, in part because he'd had a reputation, but also because… Actually, she wasn't entirely sure why. She had this silly notion of wanting to be swept off her feet, but so far none of her boyfriends had managed even a bit of light brushing, never mind a sweep. And although Mack was good looking and friendly, and he loved Skye, Duncoorie and the wild loch as much as she did, her head hadn't been turned and she'd refused all offers. Which had been a good thing, considering Freya was the love of his life.

As though he sensed her thoughts, Mack gave Giselle a swift, reassuring smile, but most of his attention was reserved for Freya, and he had eyes only for her.

Hopefully one day, a man will look at me like that, Giselle thought, and she would feel blessed if that ever happened, but until then, she was content being alone.

The music changed and the vicar ascended the pulpit.

With her head bowed, Giselle rose, along with the rest of the mourners, as the coffin was brought in. Squeezing her eyes shut, she bit her lip, willing the tears not to fall. But they fell anyway, and she grasped her shawl in twisting hands as she struggled to keep her composure.

When she opened her eyes again, her tear-fractured view of the coffin was obscured by the heads of the people in front. All she could see was the vicar.

As the hymns were sung and the vicar gave the eulogy, Giselle kept her head lowered. She was glad she was paying her respects, yet she couldn't wait for the service to end. Calan, bless him, struggled to hold his emotions in check as he said a few words on behalf of everyone who worked at the castle, which set Giselle off again. She wasn't the only one who was crying. Mhairi had been well loved and highly respected. Cal had spoken the truth when he said she'd be sorely missed by everyone.

Dabbing at her damp cheeks with a scrap of soggy tissue, Giselle was relieved when the funeral director indicated that the service was at an end. As he led the pallbearers carrying the casket down the aisle, the congregation, starting with the front rows, fell in behind. Somewhere, bagpipes started playing as the funeral procession slowly made its way out of the church.

Giselle's attention was on the polished coffin with its elegant wreath of white lilies, and it wasn't until it drew level with the pew she was standing in did her sad gaze fall on the man walking behind it, and she gasped.

She'd seen that handsome face before. *Ten years and a lifetime ago.*

Chapter 4

Stunned, Giselle gripped Freya's arm. 'Did you see that man?' she demanded.

'What man?'

'The guy walking behind the coffin.' She must have been mistaken. It was someone who looked like him, that's all. It couldn't possibly have been Rocco. Giselle rose onto her tiptoes to peer over black-clad shoulders. 'Do you know who he is?'

Freya said, 'One of the funeral directors, maybe? I didn't really notice.' She turned her attention to Mack. 'Poor Cal. He's devastated. Try to get him to talk about it, if you can – it might help.'

Mack, his wild sun-streaked blonde hair tied back with a black band and his beard neatly trimmed, said, 'I'll try, but I'm not holding my breath. He was closer to her than anyone except for Cook. Are you OK?' he asked Giselle.

Giselle gave a vague nod and shuffled impatiently, desperate to squeeze past Freya and Mack and into the aisle, but she refrained, not wanting to draw attention to herself, so she waited until everyone else had exited the pew.

Emerging into the sunlight, she blinked and shaded her eyes with her hand, but all she could see was a vastly reduced funeral party, headed by the vicar, making its way towards a mound of bright-green fake grass under which undoubtedly lay a pile of freshly dug earth.

When she made to follow, a softly spoken woman wearing a top hat and a regretful expression prevented her. 'I'm sorry, it's family members only at the graveside.'

Giselle looked past her, but the man she wanted to see was partially obscured by a large stone angel on a plinth.

The top-hatted woman continued, 'If we could give the family some privacy at this most distressing time, it would be much appreciated.'

Giselle felt a hand on her arm, and she jumped.

It was Freya. 'Are you coming to the wake?'

'I hadn't been planning to, but I think I will.' She could do with the company. The service had been even sadder than she'd expected, and she didn't want to be on her own right now.

'It was a beautiful service,' Freya said, as she fell into step beside her. Mack slung an arm around Freya's shoulders as she added, 'I think the whole village has turned out for it.'

'I'm going to miss her.' A lump formed in Giselle's throat. 'The castle won't be the same without Mhairi.'

She spied Avril, her friend's face tear blotched as she waited for Giselle to catch up, and when she got close enough, Avril linked an arm through hers. 'I looked for you earlier, but I didn't see you.'

Giselle glanced over her shoulder at the small, intimate service taking place amongst the lopsided headstones and moss-covered monuments. 'I was at the back.'

Avril said, 'I've got some news. The castle's new owner arrived last night. I don't know anything about him – no one does. I know his name, but I only know that because I saw it on the register this morning. He's the castle's only guest at the moment, although I don't suppose he really *is* a guest, since he owns it.'

Just then, the man in question glanced around and Giselle's mouth dropped open. His gaze locked onto hers, his eyes widened and time stopped for several interminable seconds as memories swept through her.

It *was* him! The man who she'd spent one glorious night with in Venice.

What the hell was *he* doing here? Then suddenly it fell into place, even as Avril said his name.

Rocco was Coorie Castle's new owner.

—

Surely not? Rocco's eyes narrowed as he peered across the graveyard, wishing he was wearing his sunglasses, the light too bright to see clearly. It couldn't be the girl he'd met in Venice, could it?

Then she was gone, and he reluctantly dragged his attention back to the vicar as he said some final words. An elderly woman, stout and with short, curly grey hair, was glaring at him accusingly. He gave her a tight-lipped smile.

When the funeral director had said, 'Close family and friends only, for the committal,' Cal had quickly introduced him to the woman as Coorie Castle's new owner. She hadn't been pleased.

Rocco didn't care. He wasn't here to make friends. He was here to pay his respects to a woman he'd never met but who nevertheless had left him a substantial amount of money – albeit in the form of a castle – and to find out all he could about said castle in order to sell it. Part one was complete, so now it was time for part two. Maybe he should have arrived a day earlier, so he could have met Mhairi's employees. Being introduced to them at the graveside wasn't ideal, but he was already taking enough time out of his busy schedule, and he hadn't wanted to take any more. However, if he'd arrived on Saturday evening instead of Sunday, he might have found out who the blonde woman was.

As he sat in the back seat of the funeral car for the brief journey back to the castle, his thoughts were on Giselle. He was convinced the woman he'd just seen was her.

Eager to discover if he was right, Rocco exited the car with unseemly haste for the recently bereaved and hurried inside. A guy on reception checked out his suit and black tie, assumed Rocco to be a mourner and directed him towards the great hall.

The hall was the size of a ballroom, reached via a series of interconnected rooms, and was thronging with people, most of whom had drinks in their hands. A long table along one end bore platters of finger food. Rocco would have flinched at the sight if he'd been footing the bill, but Mhairi had set aside a sum of money to cover her funeral expenses and the subsequent wake, so it wasn't coming out of his pocket, thankfully.

As he wove through the crowd, he scanned the room for familiar faces, looking for one in particular. Even though he hadn't seen Giselle for a decade, her face was indelibly imprinted on his mind.

He didn't see her, but he did spy Fraser. Conscious of more than a few curious glances in his direction, Rocco made his way over to him.

The man looked surprised. 'I thought you were giving the wake a miss?'

Rocco ignored the comment. 'Do you know a woman of around thirty years old with long, white-blonde hair? She attended the funeral.'

Fraser blinked. 'That sounds like Giselle.'

Bingo! Rocco nodded to himself. 'Is she here?'

Fraser's gaze roved around the room, curiosity rolling off him in waves. 'I can't see her. Avril might know; she's one of our reception staff.' He caught her eye and beckoned her over. From her cautious expression, Rocco assumed she knew who he was.

She said politely, 'Hi, Cal,' but her gaze was on him, her expression curious.

Fraser glanced at him, and Rocco gave a small nod. It was time people knew about him.

Fraser said, 'Avril, this is Rocco Moore, Mhairi's relative and Coorie Castle's new owner.'

A professional smile appeared on her face. 'Nice to meet you, Mr Moore.'

Fraser said, 'Do you know where Giselle is?'

'Um...' Avril's eyes flickered. 'I'm not sure.'

'Is she at the wake?'

'She is. Would you like me to find her?'

Rocco broke in. 'No need.' He'd spotted a bright head of silver hair, a beacon amongst the sea of funereal clothes. Giselle scanned the room, then their eyes locked for a second time and he faltered.

He'd only caught a glimpse of her in the churchyard, but now that he could see her properly he realised she hadn't changed a bit. And along with the realisation came a stirring which was entirely inappropriate, given the time and the place.

For a second, Rocco was transported back to a time when he'd been young, carefree, without responsibilities.

A time when he'd met a shining elvish woman in a magical faraway land.

Real life, in the form of Fraser clearing his throat, brought Rocco back to earth.

Giselle hadn't moved. She looked like a startled deer ready to flee. Then she seemed to shake herself, and he realised Fraser had gestured for her to join them.

'Hi, Cal,' she said, but like Avril, her attention was on him, not Fraser.

Fraser said, 'Giselle, this is Rocco Moore. He's the castle's new owner.'

'We've met, many years ago. How are you, Rocco?'

Her lips were as full as he remembered, pink and luscious, without the slightest hint of lipstick, and his gaze was drawn to them. She was even more gorgeous now, and desire stirred.

He turned to the estate manager. 'Would you give us a moment? Actually, Fraser, is there somewhere Giselle and I can talk?' He wasn't entirely sure what he wanted to talk to her about, but whatever it was, he didn't want to say it in front of this pair.

Giselle's eyebrows curved upwards. '*Fraser?* He's got a first name, you know.'

'I'm aware of that.'

'Why don't you use it? Or do you call everyone by their surnames?'

Fraser opened his mouth, but Rocco didn't give him the opportunity to speak. 'What's *your* surname?' he asked her. He couldn't believe he didn't already know it, but back then they'd had other things on their minds.

'Ellis.' Her tone was defiant, and a light blush infused her cheeks.

'OK, Ellis, let's go. Fraser, where can we go?'

The man said, 'How about Mhairi's parlour? *Your* parlour now, I suppose.'

Rocco took a step, but Giselle held her ground. 'No,' she said.

Fraser touched her lightly on the arm. 'It's all right, Giselle. It *is* Mr Moore's parlour.'

'It's not that. Rocco, please call Cal by his first name and not Fraser.'

'Giselle,' Fraser warned, shaking his head slightly.

Giselle ignored him, not taking her eyes off Rocco. 'We're one big family here,' she told him. 'That's what Mhairi used to say, and she was right.'

Rocco was tempted to retort that Mhairi was gone and as he already had a family, he didn't need another, but he let it slide. There was no point in ruffling feathers; they would be ruffled enough when they found out that the happy family might well be disbanded when the estate was sold.

'In that case,' he said graciously, 'Cal it is, but I may still call you Ellis, anyway.' He smiled lightly to show he was teasing, then sobered as he abruptly remembered he was at a wake for his dead relative and was surrounded by the people who had known and loved her.

'Do you mind if we don't go to the parlour?' Giselle asked.

Rocco didn't mind at all. The castle was large enough to find a quiet corner, although at this precise moment, he had no idea where that might be. And he was also beginning to regret asking to speak to her alone. They could have caught up another time. But he'd made a point of it now and he didn't want to backtrack, so he said, 'Of course not. Where do you suggest?'

'The loch has a jetty. We can go there.'

Rocco's eyebrows shot up. Out of the blue, he had a vision of another jetty where they'd caught the *vaporetto* from Murano Island back to Venice.

'Let's go.' He gestured towards the open double doors with a jerk of his head. 'I'll be back later,' he said to Fraser, ignoring the significant look that passed between Giselle and the receptionist.

Oh, well, he should expect gossip. He was an unknown quantity, even to Giselle. One night ten years ago didn't count for anything.

He waited until they were outside before he attempted to speak, but she beat him to it.

'It's a glorious day,' she said, leading him towards a narrow lane between the castle and a sizeable outbuilding.

Small talk? Really? OK, he could do small talk, if that's what was needed to break the ice, but what he actually wanted to ask was whether she'd found her vocation and what she'd been doing with herself. But why he was so interested wasn't a question he had the answer to.

'It is,' he agreed.

'It doesn't seem right to bury someone on a day like today.'

He supposed it didn't. 'Were you close?' It suddenly occurred to him that he knew absolutely nothing about her.

'I liked her a lot and respected her even more. She'll be sorely missed.'

'I'm sure she will be.'

Giselle's face was pale in the bright sunlight, like bleached bone or fine porcelain. Her eyes glimmered with unshed tears. Despite her grief, she was gorgeous, and he had an entirely inappropriate urge to kiss her.

'I'm sorry for your loss,' he said awkwardly.

'It was a heart attack.'

'I know.' The solicitor had informed him of this.

The tears spilt over to trickle silently down her cheeks. It was like watching an elf or a fairy cry. Should he try to comfort her? The thought of holding her made his heart leap. He really needed to get a grip on his emotions. Desire had no place here.

'It was my fault,' she announced miserably.

'Excuse me?'

'I was late. If I'd been on time, I might have been able to—' She broke off, pressing her lips together, and didn't say anything further until they rounded a corner and the loch came into view between the trees.

A small cottage lay directly ahead, and beyond it a sliver of beach and a wooden jetty. He could smell the tang of salt and seaweed. The midday sun was bright through the dappled leaves, and he could hear the cries of gulls along with the tweets and chirps of smaller birds in the branches overhead.

Then they left the trees behind and were walking on coarse sand, and he felt incongruous in his suit and tie as his polished black shoes sank into the golden grains beneath his feet.

'Do you want to tell me what happened?' he asked.

In another life he might have removed his jacket and tie and slipped out of his shoes. But not in this one. He wasn't here to play in the sand. Actually, why *was* he here, on this beach with Giselle? Why had he wanted to speak to her alone? Was it to ask her to be discreet about their prior relationship? If so, from the look Avril the receptionist had given him, that boat had already sailed. And what did it matter if they'd known each other briefly a decade ago? He'd been young, they both had, little more than teenagers on holiday. Who would care?

He should go back. He had work to do. No doubt there was a slew of emails in his inbox, and a plethora of messages on his phone, not to mention a report he really should have completed yesterday.

His hand crept to his trouser pocket, then dropped to his side without taking his phone out, and he followed Giselle onto the rickety wooden jetty instead.

She was in profile, staring out over the water, the sun turning her hair to platinum, the braid lying over her shoulder like thick rope, and he remembered digging his fingers into the silken strands.

Rocco inhaled deeply and let his breath out in a slow trickle. He could do without such memories invading his thoughts.

Woodenly, she said, 'I was supposed to be having coffee with her, but I was late. Too engrossed in my work. I lost track of time. Only for ten minutes. But those ten minutes could have made the difference. Between life and—' She spoke in disjointed sentences, and he could hear the pain in her voice.

Without meaning to, he found himself saying, 'My father died. Eight years ago. Car crash.' The words came out, bald and abrupt. They made her pause.

'I'm sorry. That must have been rough.'

He shrugged. It had been. Extremely.

Not wanting to talk about it, he changed the subject. 'It was a surprise seeing you at the church. I thought you were from... East Kilbride, was it?' Near Glasgow, he remembered her saying.

'I'm from Skye originally, born and bred. But we moved to East Kilbride when I was in my late teens. I live here now.'

'When you say *here*, do you mean Skye in general or Duncoorie in particular? Surely you don't live at the castle?' Might she be a member of staff and, as a consequence, live on site?

His time with Fraser – sorry, *Cal* – had been limited this morning and it hadn't been a question he'd thought to ask. He would ask it soon, though, because he wasn't sure where he stood when it came to property, tenants and eviction notices. That would be one for his lawyer.

She said, 'Technically, I live in Duncoorie, but my bothy is nearer to the castle than the village.'

'Bothy?'

'Cottage.'

Ah. Another Scottishism, along with 'kirk'. It was like a foreign language, one he had no intention of learning. 'Why did you return to Skye?'

'I never wanted to leave, but my dad got a job in Glasgow. I doubt you'll remember, but I have a twin sister. She was happy about the move – she enjoyed being able to travel into Glasgow – but I wasn't so keen. When I got the chance to come back, I took it.'

Rocco remembered her telling him she had a sister. There was nothing about Giselle and those days in Venice that he'd forgotten. Saying that, he forgot very little. His memory was one of his strengths, especially when it came to business.

'What do you do, jobwise?' he asked.

'I've got a studio at the craft centre. Didn't you know?'

'There's a great deal about Mhairi's affairs that I don't know.'

'I expect it's a lot to take in, but don't worry, Cal knows what he's doing. He'll keep the place going until you're ready to take up the reins.'

'I'm not here to take up the reins. I'm here to assess the estate with a view to putting it on the market.'

'You're *selling* it?'

'What else am I supposed to do with it? I have no use for a castle in the backend of nowhere, no matter how pretty the scenery. But someone will. There'll be an American or two who'll fancy themselves the lord of their very own Scottish estate.'

Giselle inhaled sharply and her navy eyes widened in dismay. 'But… but… what about the craft centre?' she stuttered.

'I'll have to have a good look over the books with my accountant, but I highly doubt the estate will be sold as a going concern. I mean, if you were buying this as a Scottish holiday home, your own slice of Highland heaven, you wouldn't want a bunch of tourists traipsing over it, would you?'

She was shaking her head in disbelief.

'Don't look at me like that,' he said. 'It makes perfect sense to sell it.'

'To you maybe. But not to me.' And with that, she whirled around and darted up the jetty.

Then she was gone, leaving him to find his own way back.

He stared after her, irritably, and it took him a while to realise that his ire had been joined by an equal measure of desire and intrigue.

His brief stay here could well be an interesting one.

Chapter 5

Giselle tore up the lane and dashed into the castle, only slowing when she entered the great hall. There were even more people here now than there had been fifteen minutes ago, and it took her a moment to locate Avril. Her friend had a glass in one hand and a plate in the other and was talking to Jinny.

'Psst!' Giselle hissed in Avril's ear.

Startled, Avril jumped, almost spilt her drink and had to do some nifty handwork with the plate to prevent the canapes from tumbling to the floor. She stared at her. 'Are you OK?'

'No,' Giselle said. She took the glass and the plate out of Avril's hands and put them on a nearby table. 'Come on.'

'Where are we going?'

'My studio.'

'Why?'

'I'll tell you when we get there. We'll go out the side door. I don't want to risk bumping into *him*.'

'Rocco Moore?'

'Shh!'

Avril lowered her voice. 'What's he done?'

'Nothing yet. It's what he's *about* to do.' Giselle grabbed her friend's hand and towed her out of the room towards the kitchen. The castle was a rabbit warren, but both knew their way around it, Avril better than Giselle.

Once outside, they skirted around the castle's eastern wall, Giselle bringing them to a halt as she peered around a corner.

There was no sign of Rocco, but the route to her studio was across the car park. Easily spottable. But there was no choice. She didn't feel safe in the castle, knowing he could appear at any moment. After all, the place belonged to him now, and he'd have every right to go delving into rooms. Even the guest bedrooms, since there weren't any guests at the moment, not with Mhairi's funeral taking place. And although the ladies' loos should be safe enough, Giselle didn't want to risk being overheard.

There was nothing for it: they'd have to make a run for it.

'One, two, three, go!' Giselle cried, tugging Avril into the open.

'Hang on, not so fast!' Avril protested. 'I'm wearing heels.'

Giselle showed no mercy, only letting go of her when they were safely through the studio door. She locked it behind them and wished there was a blind or something she could draw.

However, without the lights on, it wasn't easy to see inside, and the window display provided a decent barrier to curious eyes. Giselle didn't think Rocco would come looking for her, but one never knew. After all, he'd wanted to speak to her alone, and she wasn't entirely sure why.

'What happened?' Avril asked, dropping onto a low stool and easing off a shoe. She massaged her toes with a wince.

'He's selling Coorie Castle,' Giselle blurted.

'He *told* you that?'

She nodded. 'He said, and I quote, "I have no use for a castle in the backend of nowhere", or something along those lines.'

She was still in shock and wished she hadn't taken the glass of whatever it was away from Avril. They could have shared it; she could do with a drink right now. Whisky would be good. Several glasses should do the trick. And it wasn't just the shock of the castle potentially being sold. The shock of seeing Rocco, and the intense physical reaction she'd felt, had knocked her for six. Every part of her thrummed with remembered desire, and she was thoroughly ashamed for feeling that way on the day of Mhairi's funeral.

Avril slipped her shoe back on. 'We kind of expected something like that, though, didn't we? That whoever inherited the castle might want to sell it. It's not a total surprise that he does.'

'It's *who* he's thinking of selling it to which worries me,' Giselle said, her gaze flicking to the window and the castle beyond. Still no sign of him. Maybe he'd fallen off the jetty and drowned. It was a nice thought, but they wouldn't be that lucky.

'Who?' Avril demanded.

'An American.'

'Which one? There are a good few million of them.'

'Very funny – not. One with loads of money. One who wants to pretend he's a "Scottish laird".' She mimicked Rocco's posh English accent. 'One who wouldn't want tourists traipsing all over his property. He said that the craft centre will probably close.'

'*What?!*'

'Exactly.' Giselle slumped into the plastic chair she sat in when she did her paperwork. It was hard and uncomfortable, which might be why she disliked VAT and tax returns so much.

Avril's mouth was open in shock. Closing it, she said disbelievingly, 'He isn't going to sell it as a going concern?'

'Apparently not.'

'But the business is doing OK, I think. I mean, Mhairi seemed happy. Not that she ever discussed finances with me, but I never got the impression there was any reason to worry.'

'The first couple of years were a bit dodgy,' Giselle reminded her.

'But that was before the craft centre was properly established,' Avril replied. 'It's a real draw for tourists now.'

'Yeah, that's what Rocco doesn't seem to like.'

'How well did you know him? Where did you meet? Why haven't you told me any of this?' The last bit came out as a wail of indignation.

'Not well at all. Remember me telling you that I went on holiday to Milan with Izzy and some of her friends when we were nineteen? While they were doing the rounds of the fashion houses, I took the train to Venice. I met Rocco there and we explored the city together.'

And they'd also explored each other. That night was seared into her brain. *Well, it would be, wouldn't it*, she thought. A girl does tend to remember her first time, especially when her virginity is taken by an incredibly handsome man in one of the most beautiful cities in the world. Nothing since had compared to that experience, which was probably why she was still single. None of the dates she'd been on had been half as romantic as that. Nor the men half as... Charismatic? Sexy? Handsome? It had been a fairy-tale encounter with a gorgeous stranger, full of magic, mystery and lust. For a first sexual experience, a woman couldn't wish for anything better – unless you added love into the mix. Then it would have been perfect. But it had come pretty close, even without the emotional connection.

Afterwards, Giselle had worried she'd been too hasty, too easy, which was why she hadn't confided in Izzy. She felt guilty for not telling her sister, but they'd never been joined-at-the-hip twins, and besides, she'd had a kind of feeling that talking about it would diminish it somehow. Then there was the sea glass heart…

'There's something you're not telling me.' Avril squinted at her accusingly.

Giselle sighed. 'I slept with him.'

'Och, I don't blame you! He's hot. Unless he wasn't hot back then, but was weedy and spotty, with a basin haircut and jam-jar glasses.'

Another sigh. 'He was gorgeous.' It was her own fault she compared every man who'd ever asked her out to him since, and had found them wanting. *I mean*, she thought, *who could compete with Rocco and the red sea glass heart he gave me?* Inadvertently, he and the heart had been the beginning of the start of her adult life. When she'd returned to East Kilbride, she'd had renewed purpose, renewed faith in herself and the determination to follow her dreams.

Avril continued to study her. 'There's something else. You're not telling me the whole story.' She clapped a hand to her mouth and gasped. 'Don't tell me you fell in love with him? Or—?' She paused dramatically. 'He got you pregnant?'

'Neither of those.'

'He gave you a nasty disease? Stole your money and your passport? Had a wife?'

'He was only twenty-one!'

'So? He might have settled down early. That makes him... thirty-one now,' she added thoughtfully.

'And to think you worked that out without a calculator.'

Avril glowered. 'Tell me.'

Giselle rose and went over to the cabinet of slim drawers and took out the red heart. 'He gave me this. We were on the island of Murano, where the famous Venetian glass comes from, and we were sitting on some steps at the base of a lighthouse. We'd just eaten a picnic and were waiting for the ferry to take us back to San Marco, the main island.'

'It sounds so romantic,' Avril said dreamily.

'It was.' Giselle could almost feel the hot sun on her skin, smell the brine, hear the chatter of the people in the bars and cafes behind. Feel his lips on hers...

'Then what?'

Giselle blinked. 'He found this in the rocks near the lighthouse. There was no beach, just rocks and pebbles, and not a lot of those. This is my very first piece of sea glass.'

'And?' Avril prompted.

'It's because of him I knew I wanted to make sea glass pictures.'

'Is that it?'

'It's enough,' Giselle snapped. 'If it hadn't been for Rocco and the sea glass he gave me that day, I wouldn't be here now.'

'He who giveth can taketh away,' Avril murmured. 'Or something like that. How ironic.'

'It's not ironic – it's awful. You'll be out of a job too, you know.' Giselle felt sick. How on earth would she manage if the craft centre closed? Her mortgage was eye-wateringly high, and although she was able to keep her head above water by selling her pictures in the gift shop, if she no longer had that option, where would she sell them? The thought of trawling around all the shops on the island, trying to persuade them to carry her stock, made her stomach churn.

Avril's expression was equally concerned. 'I'm going to have to update my CV, aren't I? Unless…'

'Unless what?'

'You could persuade him to change his mind about selling the castle.'

'How do you suggest I do that?'

'Make him fall in love with you and beg him to give you the castle as a wedding present?'

'There isn't going to be a fairytale ending, you know. He isn't Prince Charming and I don't have a glass slipper or a fairy godmother.' Giselle slumped back in her seat, close to tears again. 'It's all my fault. If I hadn't been late, I might have been able to save Mhairi, and none of this would be happening.'

'Giselle, you've got to stop blaming yourself. Remember that Cal said she'd been dead for at least an hour. If anyone should blame themselves, it's me.'

Giselle stared at her through watery eyes. Avril's were equally damp. It didn't matter what Avril said, Giselle couldn't shake off her guilt. And now she had an additional load of it to carry: Rocco and his plan to sell the estate.

To think that for all these years she'd been measuring boyfriends and potential dates against an idolised version of a man she'd known for less than forty-eight hours!

What a waste. And what a disappointment. They say you should never meet your heroes, and they were right.

She'd thought of Rocco as a romantic, in love with beauty and history, but from the brief chat with him today, he clearly wasn't interested. For goodness' sake, he hadn't even noticed the breathtaking scenery when she'd taken him to the jetty just now!

He was still handsome – more so, if that was possible – and she still felt a visceral draw to him that had everything to do with her hormones and nothing to do with her intellect and common sense, but at least Giselle now knew one thing with absolute certainty: she could never fall in love with anyone who didn't love Skye, Duncoorie and this wild Scottish loch as much as she did.

Chapter 6

If Rocco had ever imagined meeting Giselle again (which he hadn't), it wouldn't have been at the funeral of a distant relative whom he'd never met, while he was planning on selling the property she'd left him, which would have a direct effect on Giselle herself. *Honestly*, he thought, *you couldn't write this stuff.*

Feeling aggrieved, he strolled back to the castle and immediately went to his room. He should have stuck to his original plan of not attending the wake, but he hadn't been able to resist the lure of speaking to her. He'd felt as though the spirit of their carefree youth had come back to him at the sight of her.

But you can't go back, can you? And it would be a fool's errand to try…

Taking off his jacket, he loosened his tie, flopped onto the bed and took out his phone, eyeing the laptop on the small desk under the window with disgruntlement. He wasn't in the mood to work, but he knew he should. It was also lunchtime, and he was hungry, so he phoned reception and asked for room service. But apparently such a thing didn't exist.

'Are there any staff in the kitchen today?' he asked, reining in his irritation.

'They're at the wake, Mr Moore.' Was it his imagination or was there an unspoken censure to the man's answer – that's where *you* should be…

'Can you find someone to rustle me up a spot of lunch?' Then he added, as an afterthought, 'Please.'

'I suppose I could ask Cook?'

'Good idea. Something light, a salad perhaps. And bring it to my room.' As he was replacing the receiver he heard the receptionist say, 'Certainly, sir,' and Rocco felt a little guilty at dragging Cook (who, he'd now discovered, had once been Mhairi's cook for as long as anyone could remember, and Cook wasn't her surname but her title) away from the wake, but he could hardly be expected to sort out his own lunch.

According to Cal, guests were booked into the hotel from tomorrow, so normal service should hopefully be resumed. Which reminded him: he needed to ask Cal about the occupancy situation with a view to agreeing on a date beyond which no new bookings would take place. Or should he instruct the man to operate the estate as normal until the castle had a confirmed buyer? At least the paying guests and tourists visiting the craft centre would continue to provide a steady income, which would ensure the estate wouldn't fall into a state of disrepair. It could pay its own way while it was up for sale. Decisions, decisions…

His instinct was to wind things up as quickly as possible, to get rid of the estate so he could bank the money, but he didn't want to let it go for a song simply because he couldn't be bothered with the inconvenience of having to deal with it until such time as a buyer was found.

Rocco was at the window admiring the view again when a knock on the door informed him that his lunch had arrived. Instructing the guy to put the tray on the table next to his laptop, he decided he'd better make some inroads into his undoubtedly overflowing inbox while he ate.

The ever-efficient Nora had deleted the irrelevant, forwarded that which could be forwarded and starred those emails needing his attention. She'd also sent him several emails of her own, each with a succinct subject line.

Pleased to see there was nothing time critical, Rocco worked his way through them, responding where necessary, and he'd just eaten a final mouthful of Caesar salad when he realised it was time for the tour of his property so he could take a look at what he'd inherited. And as he changed into something less formal, he hoped he might see Giselle, for no other reason than she reminded him of a time when he'd been free to just *be*.

As Cal showed him around the estate, Rocco learnt that the castle specialised in crafting breaks and that most people who stayed in one of its sixteen guest bedrooms enjoyed making pots or blowing glass or other such arty stuff, and that it catered to the upmarket crowd who were happy to pay for exclusivity.

The rest of the estate's inventory was impressive: as well as Mhairi's private suite, there was a dining room and a guest lounge, a drawing room, a parlour (aka Mhairi's office), a staircase inside a turret, a great hall (where the wake had been held), a library… And that was just the castle itself. Rocco also owned a converted boathouse, the cottage Cal and his partner lived in, the jetty where he'd stood with Giselle earlier, a maze, a duck pond, gardens, woodland – and the craft centre. Rocco didn't ask Cal to show him around each studio (he wasn't overly interested, to be honest) but he took a keener interest in one of them when Cal told him it was rented by Giselle.

Well, well, well… Sea glass, eh?

He had a flashback of scorching sun, the smell of seawater and coffee, waves lapping at the rocks at the base of a gleaming white lighthouse and a beautiful girl lounging on the steps of it, like a silver-haired siren. And a heart-shaped piece of frosted red glass. When he'd given it to her, her eyes had lit up, and he'd kissed her under the hot Venetian sun until he hadn't been able to kiss her anymore.

So she found her vocation, he mused, peering through the window at the display.

'Would you like to see the gift shop?' Cal asked.

Rocco would have liked to see Giselle instead, but the studio's lights were off, and as there was no one inside, he agreed. He was quietly impressed with the items for sale in the shop. Clearly the crafters were a talented bunch of people.

He skirted past a display of three doll's houses, remarkable for their attention to miniature detail, and came to a halt in front of a sizeable picture of the loch, the castle and the mountains flanking it. It was skilfully done, if a tad twee for his taste, the scene captured in various shades of sea glass, tiny pebbles and small shells.

It looked good hanging on the white wall of the shop.

The price tag made him raise an eyebrow. It didn't seem nearly enough for the amount of work that must have gone into it. He would have paid double that, if he liked that kind of thing. He could see the appeal to tourists, though, and taking something like this home as a memento of a Scottish holiday was better than a tea towel printed with 'I♥Skye'.

'I've seen enough,' he declared, and didn't miss the expression of relief that flickered across Cal's face before he masked it.

Feeling a little wicked, Rocco said, 'How long will it take to clear Mhairi's suite of her personal possessions? I'm thinking of moving in there for the duration.'

'The duration?'

'I'll be staying a little longer than planned. I won't be leaving tomorrow after all. Will that be a problem?' He hadn't realised the estate was so large, and it would take more than today to get to grips with it.

He could sense the man itching to ask how much longer, but all Cal said was, 'Not at all. I'll get someone on it straight away. What would you like me to do with her things?' He swallowed, and Rocco felt a dart of remorse.

'Actually, never mind. My current room is fine, as long as it's not needed. But her personal effects will have to be gone through and disposed of at some point.'

'Charity shops?'

'If you like. But let me take a look first.' Rocco wasn't bothered about what happened to her clothes. He'd only had a glance at the bedroom, sitting room and bathroom which made up Mhairi's private rooms, but he was confident there would be some things that shouldn't be given away, like her jewellery, for instance. And the photos he'd glimpsed.

He had to admit to being curious about this particular branch of his family tree. His great-great-grandfather, Tandy Gray, had produced two children: Mhairi's father, who had inherited the Scottish estate from Tandy, and Rocco's great-grandmother, who'd been married off to a man by the name of Moore. Mhairi had never married, and the Moores hadn't been particularly fecund, only producing Rocco's grandfather, who had married an Italian woman. Rocco had his *nonna* to thank for his Mediterranean colouring and his grandfather to thank for his smoke-grey eyes. Rocco's father had been an only child too. However, Rocco did vaguely remember being told stories of a relation who lived in a castle in Scotland, but he'd taken little notice. Until his mother had called him into her office.

And now here he was, for the first time in possibly forever, contemplating his roots.

Did he feel any connection to this land, this castle, where he presumed his great-grandmother had been born and raised?

None whatsoever, but if there were private papers and photos, he thought it best to keep them for posterity, so to speak, and also because he was interested in history, which was one of the reasons he'd wanted to visit Venice all those years ago.

He and his mate had also trailed around Paris, Rome, Prague, Vienna and numerous other places, until one historic building had begun to look like another, and the cities had blended into one.

Apart from Venice. Venice had stood out in his memory because of Giselle.

As Rocco climbed the staircase to his room, he smiled to himself. An erotic and passionate night with a gorgeous girl was bound to stick in any guy's memory. How ironic he should meet her again here, of all places.

As he reached his door, he changed his mind about doing some work and turned on his heel, heading to the south-west turret and Mhairi's rooms instead. He may as well get started, and there was no time like the present. After all, that was the reason he was here, to sort things out, not take a trip down memory lane or immerse himself in Mhairi Gray's past.

But as he pushed open the door, his phone rang, startling him.

'How is the mouldering old pile?' his mother asked.

'Old but not mouldering.' He was surprised to discover he felt a little defensive about it being called *mouldering*. 'It's quite impressive, actually.'

He glanced out of the window, his gaze drawn to the boathouse and jetty, and the white-tipped waves. The wind had picked up, he noticed. It looked choppy out there, and he didn't envy anyone out on it. He wasn't the best of sailors; the ferry from Venice to the town of Poreč in Croatia was the last time he'd been on a boat, and he'd been sick for the whole of the three-and-a-half-hour crossing. He much preferred planes as a mode of transport, but cars were his passion, especially his Aston Martin DB9 in midnight blue.

Beverly asked, 'What are your thoughts?'

He assumed she was referring to the estate's value. 'Several million, but exactly how much is yet to be determined.'

'You should have let Claire come with you. Or you could have handed it over to Jermyns. I'm sure they can find a rich American with Scottish heritage who would kill to own a piece of history. You needn't have bothered going all that way.'

'I wanted to see it for myself.' He hadn't wanted to hand it over to the estate agent to sell sight unseen, and he definitely hadn't wanted Claire to accompany him. This was his issue to deal with and nothing whatsoever to do with the business, although he may well ask her advice if he needed to. He'd speak to Jermyns soon, though, because their reputation for selling upmarket property was second to none, and besides, he would need it valued for probate. Anyway, it wasn't every day one came into possession of a castle, and part of him (the little boy who'd once owned a wooden fort and a boxful of toy soldiers) wanted to revel in its ownership, even if it was only for a short while.

Changing the subject, Rocco filled her in on a development with one of their clients, but as he spoke, his mind was only half on the job. The other half was bubbling with increasing excitement. It had been easy to be objective and clinical about this unexpected inheritance when he'd been the best part of seven hundred miles away, but now he was within its walls, the reality of owning it was beginning to sink in.

Thank you, Mhairi, he thought.

'When are you due back?' Beverly asked.

'Not sure. I'd originally planned to fly back tomorrow, but I might stay a little longer. There's a lot to get through. If that's all right with you?'

He could sense her exasperation as she asked, 'How much longer?'

'Three days?' He wished he didn't sound as though he was asking her permission. 'Don't worry; I can work from here.'

Her voice was sharp. 'This really is quite inconvenient, Rocco.'

He wanted to retort that it wasn't his fault Mhairi had popped her clogs and left him a bloody great big castle at the other end of the country, but there was no mileage in annoying her.

All he said was, 'I appreciate that, but there's a significant amount of money involved. *My* money.' Or it would be his money once the property was sold.

She said shortly, 'Let the professionals handle it – that's what we pay them for.'

'Don't worry, I will. But you're the one who says to dot the i's and cross the t's. That's what I'm doing.' She could hardly argue against her own advice, could she?

She didn't. 'Very well. Keep me appraised.'

'Don't I always, Mother?' he teased, hoping to lighten her mood and vowing to do his best to ensure his absence had minimal impact. As long as the internet connection remained fast and stable, he shouldn't have any problems maintaining his usual work schedule.

'Don't let the staff hear you call me that or they'll think we're related,' she shot back, and he chuckled. Mission accomplished – her mood had been suitably lightened. 'Am I going to have to call you *my laird* when I next see you?' Her laugh tinkled in his ear. It was something he'd not heard often since his dad died and Beverly had been forced to run the business by herself.

'I don't believe a title came with my inheritance,' he told her.

'That's a pity.' Then she was all business once more. 'Keep me updated,' she reminded him, and he heaved a sigh of relief when she ended the call.

He enjoyed what he did – keeping his father's company alive and thriving – but sometimes he could do with a break.

Like now, for instance. He couldn't remember the last time he'd been on holiday, had taken some time purely for himself.

As he turned his attention back to the room that had once belonged to Mhairi Gray, Rocco felt a frisson of something. He just hoped it was curiosity, and not her ghost coming to remonstrate with him for selling off her home.

Chapter 7

Yet another day dawned with Giselle ensconced in her chair outside the bothy, having slept poorly. She was trying to work out how she was to make a living once the castle changed hands. She'd attempted to look on the bright side, that someone might buy the castle and craft centre as a going concern, but she knew she was clutching at straws. With Mhairi's passing, an era had ended and nothing would ever be the same again.

Giselle wished she could summon the energy to make her usual early morning trek to the loch, but she felt too sad, too despondent. What was the point? Very soon she might be packing up the contents of the studio and handing back the keys. And most likely, she'd also be packing up the bothy and handing those keys back to the mortgage company as well.

Damn Rocco Moore.

She sat for a while longer, hoping the peace and beauty of the morning would soothe her, but when her phone rang she was glad of the interruption to her melancholy thoughts.

'Where are you?' Izzy demanded. Her sister's face beamed out of the screen, lightly tanned and perfectly made up. She looked so together and so gorgeous that it made her heart ache.

Giselle felt self-conscious, wrapped in an old blanket with her hair a tangled mess. 'At the bothy.' She turned the screen to show her twin the view.

Izzy did the same. She was walking along a busy street and the backdrop to Izzy's voice was rumbling engines and honking horns. 'I thought you'd be rock scrabbling or dibbling about on the beach,' she said, her face once again filling the screen. 'It looks like a nice day in Duncoorie.'

'It is.'

'Then why aren't you annoying the crabs and seagulls?'

Giselle managed a small smile at her sister's teasing. She knew Izzy was immensely proud of her and very supportive, just as Giselle was of her. 'Why aren't *you* designing something fabulous instead of stomping along the street?'

'Because I'm phoning *you*, silly. Anyway, I'm on my way to work right now. Why aren't you?'

'Didn't feel like it.'

'Oh, Zelle, was the funeral really bad?'

'No worse than expected. The service was lovely.'

'There's no need to be brave about it. I know how much Mhairi meant to you. I only met her a couple of times, but she was such a lovely woman.'

'She was.' Giselle paused. 'The new owner was there.'

'Who is it?'

'A cousin, apparently.'

'What's he like?'

As gorgeous as I remember. 'He's going to sell the castle.'

Giselle watched Izzy cross the road before her twin replied. 'In a way, you can't blame him. If someone handed me an old castle, I'd sell up, too.'

'I know, but...'

'You're worried,' Izzy finished.

That was an understatement. 'Just a bit. He thinks it'll go to a wealthy American with Scottish heritage, who won't want busloads of tourists traipsing through the castle grounds.'

'It might be sold to someone who *likes* tourists. They mightn't keep the castle going as a hotel, but the craft centre is a good little earner, I bet.'

'Hmm.' Giselle wasn't convinced. She'd worked so hard to make a life for herself on Skye – a life she loved – that anything which threatened it was going to worry her. It was the uncertainty that was the worst. At least if she knew for definite one way or the other then she could plan. Although *what* she would plan was beyond her ken right now.

'I wish I was there to give you a hug,' Izzy said. 'You look as though you need one.'

'I do. Please say you'll visit soon.' Izzy had more disposable income than Giselle, so it was far more likely that her sister would come to Skye than it was for Giselle to go to Milan. She played her trump card. 'Mum and Dad would love to see you.'

'I'll try, but work is so hectic at the moment. It's not long until Fashion Week.'

'It's always Fashion Week,' Giselle grumbled.

'Only twice a year.'

'Aye, in *Milan*. What about New York, Paris, Berlin…?'

'You forgot London.'

'That was in June, and Mum and Dad went there to see you. You didn't come to Scotland.'

'I know, Zelle, and I'm sorry. You should have come with them.'

Giselle would have done if she could have afforded it. Their parents would have paid if they'd known how strapped for cash she was, but she hadn't wanted to worry them. She was almost thirty: she should be able to stand on her own two feet without accepting handouts. She'd contemplated trying to get a part-time job for a few weeks to supplement her income, but the tourist season in Skye took off in April, so all her energy had been focused on her art and the studio. And, as a rule, she got by on what she earnt. It was just the extras she couldn't afford — like expensive trips to London.

Izzy broke into her thoughts. 'Keep your chin up, Zelle. Gotta run, speak later. *Ciao*.'

'Bye,' Giselle said to a blank screen. Reluctantly, she got to her feet. There was no point sitting here fretting. She may as well go to the studio and make some more pictures, while she still could.

Rocco stretched, the vertebrae in his lower spine clicking as he did so, making him wince, and surveyed the damage. Piles of papers, letters and photos were dotted around Mhairi's sitting room, but at least they were in some kind of order. Sort of. Without going through them with a fine-toothed comb, he wouldn't know what to keep and what to throw out, but he didn't have time for that now. He would have them boxed up and arrange for them to be sent to his house in London, where he could pick through them at his leisure. Or put them in the attic. He had an inkling he'd do the latter. Life was too busy to be spent reading crinkle-cornered letters and studying black-and-white photos of people he wouldn't have a hope in hell of identifying.

Mhairi's sitting room sported a kettle, a solid earthenware teapot and a tin of loose-leafed Lady Grey tea. He preferred coffee to tea, but he'd been working for most of the day and was thirsty, so he made himself a cup.

As he waited for the kettle to boil, he strolled over to one of the wide windows.

This, he decided, must be the best room in the castle. With a double aspect, it had views to the south and the west, and all of it was of sky, mountains and water, with a few trees to frame it.

He watched the play of sunlight and cloud across the loch and the purpled hills beyond, and couldn't decide whether it was shortbread-biscuit-tin pretty or wild and untamed.

He supposed it depended on one's perspective – and the weather. Yesterday and today had been bright and sunny, a bit breezy at times, but warm. He imagined it would be very different in the throes of a gale, or in the depths of winter. Right now, the scene was a calm one, with several boats on the water.

Movement near to the castle caught his eye and he glimpsed someone walking down the lane, the figure partly obscured by the trees as it headed for the shoreline.

It was unmistakably Giselle, and his heart gave a jolt.

Without stopping to consider what he was doing, Rocco bolted to the door and careened down the winding staircase.

By the time he found his way onto the lane, she was nowhere in sight, so he carried on walking in the direction he'd seen her heading.

Past the former boathouse, past Cal's cottage, the narrow sliver of beach was empty, the jetty devoid of life apart from a large white gull with a wicked beak and a gimlet stare, who watched him with wary anticipation. Rocco eyed it suspiciously, thankful he didn't have a portion of fish and chips in his possession, as he might have had a battle on his hands. The seagull looked like it could hold its own in a fight. It flew off with a coarse squawk, and Rocco turned his back on it to gaze along the shoreline, one hand shielding his eyes from the sun's glare.

A silhouette shimmered in the distance, picking its way over the rocks at the far end of the beach, and he recognised Giselle. Every so often she would bend over and peer at the ground. He assumed she was looking for fragments of sea glass and pretty pebbles, but she could just as easily be collecting whelks for her lunch or searching for washed-up pirate treasure, for all he knew.

Without knowing what he was going to say to her, he began to follow.

It was easy at first, over the soft sand, becoming more difficult when the beach petered out. He found he had to watch where he put his feet, and he wished he was wearing shoes with better soles. His tan brogues weren't designed for rock hopping.

Little pools contained stranded clumps of kelp, and the occasional darting fish no longer than his finger, which were almost translucent. Another pool held a crab the size of his palm, with wicked-looking pincers. And everywhere there were barnacles or whelks clinging to the damp rocks. And seaweed. Lots of seaweed.

'Found anything interesting?' Giselle's voice startled him, and he looked up from his rockpool gazing to find her regarding him quizzically.

'A crab,' he said. 'And little fish.'

'There's a starfish in that one.' She pointed, and he noticed a five-fingered (legged? tentacled?) starfish, coral-coloured against the dark rock.

'Oh, wow.' The small boy that he'd once been longed for a bucket and a net. Rock pooling, that's what it was called, and he remembered the excitement and anticipation of turning over a pebble and seeing what wonders hid beneath.

'Look.' She held out a hand. A piece of dull blue glass sat in her palm. It didn't look particularly exciting, but from the shine on Giselle's face she was thrilled. 'It's probably from an old Milk of Magnesia bottle or Vicks VapoRub, or even from an old poison bottle.'

'Poison?'

She nodded. 'At the start of the twentieth century it became law to sell poisonous substances in easily recognisable bottles, and because so many people were unable to read, the bottles had ridges or were hexagonal in shape, so they couldn't be mistaken for anything else, not even in a dark cupboard. Some even had things like a skull or crossbones on them. And the most popular colour for a poison bottle was blue.'

He studied her face as she spoke, the spark in her eyes stirring something within that he didn't have a name for. Envy, maybe? Or lust? It was more likely lust.

'You found your passion.'

'Yes.'

'I saw your pictures.' She said nothing, so he added, 'The one in the gift shop, the big one of the loch, is impressive.'

'Just the one?'

'They all are. You have a talent.'

'Thank you. What's yours?'

'Making money,' he replied, without thinking.

'It sounds like a curse.'

'It is if you don't have any,' he retorted.

'I doubt whether you know what that's like.'

She had a point; he didn't. But his father had worked bloody hard to make his asset management business a success, and so had his mother, who'd had to take over the reins after his father died. They hadn't had it as easy as Giselle assumed. Yes, they were relatively well off, but it hadn't always been the case. And Rocco hadn't had everything handed to him on a silver platter, either. Apart from this castle, which had been a totally unexpected windfall.

'Money makes the world go round,' he countered.

'Wrong. Love does.'

'Love doesn't put food on the table or a roof over your head.'

'Money doesn't buy you happiness.'

'Maybe not, but you'll be a damned sight more miserable without it.'

'When is enough money enough? Or do you just keep making it, ad infinitum?'

'I don't make it for me. I make it for my clients.'

'Is that what asset managers do?'

'You remembered?' He was surprised.

'You said you had a job to go to in January.'

'I did. My father's firm. He owned an asset management company.'

'Do you own it now?'

He could see her assessing him and finding him lacking, but in what, he wasn't sure. 'No. My mother does; I work for her.' Technically true. He did. But he was also a director and a shareholder, and the business would be his one day.

'Oh.' She subsided a fraction, and he resisted the urge to stick his tongue out at her. She quickly rallied. 'You won't be short of a penny or two when you sell the castle.' She made it sound as though having money was a cardinal sin.

Anger flared. 'I suppose you'd like to help me spend it?' he snapped. 'Exotic holidays, fine restaurants, designer labels?'

She looked pointedly at his leather brogues, now damp from the salt water. 'Hardly! I don't need an exotic holiday when I've got *this* on my doorstep.' She swept a theatrical arm at the loch. 'And what use are designer labels on a beach?' Another glance at his shoes.

His anger ebbed as swiftly as it had arrived, and he felt amusement stirring. 'How about fine restaurants?'

'I prefer fish and chips from the chippie,' she replied loftily.

'So, if I invited you to dinner at the castle, you'd refuse?' His lips twitched.

'Actually, I would.'

Her answer surprised him, but he wasn't entirely certain she wasn't calling his bluff. 'Dine with me tonight,' he urged.

'No, thanks. I'm not joking: I really do prefer a portion of chips and a piece of cod from the chip shop.'

'Fish and chips it is, then,' he said. 'I'll pick you up at seven.'

Her mouth opened and closed like the fish in the rock pool, before she finally said, 'You can't; you don't know where I live.'

'I can find out. Your address will be on the studio's lease agreement.'

'That's cheating.'

'I call it ingenuity. See you at seven.' He didn't give her the chance to refuse, striding away over the rocks and hoping he wouldn't twist an ankle.

He also hoped she would be in when he arrived to pick her up, because from the look on her face, he wasn't entirely sure she would be.

Chapter 8

Giselle seriously contemplated hiding from Rocco that evening. The bedroom area on the mezzanine floor would work. No matter how many windows he peered through, he'd never see her up there if she stayed low.

Or she could simply not be in. That was the easiest option. She could go for a walk on the hillside above the bothy. It was a nice evening, the earlier breeze having subsided, and she wasn't unduly hungry despite having eaten little at lunchtime, as her appetite seemed to have deserted her somewhat since she'd found Mhairi in the parlour. And discovering that Rocco intended to sell Coorie Castle hadn't helped.

She didn't want to see him or speak to him. Even though she could kind of understand why he would want to sell it after talking to Izzy, but understanding didn't make it any easier to bear. She tried to take heart from her sister's suggestion that he might sell it to someone who would keep it open. But she still didn't want to see Rocco.

Avoiding him shouldn't be too difficult. According to Avril, he'd be leaving in a day or so. She'd simply stay out of his way tomorrow and possibly the next day, then he'd be gone.

At six thirty, she had her hiking boots in her hand and was about to put them on when Jinny phoned.

'How are you, hen?'

'I'm fine.' It was her stock answer.

'Is everything all right with you and our new boss?'

'Why do you ask?' she replied cautiously, hoping Avril hadn't told everyone about her history with the man.

'Because he wanted to speak to you somewhere private yesterday, after the funeral. What was all that about?'

Giselle knew she couldn't keep it secret, and anyway, she'd done nothing wrong and had nothing to be ashamed of – not when it came to her past association with Rocco. However, she continued to feel that it *was* her fault he was here. Ten minutes could have made all the difference...

She said, 'He recognised me. We met years ago when I was on holiday in Venice.'

Before she could say anything further, Jinny cried, '*Ooh!* A holiday fling! I don't blame you, he's scrummy.'

Avril, bless her, had kept Giselle's promise, despite her job being on the line as much as anyone's.

'Don't get your knickers in a twist. It wasn't like that.' The word 'fling' grated a little. It had been far more romantic than a fling. Or so it had seemed at the time. 'Fling' just sounded sordid, but she supposed that was precisely what it had been, especially now, with what she knew of the man. Not that she knew a lot, but it was more than she'd known back then.

Jinny continued, 'You missed a trick there. If I wasn't happily married...' She heaved an overly dramatic sigh, then collected herself. 'You still haven't said why he wanted to talk to you in private.'

'Bloody hell. You're like a dog with a bone,' Giselle grumbled.

'Seriously, is everything OK?'

'Not really. He happened to let slip that he's planning on selling Coorie Castle.' Giselle didn't want Rocco's plans to come as a surprise to the others, and she doubted whether he'd have the courtesy to tell them himself. He was probably regretting telling *her*, because until he actually sold the place, he would no doubt want it to carry on bringing money in. A nice little earner, as Izzy had put it.

Jinny whistled through her teeth. 'More change, then. Let's hope someone nice buys it, although there'll never be another Mhairi.'

'He mentioned selling it to someone who'd want it as a private home.'

'They'll need to have deep pockets,' Jinny said. 'Mhairi found that out, which was why she turned the outbuildings into a craft centre and began hosting crafting breaks.'

'He mentioned an American with Scottish heritage.'

'He mentioned quite a bit, did your Rocco.'

'He's not my Rocco.'

'Do you think he's already got a buyer in mind?' Jinny sounded worried now.

'I don't know.'

'Can you find out?'

'I doubt it.'

'Try? *Please?* Cal is being close lipped, probably because he's been ordered to be, but the new boss seems to talk to you.'

Giselle stared at her hiking boots and pulled a face. Was there any point in finding out? It wasn't as though they could do anything about it even if they *did* know. But she owed it to Jinny and the others, so she swapped the boots for ballet flats and declared herself ready for a fish supper with a man she still fancied but wasn't sure she particularly liked.

Rocco's car might have been a rental (he'd flown to Inverness, she'd been informed, and had driven to Skye from there) but it was a top-of-the-range rental. Not that Giselle knew much about cars, as she simply wasn't interested. She'd passed her driving test at eighteen, but she didn't own a car (she couldn't afford to keep it on the road, let alone buy it) and used public transport if she couldn't walk to where she wanted to go.

Rocco arrived on time, bumping the silver saloon over the potholes in the dirt track leading to the bothy. When the vehicle was close enough for her to see his face, she smiled to herself as he winced each time a tyre sank into one of the mini mine shafts.

'You could have warned me I'd need a tractor,' he grumbled as she got in.

'You didn't give me a chance. Anyway, it's not that bad.'

His brows rose in disbelief. 'My spine will never be the same again. How do you stand it? Or do you actually have a tractor?'

'I walk.'

'Pardon?'

'You know, using your legs and putting one foot in front of the other until you arrive at where you want to be.'

'Is that sarcasm?'

Her smile was forced. 'I'm never sarcastic,' she replied sarcastically.

'You walk? You don't have a car or a motorbike?'

'I have a bicycle, but the chain's rusty and the tyres are flat.'

'I can get someone to fix that, if you want.'

'I *don't* want.' Her tone was sharp. She neither wanted nor appreciated his charity. Besides, she hated that bloody bike. The damned thing might get her from A to B faster than her feet, but the cost to her behind on the knife-edge saddle was unacceptable. The last time she'd used it to go to Portree, she hadn't been able to sit down for a week. If she could have afforded to buy and run a car, she would, but as she couldn't, she walked. Or caught the bus.

As she buckled her seatbelt, she was aware of Rocco sneaking a look at her out of the corner of her eye.

'I don't care for bikes,' she explained, in a less acerbic tone. He was only trying to help, she reasoned. Or he was flashing his cash around. Either way, he owned the estate, and she was renting a studio from said estate, so was there really any point in antagonising him, even if he wouldn't be her landlord for long?

As he gingerly drove down the track (with more wincing and several muttered oaths) Giselle took the opportunity to examine him properly while his concentration was on his driving.

Same aquiline nose, same strong jaw, shorter hair but with a hint of the curl she remembered. Smoky grey eyes, long lashes, nicely shaped lips and a light tan that she knew was his natural skin tone. *All* over.

A blush whooshed into her cheeks, and she hastily looked away.

'Well?' he asked, his eyes straight ahead. 'What's the verdict?'

'Excuse me?'

'Have I changed much?'

For a second, she feared he'd been asking whether she liked what she was seeing. For the record, she did. Jinny was right, he *was* scrummy. As scrummy as he'd been all those years ago. But whereas at twenty-one he'd still had an air of youth about him, a decade later he was all man. Fit, sexy man.

Giselle was disconcerted to find she was as attracted to him now as she'd been back then. She'd have to keep a lid on that, for several reasons, all of them as valid as each other, but the main one was that he owned the castle and her future rested on that. Besides, even if that hadn't been the case and he was in Duncoorie for a holiday, he lived in London and she lived here. He liked the finer things in life, and she didn't care for them – he'd worn leather shoes to go rock pooling, for goodness' sake! In every aspect, they were total opposites, including looks. If anyone saw them together, they'd think he was yin and she was yang. Black and white, dark and light, Italian and Scandi blonde—

He cut into her thoughts. 'I take it from your silence that I have changed and not for the better.'

'You're putting words in my mouth.'

'Only because you don't seem to have any of your own,' he countered.

'Do you know where you're going?'

'The Codfather. We did say fish and chips from the chip shop, didn't we?'

'*I* didn't – *you* did.'

'If I recall, it was *you* who said you preferred it to dining at the castle.'

'That's not what I meant.'

He raised an eyebrow, the corners of his mouth lifting in a smirk. She wanted to wipe it off his face, and she would have done if she'd been able to think of a suitable retort. She *had* said that, and it was true, she did prefer it.

'Did you visit Paris?' he asked.

The change of subject took her by surprise. 'No, but maybe one day.'

'You liked history, I seem to recall.'

'You seem to recall a lot,' she retorted.

'That's because I haven't forgotten *anything*.' His emphasis on the last word and what that might entail sucked the air from her lungs, especially when he followed it up with a sweeping glance that travelled down the length of her body and back up again until his gaze met hers.

'Keep your eyes on the road,' she snapped.

He smirked again, but did as she asked, and she was relieved beyond measure when the car glided to a halt outside the chip shop. She was out of her seat and on the pavement before he could unclick his seat belt.

'Fish supper?' she asked, feeling a little breathless. 'Or do you prefer a pie or a portion of chicken?'

'What's a fish supper?'

'It's what we call fish and chips.'

'I'll go with the fish supper.' He got out of the car, saying, 'This is my shout. After all, I did invite you to dinner.'

'I can pay my own way.'

'I'm not suggesting you can't.'

'Halfsies?'

'You mean go Dutch?'

'Yes, that's what I said, halfsies.'

'I'll have to pay, and you can owe me. I don't have any cash on me.'

'Of course you don't.'

'And you do?'

She patted her chest, and he guffawed. 'Please don't tell me you still keep your money down your bra!'

'It's the safest place for it. Money can fall out of pockets.' She also had her house key in the left cup, but she wasn't going to tell him that.

'What about your mobile phone?' he asked.

'I didn't bring it with me.'

'You're not some hippy chick who lives off-grid, are you?'

'Hippy chick? How 1960s of you. No, I'm not. I just don't see the point in carrying it everywhere.'

From the pained expression on his face, she assumed his phone was surgically attached to him. 'That must be… freeing,' he said after a pause.

'It is. You should try it sometime. Do you want a can of pop?'

His lips twitched. 'I suppose I'd better have something to wash my fish supper down, since I doubt they'll have champagne.'

She didn't flinch at his barbed comment. 'No champagne, but they'll probably give you a wee dram of whisky, if you ask nicely.'

His loud guffaw made her jump. 'I'll stick to cola, since I'm driving.'

There was a mild tussle when it was time to pay, which Giselle won because she told Shawn, who owned the place, that Rocco's card was probably stolen and that he'd be better off insisting on cash only. Shawn gave her a dubious look, followed by an even more dubious one aimed at Rocco.

'That's my reputation in tatters,' Rocco joked as she handed over some notes.

'I wouldn't worry about it. You won't be here long enough. Aren't you leaving tomorrow or the next day?'

'No.'

'When?' Her heart skipped a beat.

'Friday, probably. There's a great deal to go through.'

She should be able to avoid him for two more days. Mind you, she wasn't doing too well so far, was she? She blamed Jinny for asking her to find out whether Rocco already had a buyer in mind.

'Where shall we go to eat this?' he asked, hefting the paper-wrapped parcel containing his portion of fish and chips. 'The car?'

'Good grief, no!' Far too intimate. It had been bad enough sitting so close to him for the five-minute drive from her house. Talk about feeling trapped and claustrophobic! Ignoring the voice in her head arguing that it wasn't *trapped* she'd felt, she said, 'Let's go down to the loch.'

There was a pretty place at the far end of the village where the burn trickled into the sea. It sported a couple of picnic tables and a view of the water. Giselle couldn't think of anywhere nicer to eat her supper, even if she was forced to eat it with Rocco.

She plonked her bottom down on one of the benches, expecting him to sit opposite, but he squeezed in next to her, his jean-clad thigh almost touching hers. She scooted over a bit, disconcerted at his nearness when there was all this space around them. Was he deliberately trying to unsettle her, she wondered, determined for it not to work.

As she unwrapped the fragrant parcel, the aroma of vinegary chips and hot batter wafted up her nose and her stomach rumbled. Realising she was hungry, she popped a piping hot chip into her mouth and tried to cool it by sucking in air around it.

' 'Ot,' she mumbled, desperately wanting to chew but scared of burning her already scalded tongue even more. She fanned her open mouth, embarrassment whooshing through her. She'd been a klutz when they'd first met, and it looked as though she still was. How galling.

When her face had cooled, along with the chip, she proceeded to eat her supper with a little more caution, pondering how best to broach the subject of potential wealthy buyers waiting in the wings for a castle to come on the market.

'I bet it isn't as stunning as this where you live,' was her opening gambit.

'Nowhere near it.' His attention was on the view, and she suddenly understood why he'd chosen to sit next to her, rather than have his back to it. He continued, 'No wonder so many people come here. The scenery is outstanding.'

'And many of those people pop into the craft centre,' she said. Subtle? No, but she didn't think beating around the bush would do it.

'I noticed. Cal reckons there are at least three or four coach trips a day, plus the motor home and caravan lot, as well as the cottage renters and the bed and breakfasters.'

She was nodding vigorously, until he added, 'I bet it's not half as busy in the winter. In fact, I know it's not.'

About to ask him how he knew, she realised he'd probably viewed the accounts. 'Is that why you want to sell it to a wealthy American?' she ventured, licking her fingers.

'I don't care what nationality the buyer is, as long as they can meet the asking price.'

'You don't have anyone lined up?'

'No.'

He shuffled around on the bench to face her. His lips glistened with salt, and her eyes were drawn to them. When his tongue flicked out to lick the crystals away, she swallowed hard.

'Look, I didn't know Mhairi,' he began. 'I knew I had a distant relative in Scotland, but I thought she'd died years ago. Inheriting her estate was as much of a surprise to me as it was to you.'

Hardly, she thought. Giselle hadn't even known his surname until Avril had told her in the churchyard on the day of the funeral.

'I've got no use for a castle,' he added gently. 'I've got to sell it. I'm sorry.'

So was she. Sorrier than he'd ever understand.

Chapter 9

By Wednesday afternoon, Giselle was congratulating herself for keeping out of Rocco's way. She'd heard rumours from Avril and Tara that he'd cleared Mhairi's private suite, and if he wasn't busy in there, he'd been holed up in her parlour. *His* parlour, she corrected, but the phrase didn't sit right with her. The word 'parlour' conjured up open fires, tasselled table lamps, bone china tea services and chenille cushions, and she imagined him in more of a boardroom-type setting. Or in a glass and steel box of an office, with a computer slimmer than a *Vogue* model and a mini fridge filled with sparkling Perrier water.

It was nearing the end of the day and Giselle was putting the finishing touches to the picture she was working on when the door opened.

She didn't need to look up to know who it was. The air hummed with an electrical charge that sizzled along her nerve endings, making her skin tingle. It wasn't unusual for her to be observed while she worked – that was the beauty of these studios: they were accessible to the public, with only a counter separating the visitors and her workspace – so she carried on doing what she was doing, as calmly as possible. But she hadn't expected to be observed by *Rocco*.

Ignoring him wasn't easy. Every part of her was acutely aware of him, her body reacting despite her brain's reluctance to engage. His nearness made her feel like the nineteen-year-old she'd been when they'd first met, and under different circumstances she might have relished it. But not right now.

Her concentration irritatingly scattered, she tried to focus on the simple, yet effective picture coming to life on the canvas in front of her. She'd painted a bare-branched tree using watercolours and was now choosing tiny fragments of glass for the individual leaves. Green frosted glass – emerald, lime, olive, chartreuse, sage, teal – was interspersed with the occasional citrine, amber, brown and opal, each granule carefully chosen for its shape and delicately arranged on a branch or twig.

'You make it look easy, but I'm betting it isn't,' he said, as she glued the first piece in place when she was finally happy with the way the picture looked. Arrange first, glue later, was the general rule.

'I've had some practice,' she replied modestly, still not looking up from her work.

'Can anyone do it?'

Now she did look up. 'Why? Do you want to have a go?'

'Me?' He barked out an awkward laugh. 'I'm not in the least bit arty.'

'Yes, anyone can do it. It's sticking bits of glass onto paper, basically.'

'I'm sure there's more to it than that. What I meant was, you don't have to have any special equipment?'

'Just the mermaid tears.'

'The *what*?'

'Legend has it that sea glass is mermaid tears.' If that was true, she ought to thank those sad mermaids because their tears had brought her joy.

'Romantic,' he said. 'Is there anywhere in particular you find them?'

'In the sea?'

One side of his lip quirked up. 'You've not lost your sass.'

Surprised, her hand hovered over the next leaf to be stuck down. 'I didn't realise I had any to lose.'

'Mind if I take a closer look?' He pointed to her newest creation.

'Be my guest.'

She wasn't sure she wanted him this side of the counter, but neither did she want to be rude since, technically, he owned it. And neither did she want him to suspect that his nearness might bother her.

He unlatched the half door set in the counter and stepped through it. When he came to stand by her shoulder and peered over it, she tensed. Wood, spice, citrus… His scent invaded her, holding her hostage to a more earthy urge than the creation of a pretty picture. How was it possible to hardly know someone, yet desire them so much? That she'd been in an identical situation in Venice wasn't lost on her, but somehow it had been different. They'd been young, on holiday, ships in the night, just enjoying the experience for what it was. But this…? This felt heavier, more real. It didn't escape her notice that if they wanted, they could recreate Venice here on Skye. Rocco's presence was transient. He'd be gone in a matter of days. They could enjoy a brief fling – wasn't that the word Jinny had used? – then they'd be out of each other's lives a second time.

Giselle bit back a derisive laugh as the thought occurred to her that maybe they could meet up again in another ten years, make a regular thing of it. Although by then, one or both of them might be married or have kids.

'Is there a Mrs Moore?' she blurted, without stopping to think.

Rocco took a step back. 'There is.'

Oh. She might have guessed. He was thirty-one. It was to be expected that he'd be in a relationship. 'How long have you been married?' she asked, careful to sound neutral and unconcerned.

He shuffled, then issued a rumbling laugh. 'We're not married. Beverly – Mrs Moore – is my mother. I thought you were referring to the business.'

'You call your mother *Beverly*?'

'It sounds more professional at work than Mum. And it's easier to call her Beverly all the time, rather than just sometimes, because I'll only forget and slip up.'

Giselle pressed a piece of sea glass down with her little finger, holding it in place for a second. 'Don't tell me, you called your teacher Mum once.' Glancing up at him over her shoulder, she saw him grinning.

'More than once. I've never been able to shake the embarrassment.'

'And do you slip up at work?'

'Rarely. She's more Beverly than Mum now. Occasionally, when we disagree or I'm winding her up, I'll call her Mother, but never in front of anyone.'

To Giselle it sounded bizarre, but what did she know? She'd never worked with any of her family members.

'Why do you want to know?' he asked, and she immediately regretted asking the question.

'Just curious.' Her shrug was off-hand, but she didn't feel off-hand in the slightest. Then she added lamely, 'If you did have a wife, I was wondering how she'd feel about you owning a castle, that's all.' It was the only explanation she was prepared to give him.

'We'll never know. Is it done?' He was looking at the picture.

'Yes. I'll leave it to dry, then frame it.'

'Do you make your own frames?'

'I buy them ready made. Carpentry isn't my forte.'

'Where do you get your ideas?'

'From nature, mostly.'

'And your glass comes from the shore around the loch?'

'Some of it. There's usually something to be found at every low tide.'

'What happens if it runs out? Can you use ordinary glass?'

'Definitely not. There are machines that will grind ordinary glass, but it's easy to tell real sea glass from fake. Genuine sea glass has pores and a texture to it that machine-ground glass can't mimic. Under a macro lens it's easy to see the difference – proper sea glass has C-shaped abrasions on its surface and an uneven texture due to being worn down by different sizes of sand and gravel. Also, real sea glass is frosted, like this—' she held up a piece for him to see '—caused by seawater altering the structure of the glass itself. And no, it doesn't run out, as such. There are plenty of places to find sea glass, although some are better than others.'

'You promised to show me Skye,' he reminded her.

Feeling at a disadvantage now that her hands were no longer occupied, Giselle got to her feet. He was close enough to touch, if she felt the urge. Actually, she *did*, but she wasn't going to act on it. 'Are you asking me to show you where to find sea glass? Aside from Duncoorie?'

'Is that possible?'

It was possible, yes. But did she want him with her? Searching for sea glass was a solitary occupation, a chance to let her thoughts roam, when she let nature in and kept the rest of the world out. Which was why early morning was her preferred time, especially a wild and stormy winter morning, when most of the island's human visitors had flown south like the swallows, or were huddled indoors.

'I go in the mornings,' she said. '*Early.*'

'How early?'

'Five a.m.' She knew it sounded like a thrown gauntlet.

'Sounds good to me.' His eyes narrowed. 'How do you get there, if you don't mind me asking, since you don't have a car? Do the buses run that early?'

'Buses don't run to where we're going.'

'And where's that?'

'You'll see. Meet me on the road outside the castle and wear comfortable shoes, ones you can walk in over rough ground.' Her gaze dropped to his feet. She'd bet her right arm that he had nothing less formal than the leather loafers he was currently wearing.

'Like trainers? It's lucky I brought a pair with me. A nice long walk in the fresh air will do me good. See you bright and early in the morning. Oh, and Giselle?'

'What?'

'You've got paint on your nose.'

Crossly, she blew out her cheeks as she watched him saunter across the car park. *Trainers, my backside. I bet he'll be off to Portree to buy a pair the second my back is turned*, she thought. And she had a feeling that Mr Moore wouldn't know what a hiking boot looked like if it kicked him in the bum.

—

If Giselle thought an early start and a long walk would put him off, she was mistaken. As a matter of fact, Rocco *did* have a pair of trainers with him, along with a Lycra vest and a pair of shorts, in the hope that he'd fit in a couple of runs. So far, he hadn't managed a single one, and he was beginning to feel the lack of exercise.

Normally, he visited the gym five or six times a week, and early starts were something he was used to, as well as late finishes – Beverly expected it. A good workout on the treadmill followed by twenty minutes of weights set him up for the day. He'd hardly run a step since he'd arrived in Duncoorie, and the heaviest thing he'd lifted was a fork to his lips, so fresh air and exercise would do him good.

Rocco was waiting outside the castle as instructed, on the dot at five o'clock the following morning.

It was already light but somewhat chilly, the sun not having yet poked its head above the mountains. The air had that peculiar still quality he associated with the dawn, despite the chirping and tweeting of numerous small birds in the surrounding trees and bushes.

A slim figure came into view, striding along the road, and his heart skipped a beat at the sight of her. He found it annoying the way it kept doing that, but he couldn't seem to help his reaction every time he saw her. It didn't help that today Giselle was wearing shorts, and when his eyes were drawn to her slender legs, he had a flashback of those same legs entwined around his waist. Oh, God…

'Morning,' he said. His voice was hoarse.

If she was surprised he'd turned up, she didn't show it. 'What have you got in there?' she asked, nodding at his borrowed rucksack.

Cal hadn't asked why he needed one, and Avril, who'd been manning the reception desk, hadn't as much as blinked when he'd enquired about a flask yesterday evening. Cook, with a suspicious expression, had wordlessly provided him with two lots of cheese and pickle sandwiches, wrapped in some kind of beeswax cloth to keep them fresh. He'd stored them in the mini fridge in his room overnight, along with two slabs of moist sponge cake that he'd purloined from the kitchen. He hoped Giselle liked strong coffee, but if not, he had a bottle of water with him. And yes, he had been in the Scouts when he was a boy, although not for long.

'Just a couple of things that might come in handy,' he said in answer to her query, remembering how he'd ordered more food than he could have possibly eaten that day in Venice, when she'd knocked his table over.

Giselle had been (and still was) one of the most stunning women he'd ever met. With her floaty white dress, silver hair and waif-like figure, she'd reminded him of an elf or a fairy, and he'd remembered thinking that Tolkien would have had a field day. From her looks, Rocco had assumed she was Scandinavian, until she'd spoken, revealing a soft Scottish accent.

Giselle gave him a dubious look, her eyes more navy than blue in the morning light. Her hair was braided in a thick rope down her back, and her lips were shell pink.

Sod the sandwiches – Rocco wanted to eat *her* up. 'Which way?' he asked, his voice gruff.

She pointed north, towards the woodland. *His* woodland. He'd seen some of it on the first day when Cal had shown him around the estate using a golf buggy.

They set off down the track, the scent of earth and growing things filling his nostrils, along with the occasional waft of Giselle's perfume, light and flowery.

The trees soon gave way to more open heathland of tussocky grass dotted with butter-yellow gorse, as the track joined a narrow, tarmacked lane.

Rocco sniffed, inhaling deeply. 'What's that smell?'

'If you're referring to the coconut and vanilla smell, it's the gorse.'

Coconut and vanilla, that was it! 'A heavenly scent for such a spikey plant. Those thorns look lethal.'

'They are,' she confirmed. 'But wildlife love it. Birds nest in the bushes, bees love the flowers and red deer and rabbits will graze on it.'

Cal had also mentioned deer, and Rocco glanced around hopefully. 'You won't see them down here,' she told him, correctly guessing what he was looking for. 'They'll be up on higher ground at this time of year.'

'Pity. I would have liked to see one.' His tone was wistful.

'If you weren't going back tomorrow, you could have asked Cal to take you. He knows all the best places. And if you wanted to see orca or dolphins, there's a guy who runs whale- and dolphin-spotting trips. Maybe next time?'

'Maybe.' His reply was non-committal, although he was fairly sure he wouldn't be returning to Skye. It was a shame, though, so perhaps one day he would pay it another visit and see more of the island. Or perhaps not; cities and culture were more his thing if he wanted a holiday.

The lane continued to run parallel with the loch, and Rocco had to admit that the scenery was outstanding. If it wasn't for the road they were walking along, he could believe he was in the wilderness, because there were few signs of human habitation, just sky, sea, mountains and gorse.

At one point he asked, purely out of curiosity, 'How much further?' and when he was met with, 'We're not quite halfway yet,' he began to wonder whether he'd brought enough food.

He estimated it would take another fifty minutes to get to where they were going, wherever that was. Luckily (for him, at least), there weren't any steep climbs. The road was mostly undulating and tarmacked, so was easy underfoot.

But eventually the road ran out.

Beyond a metal kissing gate lay a dirt track through the tussocky grass, stony and uneven. Shaggy cows gazed at them through their fringes of ginger, chestnut or black hair, their jaws working as they chewed. Rocco eyed their long horns and solid bodies warily.

'Those are the iconic Highland coos,' Giselle said. 'They're placid enough.'

'Hmm.' Rocco wasn't convinced, and he was relieved when they went through another small gate, which meant there was thankfully a barrier between them. The track was now more of a grassy path, intersected by a small stream with stepping stones, and ahead lay a dry-stone wall with a gap in it.

Beyond the wall the ground rose, and when they reached the top of the incline he was rewarded with a spectacular view, and he halted to take it in. 'Oh, wow!'

In the distance was a crescent of beach nestled in a small bay. Emerald grass, azure sky, pale sand, and the sea was a bright turquoise where it met the beach, darkening to cobalt as the water deepened.

'That's where we're going,' Giselle said.

The stunning view was definitely worth the trek.

'And we've got it all to ourselves,' she added happily. 'It's a bit off the beaten track, so it's never heaving, but give it an hour and there'll be more people about. This is why I come here so early, because there's no one else around.' She beamed at him. 'Just wait until you see what it's made of.'

The track led downhill to the shore, the water's edge flanked by burgundy-coloured lines of seaweed along the high-tide mark, which lay on the dark volcanic rocks and pebbles. The sea was calm, its glassy surface broken only by the gentle lap of small waves, and overhead a skein of geese flew wingtip to wingtip, low enough for Rocco to hear the wind through their feathers as their haunting calls broke the silence. A hill rose behind the beach, a craggy backdrop, purple-hued with heather in the morning sun.

It was breathtakingly beautiful.

It wasn't until Rocco set foot on the beach that he realised what Giselle had meant. 'Are those shells?' he asked, peering down for a closer look. The 'sand' consisted of broken shells, some of them quite large, others mere fragments, and was crunchy underfoot.

'This place is called Coral Beach,' Giselle said, kneeling and picking up a handful to show him. 'But it's not really coral. It's the calcified remains of red coralline seaweed and millions of snail shells, crushed by wave action and bleached by sunlight. Legend has it that crofters used to use it to spread on their land to improve the soil.' She allowed the fragments to trickle to the ground, then got to her feet and dusted her palm on the seat of her shorts.

Once again, his gaze was drawn to her legs, and once again he brushed the accompanying image away. 'So, what are we looking for?' he asked. 'I know you showed me the blue glass you found, but what else should I be looking for?'

She gave him a quizzical look. 'It was you who found the sea glass at the lighthouse on Murano.'

'To be honest, I had no idea what it was. I just picked up some random stones because they looked nice.'

'OK, let's see if I can find some and I'll show you, although we'll probably have better luck among the rocks.'

Head down, eyes on the ground, he walked alongside her, so close they were almost touching, and instead of concentrating on what was underfoot, he found most of his attention was taken up with Giselle. She was engrossed, her gaze focused, and he kept shooting her little glances out of the corner of his eye. He couldn't seem to stop looking at her.

'Here's a piece,' she said, stooping to pick up a small bit of what seemed, to his inexperienced eye, to be a frosted pebble. He'd found something similar all those years ago, he recalled, and a heart-shaped red one along with some others.

She handed it to him, and he tried not to react as her fingers brushed the palm of his hand. Her touch was electrifying.

'I know it doesn't look much on its own, but you've seen what happens when several pieces are arranged together.'

'Magic,' he breathed. 'That's what happens.'

'Pardon?'

'It's awesome,' he backtracked. 'Do you ever use the coral itself?'

The bleached strands of hard seaweed looked remarkably like real coral, with their twiglet shapes, and amongst them were hundreds of tiny shells.

'Never. Taking a handful mightn't seem like much, but if everyone did it, there'd soon be none left. I don't take any shells from here, either. I occasionally use them in my pictures, but I'm really careful about taking too many. Glass, on the other hand… It's an endless supply.'

She removed the fragment of glass from his hand and popped it into her canvas bag, and they carried on walking, eyes on the beach.

Finally, after an hour and several more 'finds', one of them being a fragment of what Giselle thought was costume jewellery – not glass but paste maybe, perhaps from a brooch or an earring – she called a halt, saying, 'I hope you've got breakfast in that rucksack.'

Rocco's eyes widened. 'How do you know?'

'Avril, via Cook. Otherwise, I'd have brought a snack myself. Cheese and pickle sandwiches?'

He nodded.

'My favourite. Let's eat it up there.'

Up there was the impressive hill on the northern end of the beach.

He must have looked as apprehensive as he felt (that hill looked *steep*), because Giselle said, 'Don't worry; its bark is worse than its bite. It'll only take five minutes to reach the top, but the view is so worth it.'

Not wanting to appear a wimp in her eyes, he agreed, but even though the hike to the top couldn't have been more than thirty metres, he was puffing like a steam train by the time they got there. He clearly needed to do more work on the stepper next time he went to the gym.

But once again, the view was astounding, and Rocco couldn't think of anywhere better to eat breakfast.

Hardly able to drag his eyes away, he unpacked the rucksack. Before he ate, he took a long drink of water. It had been thirsty work hauling his backside up that hill.

'It's so peaceful,' he observed, unwrapping his sandwich.

'Shh. What can you hear?'

'Nothing, that's what—'

'*Listen*,' she urged, as he was about to take a bite.

He lowered the sandwich and did as he was told.

He could hear the wind, a gentle breeze playing about his ears, but he could also hear faint peeping sounds, and realised they were coming from the seabirds patrolling the shore now that the humans (in other words, he and Giselle) had left them in peace. The sound of the waves carried on the wind, and he was surprised at how still the sea was, the wispy clouds above reflected on its mirrored surface. A short distance offshore lay a low island, a ribbon of land sheltering the beach, and movement caught his eye, grey shapes on the darker rocks.

'What are those?'

'Seals.'

Awed, he turned to look at her. 'Wow.'

'They haul out onto the rocks to rest and sun themselves. When the tide is really low, you can wade across to the island. I wouldn't recommend staying long, though, as you don't want to get stranded.'

'Couldn't you swim back?'

'Best not. The currents can be unpredictable in the channel.'

'It really is wild,' he marvelled. 'And so beautiful.' Suddenly he was glad he'd come to Skye, and hadn't simply instructed Jermyns to sell the castle, sight unseen. He'd have missed out on all this beauty.

He would have missed out on seeing *Giselle*. As the thought slipped into his mind, he glanced at her out of the corner of his eye and faltered.

Once again something stirred inside him, but this time he couldn't put a name to it. All he knew was that he wasn't ready to leave Skye just yet.

Chapter 10

Giselle rose to her feet and dusted off the seat of her shorts, feeling self-conscious. She rarely wore them because her pale skin burnt easily despite copious amounts of sun cream, but it was early, and she'd had a hunch that the day might be warm. Maybe she'd envisioned a bit of a paddle, too – after removing her socks and boots, obviously. But now that she was here, suggesting a paddle would have made this walk feel too much like a date, which it most definitely wasn't, so she hadn't.

By the time they'd got to the top of the hill, she wished she'd taken the plunge. Hot and bothered, and very aware that Rocco, who had been scrambling up behind her, was getting an eyeful of her white legs, she had been glad to collapse onto the grass. At least the climb had been worth it. Rocco, mesmerised by the view, hadn't been able to take his eyes off it.

Skye was on her best behaviour today, parading herself in all her glorious beauty – emerald grass, turquoise water, azure sky, white fluffy clouds, dark glistening rocks and the iridescent beach, all of it bathed in brilliant early morning sunshine. And not to mention the wildlife: sea birds, geese flying overhead and the fat sausage shapes of the grey seals. All that was needed was a pod of dolphins or orcas to complete the scene.

'I'd read that Skye is beautiful, but I didn't realise just how beautiful,' Rocco murmured. He was sitting with his forearms resting on his knees, his eyes on the horizon. 'I can see why you love it so much.'

'I don't want to live anywhere else,' she replied simply.

'How about Venice? I recall you were quite taken with the city.'

The city wasn't all she'd been taken with. Heat infused her cheeks, but her voice was calm as she said, 'Nice to visit, but I wouldn't want to live there.'

'Not even for the sea glass?'

'Actually, there isn't much to be found in Venice. You were lucky.'

She caught his sideways look as he replied, 'I certainly was.'

Determined not to show how discomforted she felt, she said, 'It's unusual to find sea glass on the island. Most furnaces don't discard their waste glass; they reuse it. And there aren't exactly loads of beaches, apart from Lido, but I think those are man-made. We just happened to be at the lighthouse at low tide that day.'

'I didn't think Venice was tidal, or the Med as a whole, for that matter.'

'I believe there's a fluctuation in sea level in Venice itself of around a metre, but it doesn't happen often. When it does, it exposes that rocky area by the lighthouse.'

He grinned at her. 'We were fortunate, then.'

'Very.' More fortunate than he could imagine, since Rocco finding the sea glass had set her on the path to Duncoorie, the castle and its craft centre.

A wave of sadness washed over her as she thought of Mhairi. She really was going to miss the grand old lady, and not just because there was a real possibility that her life was about to change as a result of her passing.

'It's time we made a move,' she declared. 'I've got a studio to open.'

'And I've got work to do.' A shadow flitted across his face. 'Thank you for letting me come with you this morning.'

'You're welcome.'

They walked down the hill, soon reaching the bottom, and he fell in beside her again. His gaze swept across the landscape, and he kept slowing down for a longer look.

'I can't believe how incredibly beautiful it is.'

'It's only a small part of the island. There are places like this all over. Some are far more spectacular.'

'Do you mean the mountains? I drove past some impressive ones on the way to Duncoorie.'

'Yes, tourists flock to the Quiraing, which is probably the most beautiful place to hike on Skye, as well as The Old Man of Storr and Trotternish Ridge, and quite rightly too, as they are all impressive. The scenery is stunning, but they can get busy in high summer.'

'Like now?'

'Exactly.'

So far, they'd had this walk to themselves, but they were starting to encounter the occasional person, and she knew from experience that as the day wore on visitors to the beach would increase. Which was why she preferred getting here early. Not that she visited often because, as she'd told Rocco, it wasn't the best beach to find sea glass. But she'd wanted to show him how beautiful her island was, and she'd also wanted to make him suffer. Although that plan seemed to have backfired, because getting up early hadn't fazed him and neither had the long walk. If she was honest, she was impressed he'd coped so well with the hike, considering he was a pencil pusher, chained to his desk for hours on end.

'I get the feeling you prefer quieter places,' he said. 'Are there any?'

'Plenty, but you really should see the more touristy ones as well; they're popular for a reason.'

'Such as?'

She sent him a sideways glance. 'I know you love history, so you could go see the dinosaur footprints at Staffin, and if you want something more recent, there are plenty of brochs around – they're round towers built around two thousand years ago – and of course, you have your very own castle.'

'I doubt mine is the only one on Skye,' he replied.

'It's not. The ruins of Duntulm Castle are worth seeing. It was owned by the MacDonald clan, the same clan Flora MacDonald belonged to. Her grave is on Skye, if you wanted to visit it.'

'Where do I know that name from?'

'Bonnie Prince Charlie. She helped him evade the British after the Battle of Culloden and brought him to Skye. That's where the "Skye Boat Song" comes from.'

'The what song?'

'It's an old Gaelic song with several versions, but the most famous is the one that goes… "Sing me a song of a lad that is gone, Say, could that lad be I? Merry of soul he sailed on a day, Over the sea to Skye."' Suddenly aware that she was singing, she closed her mouth abruptly.

'You have a nice voice.'

'Och, I do not! Although I sometimes do a bit of karaoke in the pub on a Friday night. But not often. I get too self-conscious.'

'The pub in Duncoorie?'

'That's the one.'

'Is that your local?'

'Aye, since I can walk there and back.'

'That's lucky if you want to have a drink. I should imagine taxis around here are scarce.'

'You can say that again!' But even if they weren't, she wouldn't waste her money on them, not when she had two good legs.

'What's Duncoorie like? I haven't seen much of it, apart from the church and the loch.'

'It's quiet during the winter, busy the rest of the year.' She shrugged, not sure what he wanted to know. 'There's a bakery, a corner shop that's also a post office – although it's not really on a corner – a shop selling fishing gear and bait, a couple of cafes, a restaurant, several B&Bs, a teeny-weeny primary school…' She trailed off.

'It didn't look particularly big from what I've seen of it. But it does have a lovely chip shop.'

She smiled and wrinkled her nose. 'Yes, it does.'

'If you want anything more than the occasional loaf of bread or pint of milk, where do you go?'

'Portree. It isn't a big town by any stretch of the imagination, but it does have a nice selection of shops. I go there a handful of times a year if I need something in particular, and for everything else I use the corner shop. I don't need much because I eat in the craft centre cafe most days – although I have been known to dine in the parlour with Mhairi.' Sadness swept over her. 'We used to have tea and cake, sometimes a sandwich.'

'What was she like? I mean, I've been through some of her private papers and photos – she must have kept every letter and receipt – and I've boxed them up to be shipped home so I can go through them when I've got more time, but they don't give me a sense of *who* she was.'

Where should she start? 'Mhairi was regal, determined, generous, astute, well liked and well respected. She could come across as aloof, but not once you got to know her.' Giselle's smile was tremulous. 'You can tell how much people thought of her by the number who went to her funeral.'

'I noticed that there were quite a few there. One big family.'

He *did* have a good memory, she thought, recalling that she'd told him that very thing on the day of the funeral. 'That's right, we are. We look out for each other, help and support one another. We make a good team,' she added. 'We all pull together to make the craft centre work.'

'I believe Mhairi was forced to open the craft centre because the money had run out?'

'You'd have to ask her that,' Giselle replied sharply, not wanting to gossip. Then she realised he couldn't, and her spirits sank.

'It's OK; I already know the background. I was just making conversation.'

Of course he did. By now, he probably knew everything there was to know about the castle's financial situation.

'Tell me about the other crafters,' he asked. 'I haven't had a chance to meet them properly.'

Or he hadn't cared enough to. Swallowing her misgivings, she said, 'I expect you've met Tara, Cal's fiancée? She makes doll's houses and all the wee furniture and things to go in them. Then there's Fergus, who's the glassblower, and his brother Shane, who makes stained glass. Isla does needle felting; then there's…' As she reeled off the names of the people she'd worked alongside for years, she wondered what they would do if the craft centre were to close. How would they manage? She couldn't imagine it not being there, all the studios lying empty, the gift shop and the cafe silent.

The questions kept coming. 'How long have you lived in Duncoorie?'

'Three years.'

'Have you had a studio all that time?'

'Yes. It was the reason I bought the bothy.'

'When did you move to Skye?'

'Not long after Venice.' She blushed at the memory the word invoked and hoped he didn't notice. 'I lived in Portree at first, renting a room and working three jobs to make ends meet.'

'You must have really wanted to live here.'

'Some of us didn't have the benefit of working for the family firm.'

'I'm not sure whether it was a benefit,' he replied softly. 'It was assumed, and then when my dad died, it was a necessity and an obligation. My mother might own the company, but I'll be the one to carry it on when she retires.'

'That's quite a responsibility,' Giselle said, softening. 'Do you enjoy asset management?'

'Sometimes. It has its highs and lows, like any job.'

'Mine are mostly highs.'

'Is that because you work for yourself?'

'It's because I'm doing something I love. All the crafters are. It isn't easy, especially during the quieter winter months, but I can't imagine doing anything else. Are you really going to sell?' This last was blurted out, without thinking, but she had to know.

'I am.' His voice was gentle, understanding. But it didn't change the fact that soon the craft centre might be no more.

'But you could—' She stopped abruptly. What could he do? Stay here and run it, like Mhairi? Giselle knew that wasn't going to happen.

Little more was said for the rest of the way back, and when they arrived at the castle he said, 'Thank you for showing me a piece of Skye.'

'You're welcome.' Her voice was stilted.

'I'm leaving in the morning. By rights, I should have been back in London already.'

Her treacherous heart stuttered. Despite him being about to turn her life upside down, there was a part of her that was dismayed at the news of his imminent departure.

'It was nice seeing you again, Rocco.' She actually meant it. Selling Coorie Castle didn't make him a bad guy, and she could see why he'd want to sell up. Izzy was right; if the shoe was on the other foot and Giselle had suddenly inherited a substantial property in *London*, she'd have it on the market quicker than a heron snatching a fish out of the water.

It wasn't his fault that selling the castle might have such a devastating effect on her, the other crafters and everyone else who worked there. And at least he was leaving with some appreciation of the island and the castle he was so keen to get rid of.

However, the thought gave her scant comfort.

Chapter 11

When Rocco opened the heavy drapes on Friday morning, the view made him pause. He was going to miss waking up to this. He was also going to miss having it as a backdrop to his laptop when he was working, although it did sometimes prove to be more of a distraction than he needed.

It was five thirty, and he wasn't in the mood to do any work, despite knowing he should get a couple of hours in before the drive to Inverness airport. Instead, he decided to go for the run he'd been promising himself all week.

When he stepped outside, he took several deep breaths, stretching his calf and thigh muscles, then jumped up and down and jogged on the spot to warm up. As he did so, his gaze roamed over the craft centre, the woodland and the castle.

It still hadn't totally sunk in that he was here because he owned it. To him, the feeling was more akin to being on holiday, as though he'd had a pleasant mid-week break. Rocco guessed he would look back on his time on Skye with a degree of surrealism. Heck, it didn't feel real *now*, when he was actually here!

He set off along the lane leading to the small beach and jetty but veered off down a dirt track before he reached the former boathouse. The track led to the village and he jogged down it at a comfortable pace, one he could keep up for an hour or so.

With his breathing deep and even, and his feet pounding out a regular rhythm, he soaked up the serenity of the morning. It felt strange not to run with buds in his ears, but birdsong was music enough, and it was rather liberating not to have his mobile with him.

It wasn't long before the track ended and the rough ground under his feet changed to terraced pavement, but he kept on running, past the church where Mhairi was buried, past the little shop with the Post Office sign above it, past the pub where he assumed Giselle and the others would be gathering for a drink this evening. Then on past a guest house, a restaurant, a shop selling fishing tackle and a handful of pretty whitewashed cottages, until he'd left Duncoorie behind.

A stone bridge over a burbling stream marked the far end of the loch, where the sea was corralled by the land, and he crossed it, the narrow road leading upwards.

Soon he was on the opposite side of the loch to the castle, and the early morning sun was in his eyes and the wind was in his hair. Sweat trickled down his back and his chest, and his breathing became ragged as the gradient steepened. Below him lay the calm water, edged by dark rocks and framed by heather, low bushes and gorse. This side of the loch was wild and uninhabited, and the solitude was suddenly overwhelming.

Coming to an abrupt halt, he put his hands on his thighs above his knees and leant forward, gasping. The incline on the treadmill in the gym was no match for this hill, and it took him a moment or two to catch his breath.

When he straightened up, he was mesmerised by the view.

Duncoorie stretched along the loch on the opposite shore, the whitewashed buildings nestling in the hillside like pebbles in grass. And at the far end, on a rocky rise, sat the largest pebble of all – Coorie Castle.

It looked like part of the landscape, as though it had grown out of the rock, rather than being built on it, and although he knew it had changed significantly since its construction over eight hundred years ago, he could imagine the feelings of those medieval Scots when they saw it for the first time: awe, fear, envy. It had been a fortification built for defence and warfare, and still held some of that majesty in its high walls and square turrets. But now it was picturesque rather than brooding. And it was *his*.

Rocco sank into the springy heather, his behind on a tussock of soft grass, and gazed at it, drinking in every detail. He would never forget this magical sight.

Unwilling to return to the castle just yet, he sat there for a while, the sun on his face, and enjoyed the peace. It was quite freeing not to think about emails or meetings, schedules or reports, and he found his mind drifting as his gaze roamed over the distant village. Which house was Giselle's, he wondered; he'd only been there once, and from where he was sitting it was hard to work out the route he'd taken to get to it.

Was she there, or on the beach? The distance was too great to tell if anyone was walking along the shoreline.

Then movement caught his eye, but it was much nearer, and it wasn't a person.

Bounding through the tufts of heather, only twenty metres away, was a fox.

A russet-bodied, white-chested, bushy-tailed *fox*!

Rocco held his breath, willing the creature not to notice him, but when the fox turned its head, he realised the animal was well aware of his presence as it locked its pale amber eyes on his.

Unperturbed by the human's nearness, the fox continued on its way, Rocco watching until it was out of sight.

'Wow,' he whispered, feeling privileged to have seen such a stunning animal so close.

Instinctively, he reached for his phone, before remembering he hadn't brought it with him. Then he wondered who he would possibly call, if he had. Who would he tell who'd be interested? Not his mother, that's for sure, nor any of his mates.

I would tell Giselle, though, he thought.

Sighing, he scrambled to his feet. He needed to have a shower, eat some breakfast then pack. And before he left, he wanted a quick word with Cal. Then it was back to real life.

Unfortunately, the thought failed to infuse him with joy.

—

Giselle pushed the poached eggs and salmon on sourdough around her plate in a desultory fashion. Unlike Avril, who was tackling her halloumi salad with enthusiasm.

'Well, he's gone, then,' Avril declared around a mouthful of food. 'Cal doesn't seem to think we'll see him again,' she continued. 'Aren't you going to eat your salmon?'

They were in the cafe having brunch, since Giselle hadn't had breakfast yet and Avril was on her break.

Giselle pulled a face. 'I'm not hungry.'

'Can I have it?'

'Go ahead.' She pushed her plate across the table.

'How was your picnic yesterday?' Avril arched her brows.

'The sandwiches were cheese and pickle, my favourite.'

'That's not what I meant.'

'It was fine.'

'Then why are you looking so glum? Rocco looked as pleased as—' Avril gasped. 'You *didn't*! Did you?'

'Didn't what?' Giselle reached for the iced coffee and sipped it as she stared through the cafe's window. She'd watched him get in his car and leave earlier. Oddly, she'd felt melancholy.

'*Kiss him!*' Avril's fierce whisper made her jump.

'No, I did not,' she replied hotly.

'What then?'

'Nothing. We had a nice walk and chatted a bit. That's all.'

'What about?'

'Mhairi, places to visit on Skye, the pub… Just, stuff. Nothing exciting. Nothing *personal*.'

Avril looked crestfallen. 'You spent God knows how many hours alone with a hot guy in one of the most beautiful places on earth, and all you did was chat about *stuff*?'

'It wasn't like that,' she protested. 'He wanted to know where I collect sea glass, so I— Why am I justifying myself to you?'

'Because you still fancy him.'

Avril's comment took the wind right out of Giselle's sails. It was true; she did still fancy him. 'You said yourself that he's hot. I bet *you* fancy him as well,' she countered. Wasn't attack the best form of defence?

'I do, but I'm not the one who has *history* with him.'

Giselle shrugged. 'It doesn't matter whether or not I fancy him. He's gone and you and Cal seem to think he's not coming back, so I'll probably never set eyes on him again.'

'All the more reason to have snogged him yesterday. I bet you wish you had, now.'

'Actually, I don't.' Giselle stuck her nose in the air. If she had, she wouldn't have wanted to stop at kissing. The thought of what she would have liked to do with him made her face flame. Thank goodness he'd left, otherwise...

'Will you be coming to the pub this evening?' Avril asked.

Giselle didn't really feel like it, but neither did she feel like sitting at home on her own. 'Who started this silly Friday-night tradition, anyway? Don't we see enough of each other during the day?' she grumbled.

'We hardly see you at all,' Avril retorted. 'You only emerge from your studio when you're hungry, or you need more sea glass.'

'Speaking of sea glass, I'd better get back to work, and so had you,' Giselle advised. 'The cat might be away, but Cal won't let things slack.'

'I know. Cal and Rocco were in the parlour having a tête-à-tête before Rocco left. I bet he's given him a list of instructions.'

Giselle took her half-drunk coffee to the studio with her, trying not to think of Rocco, and sat at the worn, wooden table to work.

Sometimes an idea for a picture would come to her and she would source the pieces of sea glass in order to make it. Other times, the glass itself would spark the inspiration. Today was one of those times. The fragment of costume jewellery she'd found yesterday had been playing on her mind. It comprised of three small blue stones, with another five oval stones down one side, and suddenly it came to her what she wanted to do with it.

Selecting a piece of card, she placed it on the table, then opened the drawers one by one, sifting through the colours and sizes of glass until she found suitable fragments. The predominant colour was green, with a few pieces of pale blue, brown and white, and she also selected a small shell with a shimmer of pink on its shiny surface. She wouldn't use all the pieces of glass that she'd removed from the drawers, and she may well have to revisit them to find a different shape, size or colour, but the selection spread across the table was a good starting point.

Concentrating hard, she began with the scrap of costume jewellery, placing it towards the top of the card, making sure it was centred. This would form the bodice of the mermaid she was about to make, then she began arranging the brown pieces so that they looked like hanks of flowing hair. An oval of milky white formed a face, a more cylindrical one was the neck, others became a shoulder and an outstretched arm, and gradually the top part of a female form emerged.

With practised ease, Giselle sensed where a fragment of glass needed to be placed, where it would work best for maximum effect. It was as though she was putting together a jigsaw puzzle only she could see. Working deftly, mostly oblivious to the customers who wandered in to watch, she created a body and a tail, flamboyant fins echoing the mermaid's flowing hair. The finishing touch was the small shell on the outstretched hand.

Giselle sat up, straightening her spine, careful not to dislodge any of the pieces. She still had to glue them in place, but for all intents and purposes the picture was done, although she might tweak it a little later. The secret was knowing when to stop.

Now that her mind was no longer on her work, her thoughts turned to Rocco.

In her heart, she knew she probably wouldn't see him again. He'd told her he'd arranged to have everything sent to him, so she guessed he'd have no reason to return now that he'd seen the place.

With her spirits heavier than ever, she looked at the rest of the sea glass she'd collected yesterday morning. It was sitting on the draining board, ready to be put away, but she was oddly reluctant to do that. It was silly, but it reminded her of him.

Yes, it *was* silly, she acknowledged irritably, especially since she had the red heart he'd given her all those years ago.

Feeling ridiculous, she scooped up the sea glass and put it into the relevant drawers where it immediately blended in with all the other fragments of glass of similar size and colour. She had enough memories of Rocco; she didn't need any more. In fact, now that she'd met him again, she almost wished she hadn't encountered him the first time, because the pedestal she'd put him on had been smashed to smithereens. What was that saying about never meeting your heroes because you'll be disappointed?

Giselle was disappointed all right, despite still being more attracted to him than was good for her.

Feeling even more depressed than she'd been on the day of Mhairi's funeral and needing some advice but not wanting to worry her mum and dad, Giselle rang her sister.

'*Buongiorno*, Zelle,' Izzy chirped. 'Actually, is it still morning? I've lost track of time.'

'Just about.'

'Is everything all right? You sound glum.'

'I'm exceptionally glum,' Giselle confirmed, and she took a deep breath. 'I think I might have to sell the bothy.'

'No! *Why?*'

'Because if the craft centre closes, I won't be able to pay the mortgage,' she said, and went on to explain her worries.

'Come live with me,' Izzy suggested immediately.

'Milan is miles away from the sea,' Giselle pointed out. 'But thank you, anyway.'

'Do you have to live by the sea? Can't you just visit it a couple of times a month?'

She could, but she didn't want to. And neither did she want to live by any old seaside – she wanted to live by *this* one. Skye and Duncoorie were her home; it was where she belonged. This was where her heart was. She hadn't been exaggerating when she'd told Rocco that she didn't want to live anywhere else.

There was only one thing for it: she'd have to start looking for a job.

Chapter 12

Driving over Skye Bridge was like driving over the edge of the world. The road rose up in front of Rocco, soaring into the sky like a rollercoaster, the ground dropping away as the bridge arced over the open water of Loch Ash below.

A song he'd heard recently came into his head, and when he uttered a command, the haunting music of the 'Skye Boat Song' filled the car.

He glanced to his left. The sea was grey under the shade of a scudding cloud, a shaft of sunlight illuminating one of the many low islands. And then the bridge crested, the road now falling away, and his jaw dropped. All he could see was water, sky and the distant mountains.

Even as he was leaving, the beauty of this part of the world conspired to make him want to stay.

'All that was me is gone…'

As the lyrics washed over him, his heart felt heavy. He didn't want to leave. There was so much he wanted to see: Flora MacDonald's grave, the Quiraing, Brothers Point… *Giselle*.

The bridge had now become dry land; Skye was behind him, the road to real life ahead. Through the open car window, a familiar vanilla and coconut fragrance from a bank of yellow gorse wafted across his face, and he inhaled deeply. Then, an image of the fox's wild amber eyes flashed into his mind, followed by Giselle's fathomless blue ones, and he didn't pause to consider what he was doing.

Braking hard, he pulled into a layby, checked his mirrors then hauled on the wheel, executing a swift and probably illegal U-turn.

He was going back.

Rocco's spirits lifted instantly, and not even the thought of his mother's displeasure could dampen them.

'Call Nora,' he instructed, and his phone immediately obliged.

'Calling Nora,' the disembodied voice informed him.

'Rocco!' Nora sounded pleased to hear from him. 'Giles Wiltshire called; he—'

'I'm not going to make my flight this afternoon,' he broke in, cutting her off. Giles Wiltshire was always calling. The man could wait.

There was the briefest of hesitations and he guessed she was mentally working out what she needed to do to rearrange his travel schedule before she said, 'Leave it with me. I'll check out the next available flight and book you on it.'

'I'm not coming back today.'

'Oh? Tomorrow, then.'

'I won't be back tomorrow, either. Don't book anything for now; wait until you get confirmation from me.'

Another hesitation. 'How long do you expect to be away?'

'I'm not sure.'

'Is there a problem?'

'No, no problem. Got a few things to sort out, that's all.'

'OK. I'm sure I can rearrange your Monday meetings.'

'Better rearrange all next week,' he said. Nora's silence was telling. '*I'll* speak to Beverly,' he told her, and he didn't imagine her sigh of relief.

'I'll get onto it,' said his PA, with her customary efficiency.

'Thanks, Nora.'

He ended the call and was about to make another, this time to Beverly – who wouldn't be thrilled that he wasn't flying back to London today – when he thought, *Sod it*. He'd speak to his mother in a 'wee while', as they said in these parts. Right now, he needed to let Cal know what was happening. And he needed to find out where he could purchase some more clothes!

Portree, the largest town on Skye, had its fair share of tourist type shops, but it also had the gems Cal had mentioned: a couple of outlets, one selling clothing suitable for the great outdoors and the other selling clothes for a more casual lifestyle than the offices and boardrooms that usually made up Rocco's day.

It had taken him around fifty minutes to get there, and several more to park and find the first shop, and he was currently standing in front of a rack of hiking trousers, wondering which pair to go for. Would one pair be enough? He supposed it depended on how long he'd be in Duncoorie, a question Cal had also asked, and one Rocco couldn't answer. He simply didn't know. Three days? A week? Longer?

Boots! He needed boots. And more socks and boxers, and he was running out of shower gel. Cal had assured him that Mhairi's suite would be ready for him by the time he arrived. Rocco had a vision of waking up tomorrow to that glorious view, and he was filled with an inexplicable contentment.

Weighed down with bags, Rocco returned to the car, intending to drive back to the castle, but after he'd placed everything in the boot, he changed his mind, deciding to have a look around the town. A coffee and a bite to eat wouldn't go amiss, either.

Walking to the end of the main street, he caught a glimpse of the sea, and it drew him like a magnet. When he saw a sign for the harbour, he couldn't resist.

The aptly named Quay Street led him down a steep hill to a waterfront lined with brightly painted buildings that looked out onto a sheltered bay dotted with small boats.

The smell of frying fish from a chip shop made him smile as he thought of the fish supper he'd eaten with Giselle the other evening.

Strolling down the road a short way, he stopped to peer over the railings and down at the water. A pebble-and-rock-strewn beach caught his eye; *Will there be any sea glass on it?* he wondered. He was tempted to go looking, but he wasn't dressed for it, which was ironic since he had half a shop's worth of suitable footwear and clothing in the boot of his hire car.

Retracing his steps, he was soon facing the main street again, but instead of turning onto it, he carried on up the hill, past a small supermarket, a wine bar, a guest house or two, and then the road levelled off and he paused to take in the view. From up here, the row of pretty painted houses lining the quay was strung out before him, and he did the tourist thing and took out his phone.

A photo or two later, he headed back down, aiming for one of the many cafes he'd seen. Diving into the first one he came to, Rocco felt as though he was playing truant from school or throwing a sickie to have an illicit day off work. By rights, he shouldn't be here, but he was enjoying himself too much to care. When was the last time he'd explored a strange place on his own? Venice, maybe, before a certain silver-haired sprite had knocked his table over, and then they'd explored the city together – and it had been much more fun with Giselle.

Abruptly, he wished she was with him now, insisting on paying for his late lunch with a few notes wrestled from her bra.

As he ate, he wondered how she would react to his return to Coorie Castle. Would she even react at all? Maybe there'd be some mild surprise on seeing him again, and perhaps some smug satisfaction that her beloved isle had dug its claws into him and wasn't letting go easily. But nothing more. And why did that bother him?

He was just finishing a second cup of delicious coffee when his phone rang.

Scrambling to answer it so as not to disturb the cafe's other customers, Rocco's heart sank when he saw his mother's name on the screen.

'Hello, Beverly,' he said warily.

'Nora tells me you're not on the flight.'

'Er, no.' Damn. He should have phoned his mother when he'd thought about it, and he guessed he'd need to apologise to his PA since Beverly had probably given her a grilling as to his whereabouts and intentions.

'Would you care to explain?'

'Give me a moment.' He pushed his chair away from the table and got to his feet.

'I don't want to give you a moment. I want an explanation *now*.' Her anger was clear, despite her voice not being raised.

'Wait until I'm outside.'

'Where are you?'

'In a cafe.'

'Where is the cafe?'

'Portree. It's the largest— Never mind. Thanks,' he said to the woman at the till as he paid for his food, then hurried out of the door. 'Right, you can shout at me all you like now.'

'I never shout.' It was true, she didn't: her frosty tone and icy glare were usually enough to show her displeasure. 'What's going on, Rocco?'

'There's nothing to worry about. I just fancied a break.' He began walking, dodging around pedestrians as he headed for the car.

'In *Scotland*?' Her tone was scathing.

'I may as well, since I own a place here.'

'Not for long, hopefully.'

A pang caught him unawares. 'Which is why I thought I'd make the most of it.'

'And what most is there to make? Is there something you're not telling me?'

'I saw a fox this morning,' he blurted, without thinking.

'A fox,' she echoed flatly. 'Is this a joke?'

'A poor one,' he sighed. 'The scenery is stunning, and I haven't had a holiday in…' He struggled to remember.

'Nora tells me you've asked her to arrange online meetings; I'm assuming you'll still be doing some work, so it's hardly a holiday.'

'It never is.' He recalled a two-week vacation to the Maldives, where he had to pack a suit in his luggage because he'd still had to work. On his top half, the visible-on-a-computer-screen half, he'd been wearing a shirt, a tie and a jacket, while the bottom half had been sporting swimming shorts and flip-flops because it had been so hot, and all the while he'd been trying not to stare longingly at the swim-up bar just outside his chalet.

At least if he was halfway up a craggy mountain, there would be little chance of a conference call. Mind you, knowing his mother…

Mhairi's rooms no longer felt like Mhairi's. Her presence, which had been so prevalent the first time he'd entered them, was no longer there. Rocco concluded it was partly due to all her personal things having been either removed or boxed away – the boxes were still stacked neatly in the little sitting room, ready to be transported to London – and partly because he'd spent a considerable amount of time there already. And once he'd hung his new clothes in the wardrobe and placed his toiletries in the bathroom, it felt more like his – albeit his in the way that a hotel room felt like his after he'd checked in: impermanent, but his for the duration of his stay.

However long that might be.

But rather than the sense of duty that had hung over him since his arrival on Sunday, he now felt as though he was on holiday. This time, he wasn't here to sort out the castle: he was here to explore the island. He would have to do some work, but wherever he vacationed, he invariably ended up working – that was a given. But with little to do in the evenings, he would fire up his laptop then. As far as possible, the days would be for fun.

He had no intention of working this evening, though. He was going to go to the pub and eat there. He hadn't been to a proper British pub since he was a student. Trendy bars, clubs and restaurants had been his thing, not traditional pubs, and he was intrigued. And he was going to walk to it, so he could have a pint or two. Real ale, preferably. If they had it. Or cider. He hadn't had cider in years. And sod cordon bleu cooking – he wanted pie and mash, or steak and chips. Not haggis, though, assuming the pub served that kind of thing, as he didn't like the sound of it.

Rocco had a quick shower, changed into one of the new T-shirts and with his recently purchased hiking boots on his feet to break them in, he set off.

The early evening was pleasant, and he enjoyed his stroll, the path already familiar from his run this morning (had it only been this morning?), and soon he was in the beer garden with its picnic benches and view of the loch.

Deeming it too nice an evening to sit indoors to eat, he grabbed a bench and perused the menu. Gammon and chips, he decided, and ordered a pint of Feral Fox to go with it, only because it reminded him of his foxy encounter earlier.

Unsurprisingly, the pub was busy, and he people-watched as he ate. Most customers appeared to be tourists, he surmised from the snippets of conversation he overheard, as they chatted about where they'd been and where they were planning to go next.

And then he spied a familiar face heading for the pub's open door. It was Jinny, accompanied by a man he didn't recognise. Shortly after, the two glass brothers (as he thought of Fergus and Shane) arrived and went inside, then the woman who made silver jewellery, followed by Cal and his fiancée, Tara.

None of them noticed him as he sat there nursing his pint, but Giselle did.

As soon as she came into view, her gaze locked onto his and his heart faltered, missing a beat before catching up with itself in a double thud that reverberated through his chest.

Her eyes were guarded as she walked towards him.

'Care to join me?' he asked.

'No. Would you care to join *me*? *Us*, I mean. A group of us meet for a drink most Friday evenings.'

'Did Mhairi ever—?'

'God, no!'

Her shock at his question made him laugh, but he quickly sobered. 'Perhaps I'd better not. If she didn't...'

'You're not Mhairi.'

'I'm pretty sure that's not meant kindly,' he teased.

'You can take it whichever way you like.' She glanced at the open door, then her gaze settled on him again. 'Why have you come back, Rocco? Have you forgotten something?'

'Unfinished business.'

'Have you got a buyer for the castle already?'

He was dismayed by the worry on her face. 'No, it isn't on the market yet.' It would be soon, but he'd wait until he returned home to start the ball rolling. Besides, he needed to speak to his solicitor and accountant before that could happen, because there was the little matter of probate to sort out. However, he didn't want to think about such weighty matters right now.

'It'll be a while yet,' he added, hoping to reassure her. 'If I can't persuade you to join me, can I at least buy you a drink?'

'Not unless you're prepared to buy the rest of your workforce a drink as well.'

Rocco knew a challenge when he saw one. 'OK, I'll go to the bar and—'

'You should have a drink with us. It'll do a lot for employee relations, even though us crafters aren't actually employed by you. You're more like our landlord.'

'I don't want to intrude,' Rocco protested, unsure whether he'd be welcome. Beverly didn't go in for attending staff events, claiming that you can't socialise with the people you might have to discipline at some point. Or even sack. He could appreciate her reasoning, but this wasn't the same, was it?

'They'll be fine,' Giselle said, and he guessed she was correctly interpreting his reluctance. 'In fact, they'll appreciate it.' From her mischievous twinkle, he assumed his presence would give them something to talk about for a while.

He didn't begrudge them that. Anyway, he was curious about this 'one big family' thing that Giselle had mentioned at least twice. The staff at Moore Asset Management definitely couldn't be described as a family.

Cal's eyes widened when he saw Rocco enter the pub, Giselle by his side, and Rocco noticed several nudges and more than a few comments behind hands held up to mouths.

'Look who I found,' Giselle announced, and Rocco dredged up an awkward smile.

He was rapidly having second thoughts. He should've simply spoken to the bar staff and paid for a round, rather than endure this. For a man who was the owner of the establishment where they all worked, he felt like the outsider he so clearly was.

There was some shuffling and rearranging of chairs, but eventually two empty seats appeared.

Jinny, the woman who managed the gift shop, pointed to one of them. 'That's yours,' she said, 'but before you sit down, mine's a Pimm's. This lout—' she placed a hand on the knee of the man sitting next to her '—is Carter, my worse half, and he'll have a pale ale. What?' she demanded, scanning the rest of the people sitting around the tables that had been pushed together.

Their faces bore expressions ranging from incredulity to concern.

Giselle told them, 'Rocco has already said he'll get a round in, so don't be shy.'

'And no taking advantage,' Jinny warned. 'I'm looking at you, Fergus.'

'Would I?'

'Yes.' She addressed Rocco. 'If he asks for a double whisky, tell him to go boil his head. He's on lager.'

Rocco wasn't going to remember everyone's preferences, so he was relieved when Cal got to his feet, saying, 'I'll give you a hand. This lot mostly have the same drinks, week in and week out.'

As they stood at the bar waiting to be served, Cal said, 'I didn't expect to see you in the pub.'

'I thought I'd get out and about a bit, since I'm here.'

The man turned to face him. 'Why *are* you here?' His gaze bored into Rocco.

'I'm not totally sure,' he admitted. 'I was driving over Skye Bridge, listening to the "Skye Boat Song", and I realised I didn't want to go home just yet.'

'Aye, that'll do it. My heart always sinks when I go over that bridge. Skye gets under your skin and you don't want to leave her. Mind you, I can't say I've had my head turned by a song.'

'It depends who's singing it,' was Rocco's unthinking reply as his eyes flashed to Giselle before he hastily glanced away, earning himself a curious look from Cal. 'No karaoke on this evening?' Rocco asked, to distract him.

'Not in the summer. Karaoke is reserved for the quieter winter months.' Cal picked up a tray of drinks, leaving Rocco to grab the other.

Praying he didn't slop them everywhere – or worse, drop the damn tray – Rocco carefully trailed behind him. As the drinks were distributed, accompanied by a chorus of cheers and thank yous, he was aware of the tension his presence was causing.

He could understand that; he was an unknown quantity, a stranger in their midst, and crucially, by putting the castle on the market, he could be affecting their livelihoods. No wonder they weren't comfortable with him around. Apart from Jinny, who didn't seem to give a rat's arse.

Rocco made a decision. 'Cheers, everyone,' he said, taking his own drink – a small dram of whisky, because when in Rome... or should he say *Scotland*? – and downing it in one. He'd remained standing, and he placed the empty glass firmly on the table and said, 'I'll be off. Enjoy your evening.'

Then he was striding through the door into the evening air, the whisky heating its way to his stomach, embarrassment heating his face. He should never have allowed Giselle to persuade him to join her and her 'family'.

It was rare he had such poor judgement. Those people weren't his friends, and the power disparity between him and them meant they never would be.

Giselle's voice stopped him in his tracks. 'Rocco! Wait up.'

He waited.

'Why are you leaving?' she asked when she caught up with him. 'I thought you were joining us for a drink?'

'I did. I had a *wee dram*.' The assumed Scottish accent felt alien on his tongue.

'That's not what I meant.'

'I know, but it's for the best. They don't want me there.'

'*I* do.' Her eyes widened and she caught her bottom lip between her teeth.

He guessed she hadn't meant to say that. It warmed him more than the whisky. It warmed him more than it should, considering… and Rocco did some blurting of his own. 'Show me Skye.'

'Why?'

Because I want to spend time with you, he almost replied. 'Because you love it.'

'So do they.' She waved an arm at the pub.

When he automatically glanced behind, he saw several curious faces gawking out the window. 'I'm not asking them. I'm asking *you*.'

'When?'

'Tomorrow? The next day?' He wasn't sure how much longer he could stay before Beverly demanded his return. Not for the first time, Rocco wished his boss wasn't his mother. It was an uncomfortable dynamic, but he supposed anyone going into a firm run by their parents must feel the same way. And what he was feeling now was conflicted, on more levels than he could count.

Giselle was hesitating.

He said, 'Sorry, I forgot that tomorrow is Saturday. It'll be your busiest trading day. And Sunday won't be far behind.'

'Not necessarily. Weekdays are equally busy.'

He blinked, disarmed. He knew that: he'd seen the figures from the cafe and the gift shop. Although he wasn't an accountant like Claire, it was easy to see that there were only minor fluctuations in the daily takings from both establishments over the course of a week during the more lucrative summer months.

He expected her to tell him she couldn't spare the time, but instead she said, 'Pick me up at eight,' as she turned on her heel and walked away. He stared after her in surprise and a considerable amount of pleasure.

Chapter 13

The area north of Portree had some of the most stunning sights on Skye, from towering peaks and stomach-dropping cliffs, to tumbling waterfalls and fairy circles. And Giselle was going to take Rocco to see every last one of them in a whistlestop tour of the most popular tourist must-sees.

When he came to pick her up at dead-on eight o'clock the following morning, she noticed with a wry smile that he was suitably dressed for the great outdoors. There was even a brand-new rucksack on the back seat. More cheese and pickle sandwiches, she presumed. She also noticed he hadn't shaved, and she thought the less-well-groomed look suited him. He was looking more like the laid-back, T-shirt-wearing, necklace-sporting man she'd met in Venice, and a bolt of desire shot through her.

'Where to?' he asked.

Bed? The thought caught her unawares. 'How fit are you?' she asked, swiftly shoving the thought out of her head.

'Probably not as fit as I'd like to think I am. Why? What did you have in mind?'

Oh, he was fit all right, and what was going through her mind right now had nothing to do with the great outdoors. 'Lealt Falls, I think.'

'Sounds good.'

'And after that, a nice wee stretch of the legs.'

'How wee?'

'A couple of hours.'

'That doesn't sound too bad.'

We'll see, she thought with a smile. It would probably take a bit longer. Maybe twice as long. *If* he was up to it. The Quiraing was an impressive rock formation, regarded as possibly the most spectacular landscape on Skye. Was she being cruel making him hike it?

Probably!

'Why do I get the feeling I'm in for a rather full day?' he asked, after she'd given him directions. 'We don't have to do everything today; we can save something for tomorrow.'

'You expect me to entertain you *two* days in a row? I do have other things to do, you know.'

'Yes, of course. Sorry. Thank you for taking time out today.'

She shot him a glance to see if he was being sarcastic, but he seemed genuine. Relenting, she said, 'If we don't cover it all today, we'll go out again another day, if that's what you want.' Actually, it was what *she* wanted. The thought of spending another day in his company was rather exciting. It was also worrying *because* she found it exciting. Too much excitement when it came to this man wouldn't be good for her – and she had a feeling she could get very excited indeed.

Oh, dear, I must stop thinking of him that way.

Unfortunately, she couldn't help it because he was so damned sexy. And she was starting to like him again – a fatal combination. Deciding she'd better concentrate on something other than her growing desire, Giselle took to pointing out things of interest as they travelled along the A855 towards the falls.

'Slow down here,' she instructed, 'and look to your left.'

Rocco slowed and glanced out of the window, then quickly turned his attention back to the road.

'Pretty,' he said, risking another look.

'That's the Bride's Veil Fall, so called because it resembles a white veil flowing over the rocks.'

'So it does,' he agreed after yet another look.

'And up there is the mountain known as The Old Man of Storr. It's the remains of a volcanic plug of rock formed during the Jurassic period, and it got its name because its outline looks like an old man. I've never been able to see it myself,' she added, wishing she didn't sound like a badly scripted tour guide as they drove past the glowering basalt pinnacle.

She fell silent for a while, letting the scenery speak for itself as the car ate up the miles. Being without transport meant she rarely ventured far from Duncoorie, and she was enjoying the novelty of this excursion almost as much as she was enjoying being in Rocco's company.

It was a glorious day: blue sky, a smattering of white fluffy clouds, cobalt sea, with the misty Isle of Rona in the distance on the one side and the brooding mountains on the other.

'Pull over,' she instructed, pointing to a layby, and Rocco swung the car off the road and brought it to a halt.

Giselle scrambled out, glad of an excuse to put some distance between them, even if it was only for a minute or two.

Looking back the way they'd come, she said, 'That's Storr. You can see it better from here. It takes about an hour to hike to the top. And that there—' she pointed '—is the island of Rona, and beyond it, Raasay. Lealt Falls is a couple of miles in that direction.'

Rocco was gazing into the distance. 'The scenery here is stunning.'

'It is that,' she agreed.

He took several deep breaths. 'The air is so clean and fresh.'

'We've got a bit of a northerly breeze going on just now, so it's coming all the way from Greenland.' The sun might be shining, but it was a bit parky, and she shivered. Then immediately stiffened when Rocco put his arm around her.

'I've got a spare fleece in the car, if you're cold,' he told her.

'Och, I'm fine,' she replied in a high-pitched squeak. 'Shall we get going? It's still early yet. The day will soon warm up.'

It was warming up already, she thought, as her cheeks began to glow, and when he released her, her disappointment was acute. Being held by him, however briefly, had felt so good.

After they'd got back in the car, Giselle studiously not looking at him in the hope that her flushed cheeks would calm down, it only took a minute or so to arrive at the falls.

'We're here,' she said, instructing him to pull into a small parking area that already had several cars in it. The waterfall wasn't visible from the road, and if it wasn't for a wooden viewing platform jutting out from the side of the hill, there'd be little indication of anything worth seeing.

Miraculously, the platform was empty of people and Giselle skipped to the end, Rocco following at a more sedate pace. The roar of the water as it plunged down the narrow tree-covered gorge in its headlong rush to the sea filled her ears.

'Oh, wow!' Rocco exclaimed as he came to stand beside her, his face alight with wonder.

'It's quite something, isn't it? Want to take a hike to the bottom?'

'Can you actually get down there?' He gazed dubiously at the drop.

'You most definitely can. It's steep and narrow in places, but loads of people do it, even kids.'

'Are you insinuating that I'm a scaredy cat?'

Giselle smirked. 'I wouldn't dream of it.'

'Then lead on, Ellis,' he commanded with a mock frown.

The path was gravelly and well defined at first, but quickly became less easy to navigate, with a steep drop on one side. But the views were worth what was promising to be a very challenging hike back up.

The gorge was a gash in the earth, the river cascading through it, and with the mountains as its backdrop, it was breathtaking. Dropping lower, the views changed as she and Rocco traversed the rough zig-zag path, and they paused for a moment to gaze out to sea.

'How does it compare?' Giselle asked. 'I bet you've been to some impressive places.' She recalled that he'd been travelling around Europe with a friend when she'd met him, and assumed he'd seen grander sights than this.

'It doesn't.' His reply was thoughtful, considered. 'I've been to some great places – the Alps, the Pyrenees, Iceland—'

'*Iceland*? I'd love to go there!' she interrupted. 'What was it like?'

'Otherworldly, magnificent, humbling, but...'

'But, what?'

'There's something about Skye, isn't there?' His eyes shone as he turned to look at her.

He got it, he *really* got it. There *was* something special about Skye. It was difficult to put into words, but the island tugged at your heartstrings, and Rocco felt it too.

She cleared her throat, a throat that had suddenly developed a lump in it.

The rest of the descent continued in silence until they reached the rocky beach bisected by the river. Crumbling stone buildings sat on either side, the water relatively shallow because the tide was out. Above the high-tide mark was a stone structure with tumbledown walls and no roof, but a tall, metal-clad, orange-rusted chimney still stood proud.

'What did this use to be?' Rocco asked.

'I'm not a hundred per cent sure, but I believe it was something to do with the mining of diatomite, back in the nineteenth century. Diatomite is used in cat litter and toothpaste, of all things. The rock was prepared here, then shipped out on boats. Don't ask me how the chimney comes into it, though. If you go around the other side, you can actually go inside and see right to the top.'

Eagerly, Rocco did as she suggested and she followed, standing close beside him to stare up through the brick heart of the chimney at a circle of bright blue sky.

'From the road, you'd never know any of this was here,' he said, running a hand over the coarse worn bricks. 'Is it possible to get to the buildings on the other side of the river?'

'The tide is low, so we can paddle across.' She eyed his hiking boots. 'You might have to take those off, though.'

'I'm game, if you are.' He paused. 'Would you like to explore the beach? See if you can find any sea glass?'

She shook her head. 'This is your day, not mine. I can look for sea glass any time.'

'Here?'

'Well, no, not *here*, exactly.' She could get here on the bus, but it was a bit of a faff.

'Are you in a rush to move on?'

She wasn't, and Rocco seemed happy enough to dabble around on the rocky, pebbly beach. It was probably too pebbly for any decent finds, but she wasn't about to pass up the opportunity to have a quick look.

After half an hour of poking around, she'd managed to find a couple of fragments, which she carefully stowed in her bag.

'Do you still want to go to the other side?' she asked, and when he confirmed that he did, they headed upstream to find a suitable place to cross.

The water was clear, fast flowing and icy cold, as Giselle discovered when she delicately dipped a bare toe in it.

'Damn, that's freezing!' Rocco exclaimed, wading in up to his ankles.

'Changed your mind?'

'Nope. It's slippery though, so be careful. Give me your hand.'

Giselle placed her hand in his, and as he tightened his grip, she felt a tingle go right through her. But all too soon, they reached the opposite bank, and he let go of her to put his socks and shoes back on.

There was no path on this side, and Giselle guessed fewer people braved the icy crossing. Stumbling over tussocks of coarse grass, she followed Rocco as he ploughed resolutely towards the buildings.

One was still in use, as it had a rickety tin roof and contained a pile of lobster pots, but the other had been abandoned decades ago. The half-standing ruined walls showed where windows and doors had been, but Giselle was fascinated to discover an old hearth with a stone chimney. It was nowhere near as large as the one they'd just explored, but it was more atmospheric.

'Can I take a photo of you?' Rocco asked.

She'd noticed him taking a couple of snaps, but she'd been careful to keep out of shot, not sure whether he'd want her photobombing his Skye memories.

'If you want, but only if I can take one of *you*.'

Rocco laughed. 'You drive a hard bargain.'

Several photos later, his attention was captured by the rusting remains of various bits of machinery left lying around in the grass: a pulley, lengths of metal cabling, some kind of gear contraption... Every so often he would mutter, 'Fascinating,' and she smiled indulgently – he was surrounded by all this fabulous scenery and he was enthralled by bits of rusted metal?

'Ready to see the falls?' she asked, when she deemed that they'd poked around for long enough.

'I thought we'd seen them.'

'I've saved the best bit till last,' she told him, and she laughed aloud when his eyes lit up.

She was having more fun than she thought possible, showing him around her homeland and seeing the delight on his face.

It took considerable effort to convince herself that was the reason she was having fun, and not because she was enjoying being with him.

A second teeth-chattering, toe-numbing, hand-holding river crossing later (she enjoyed the hand-holding – the rest, not so much) found them on the right side of the river again, and Giselle set off along a narrow track. Then, after rounding the side of the hill, the base of the waterfall came into sight.

'Would you look at that?' Rocco breathed.

The water fell in a continuous white torrent into a large pool. At the edge, the pool was shallow enough to see the rocky bottom, but the deeper water was dark and mysterious.

They lingered for a while, taking photos, but finally they had to face the trek to the top.

Neither said a word on the way up because they didn't have the breath, but when the incline levelled off, Rocco panted, 'That was awesome.'

Giselle had to agree. She hadn't visited the falls for many years and had forgotten how magnificent they were.

'Before we go any further,' she said, 'how about we have some lunch?' She hadn't planned on being here this long and was starting to get hungry.

'Good idea. I've brought a picnic for us to share.'

'So have I.'

The wind was quite gusty at the top, blowing in from the sea and rising sharply to whip around them, taking their breath, but instead of retreating to the car, they found a sheltered spot and sat amongst the clumps of pink and purple heather to eat their lunch.

'What have you got in mind for the rest of the day?' Rocco asked, biting into a chicken wrap.

'Haven't you had enough of the great outdoors yet?'

'Definitely not.'

'How about the Quiraing? You can't visit Skye and not walk up it.'

He said, 'Isn't it supposed to be tough?'

'It's a hike, not a scramble, but there's no climbing involved, so it's not too bad, and the views are absolutely stunning.'

'In that case, I'd better fuel up,' he declared, tucking into another wrap.

Giselle wasn't far behind him. She was starving, and by her reasoning the food was better being carried in her tummy than in her backpack.

With lunch finished and everything packed away, they were ready to go.

Rocco got to his feet first, slinging his rucksack over his shoulder, then stretching out a hand to help her up.

Remembering the effect their earlier hand-holding had had on her, Giselle hesitated before taking it and allowing Rocco to haul her to her feet. She stood up too quickly and, unbalanced, stumbled forward, falling against him.

His free arm snapped around her, steadying her, and she found herself pressed against his chest.

A burst of desire exploded in her stomach like a firework, fizzing along her veins, and she gasped.

'Are you OK?' His voice was full of concern.

'Oops. I'm fine. Sorry, didn't mean to launch myself at you,' she stammered, stepping back out of his grasp. Embarrassed, she fiddled with the straps of her bag, keeping her head down and her eyes averted, then turning away, she set off for the car, but as she did so, she thought she heard him say, 'That's a pity.'

Chapter 14

Rocco gripped the steering wheel with white knuckles, praying they wouldn't meet any vehicles coming the other way. There were plenty of passing places, but the thought of having to reverse down this single-track road with its soft verges didn't appeal.

The landscape was wild and rugged, clothed in long-stemmed grass, spiky reeds and bracken, and dotted with the occasional sheep. Ahead lay vast outcrops of forbidding rock, towering into the sky.

Everywhere he looked, in every direction, was a photo opportunity begging to be taken. The only word he could think of was 'breathtaking', but in his opinion, *everything* here was breathtaking.

The road twisted and climbed ever higher, each hairpin bend revealing another jaw-dropping view, and just as they crested the top of a rise, to his relief, a car park appeared.

Once they'd parked up and settled their bags on their backs, Giselle pointed to a path on the opposite side of the road.

'We're going that way,' she said.

Rocco blew out his cheeks. 'Up *there*?'

'That's right.'

Up there was a huge cliff with stomach-churning drops, and he couldn't take his eyes off it. He didn't *think* he was scared of heights, but he had a feeling he was about to be proved wrong.

The path was gentle at first but soon became rough underfoot, and then positively scrambly (*you fibbed, Giselle*) as a small stream had to be crossed, and further on they were faced with a section of loose scree. And they kept heading ever upwards, passing needles of rock, climbing over stiles, trying not to get too close to the cliff edges, and always, *always* being humbled by the view.

The summit was five hundred metres above sea level, and Rocco was thankful by the time they reached it. And totally astounded, because below them was a spectacular tableau of flat emerald-green plateau which was surrounded by rock formations and staggering cliffs.

He'd never seen anything so awe inspiring in his life.

Shaking his head in wonder, he turned to look at Giselle, who was equally moved. Her eyes were wide, her full lips parted and she had a rosy glow in her usually pale cheeks. God, she was beautiful. So beautiful that he forgot to look at the view for several long seconds.

'Well?' she asked.

'Huh?' Damn. Had she noticed him watching her?

'Was it worth the hike?'

'Absolutely!' Of that there was no doubt. 'Thank you for bringing me.'

'I'm sure you would have found this place on your own.'

'I expect I would have, but it's so much nicer to have someone to enjoy it with.'

Not just someone: *Giselle*. He couldn't think of anyone else he'd want to be here with. To be truthful, he was beginning to think he wouldn't want to be *anywhere* with anyone other than her.

It was a sobering thought.

'Real live dinosaur footprints?' Rocco asked, incredulously.

'Not live, no. I believe dinosaurs have been dead a wee while.'

'I meant, in situ – not in a museum.'

'On An Corran beach, actually. I've never heard of "situ". Where's that? Down south?'

Rocco pulled a face, and wondered whether to tell Giselle that in situ didn't mean an actual place, when he caught the twinkle in her eye and realised she was winding him up.

'Why don't you stop making fun of me and tell me where we're supposed to be going,' he said.

'I told you, An Corran beach.'

'Who's Anne Corran and where is her beach?' he shot back.

Giselle rolled her eyes. 'Just drive. I'll let you know where to go when we get to the main road.'

'Please tell me it won't involve any more walking,' he begged.

He'd more than achieved his step count for today. In fact, he'd happily find a nice pub to sit in for a couple of hours, but he'd asked her to show him Skye, and he could hardly complain that she was doing as he'd asked. He was also worried that if he did, she might suggest they return to Duncoorie, and he wasn't ready to go back yet. Not unless he was able to spend the rest of the day with her, but he had no idea how he'd wangle that.

Great, yet more single-track lanes, Rocco grumbled to himself when Giselle instructed him to turn off the main road and head for a village called Staffin. At least they were at sea level now, so hopefully their destination wasn't far.

'There it is,' she said, pointing to a small expanse of sandy beach flanked by rocks.

He parked the car and they picked their way down onto the beach. As they did so, he glanced back the way they'd come, to see cliffs rearing above them, and to the west he could make out the Quiraing.

Rocco was now standing on a shelf of flat rock, and he wondered where to start looking. The rock was criss-crossed with cracks and furrows, and speckled with green algae and seaweed.

Heads down, they spread out and began their quest.

'What are we looking for, exactly?' he called, after a few minutes of not seeing anything obvious. He wondered whether they'd be similar to the massive, cratered footprints depicted in the *Jurassic Park* films.

Giselle was a few feet away. She was crouching down, tracing the outline of something with a finger. 'This,' she said.

Rocco hurried to her side and peered down. He still didn't see anything.

And then he did! It wasn't as big as he'd anticipated, about forty centimetres long, and neither was it as distinct an outline as he'd expected. But now that she'd pointed it out, he could see a three-toed depression. Although, if it hadn't been for Giselle, he would have walked straight past it. Now that he'd seen one, he spotted another, and another. Three in all, although he subsequently found out that there were eighteen in total.

'This island is full of surprises,' he said. 'I knew it had lots of history, but I didn't realise it went so far back.'

'Want to see some more?'

'Footprints?'

Giselle nodded. 'And other things. Staffin Fossil Museum is just down the way.'

The museum was an old stone single-storey building, a mile or so along the main road leading towards Portree.

'It's quite a small museum,' Giselle said, 'run by a guy by the name of Dugald. He's collected many of the exhibits himself, and some have been donated by local schoolchildren.'

She was right. It was small, but it had some interesting stuff. Rocco gravitated towards a display of footprints made by a creature called a Coelophysis, and a slab of rock containing fossilised shells. There was also a thigh bone as tall as a small child. The Neolithic arrowheads and pottery fragments were fascinating, and he spent a few minutes studying them before joining Giselle, who was at the far end of the room, examining something called a mangle.

Rocco had no idea what the contraption was for.

'It was used to wring out wet clothes after they'd been washed, before they were hung on the line to dry,' she said. 'People rolled them between the two rollers to squeeze the water out.'

'It looks lethal. You wouldn't want to get your fingers caught in that!'

'I believe you own one of these,' she told him.

'I do?'

'I think it was put in the cellars when the outbuildings were converted into the craft centre,' she said, and Rocco made a mental note to take a look when he got the chance, wondering what else might be down there.

It was now five thirty and the museum was about to close, so they returned to the car.

'Hungry?' he asked.

'Starving.'

'So am I.'

'Fish and chips?' she suggested.

Rocco thought he could do better than that, but he'd have to be careful how he went about it. She wasn't going to take kindly to him paying for her meal. 'I could eat some fish. We've had a busy day. Thanks for showing me your island. I've enjoyed it.'

'That was only a teeny tiny part.'

With fake surprise, Rocco said, 'There's *more*?'

'Of course, there's—' she began hotly, subsiding when she realised he was teasing. 'I really do have to get some work done tomorrow,' she said. 'This is peak tourist season, and—'

'I understand. There's no need to explain. I'm sure I can find my way around by myself.'

'I'm sure you can.'

'It won't be as much fun.'

'I doubt it will.' She sighed. 'OK, how about Monday?'

'Monday is fine.' He hid the smile creeping across his face.

'When are you going back to London?'

'I'm not sure.' It depended on how long he could get away with this impromptu holiday. He was aware that work would be building up, and there was only a certain amount he could do while away from the office, but goddamn it, he'd put his heart and soul into the business since his dad died, so surely he was entitled to some time off? His battery was in sore need of recharging, and the most telling thing was that he hadn't thought about work at all today. Not once. That had to be healthy, right? He *needed* this holiday. He'd felt more relaxed today than he'd felt in months.

'What will you do with yourself tomorrow?' she asked, her head still resting on the back of her seat.

He glanced at her to find her gazing at him. 'I suppose I could try to get some work done.'

'Are you able to work remotely?'

'I am, but not for long. Beverly isn't keen, and many of our clients prefer face-to-face meetings.' That was simplifying things considerably, but he didn't want to go into the details of the business. He didn't want to think about it at all, right now. *Sod it*, he was on holiday. He wasn't going to work while he was here. He was going to kick back, relax and enjoy himself. Preferably with Giselle.

'On second thoughts,' he said, 'I'll get out and about tomorrow. Any recommendations?'

'Plenty, but nearly all of them involve some kind of outdoor activity. If you don't want to venture too far from Duncoorie, you could go out on a boat. Mack – you met him last night in the pub; the guy who looks like a Viking? – he does whale- and dolphin-watching excursions.'

'That sounds perfect. Are you sure you don't want to come?'

She looked rueful. 'I'd better not,' she replied, then lapsed into silence.

Rocco turned the radio on for some background noise and relaxed into the drive. The pub was on the outskirts of Portree. He'd noticed it yesterday – was it only yesterday that he'd changed his mind about going home? – and had thought it looked nice. He was about to find out if it was.

'What are you doing?' she asked, sitting up straighter as the car rolled to a halt.

He switched off the engine. 'I'm about to have dinner. You can join me, if you wish.'

'Here? I thought we were going to have fish and chips?'

'I'm sure they'll have fish on the menu.'

Giselle narrowed her eyes. He noticed her nose had caught the sun, and he really, *really* wanted to kiss it.

'I can't afford it,' she stated boldly.

'I'm paying.'

'No.'

'Giselle...'

'I said no.'

'Think of it as me buying you dinner in exchange for your services as a tour guide.'

'Like a kind of barter system?' she said.

'That's right, a barter system.'

'Is everything business to you?'

'Not everything. Anyway, you bought the fish and chips last time.'

'Don't pull this stunt again,' she warned, getting out of the car.

'I won't.'

'Promise?'

'I promise.'

'And don't you go ordering too much, or loads of side dishes,' she added.

'Would I do such a thing?'

'Venice,' was all she said, stalking towards the pub's entrance.

He'd guessed at the time that she'd seen through his ruse when he'd ordered far too much *bruschette* for one.

The pub was more of a restaurant, Rocco realised, as they were shown to a table.

With drinks ordered and menus in their hands, Giselle hissed, 'I feel underdressed.'

Oh, I wish you were, Rocco thought, before catching himself. 'You look fine,' he told her. She looked more than fine: she looked gorgeous.

'My hair is a mess and I've got grass stains on my trousers.'

'So is mine,' he said, running a hand through his hair.

Her lips twitched. 'How about grass stains?'

'Do you want me to stand up and show you my backside?' Then he groaned aloud as he realised what he'd said. 'Did I just offer to show you my arse? Good grief!'

'I've seen it before,' she quipped.

'So you have. Does the fact that we knew each other years ago bother you?'

Two spots of colour appeared on her cheeks. 'A little,' she admitted.

'Me, too. Venice was lovely, wasn't it? I mean, the city, not the… although that was lovely, too. Oh, shit!'

Giselle was giggling, and Rocco started to laugh. 'I'm not usually this inarticulate,' he said. 'I'm normally quite eloquent. Or at least not as embarrassing.'

'I loved it,' she said, her eyes brimming with laughter. 'Venice, that is, as well as the…' Her laughter faded as she stared into his eyes.

Hers were navy, as fathomless as the ocean.

'Are you ready to order, sir, madam?'

The moment was gone with the appearance of a waiter, and Rocco hurriedly looked at the menu and picked the first thing he saw.

Giselle seemed equally as flustered, and further conversation was stilted and awkward, only settling when the food arrived and the conversation turned to less personal matters.

'Didn't you tell me that Flora MacDonald is buried on Skye?' Rocco asked. They'd been discussing Skye's rich history and the role the island played in the war against the English in the eighteenth century.

'She is. I've been to her grave.'

'I'd like to see it.'

'We could go there on Monday, if you like.' Giselle looked pleased. 'Most people want to see the big stuff: the mountains, the waterfalls, the castles, the jaw-dropping scenery, but the smaller stuff, the less well known, is equally important.'

Rocco was looking forward to it already.

They lingered over dessert and coffee, Giselle declaring herself to be stuffed, then Rocco paid the bill and they headed home.

Dusk was falling as he brought the car to a halt outside her bothy.

Her rucksack was in the boot, so he got out and opened it. Picking the bag up, he handed it to her, and when his fingers touched hers, the contact sent a shock up his arm.

He thought she must have felt it too, because she inhaled sharply and her lips parted.

There was a moment where their hands were touching, the rucksack between them, when he thought he was going to kiss her, when he thought he was going to lose himself in the depths of her eyes. But then she stepped back and he released his hold on the bag, and found himself saying off-handedly, 'See you on Monday,' as he closed the boot.

Unfortunately, he didn't think he could wait a whole day to see her again.

Chapter 15

Muirporth Quay, a couple of miles north of Duncoorie, was home to a handful of boats, one of them belonging to Mack, the guy who ran the whale-watching tours. Rocco was rather looking forward to this, although he would have been looking forward to it even more if Giselle had been accompanying him.

Squeezing past several people, he chose a spot to the right of the bow and settled down to enjoy the trip. The sea was calm initially, but as the boat chugged further away from the shelter of the quay, the waves grew. It was blustery out on the open water, the wind tugging at the fabric of his recently purchased Gore-Tex jacket and flecking the waves with white, as seagulls swooped overhead, wheeling through the sky on the unseen air currents with raucous cries. The smell of diesel from the engines was mixed with brine and the peculiar seaside smell reminiscent of his childhood. Feeling like a kid, Rocco revelled in the slap of the boat through the waves and the exhilaration of being on the open water.

Mack kept up a running commentary for the passengers, pointing out things of interest, and to Rocco's amusement one of them was Coorie Castle. Seeing it from this perspective made him realise anew how impressive it was, and he felt an entirely misplaced sense of pride as an elderly couple sitting next to him exclaimed over it.

'It's very picturesque,' the woman said. 'I'd love to see inside. Is it open to the public?'

'I don't think so,' her husband replied.

Rocco couldn't resist. 'Sorry, I couldn't help overhearing. The castle has a craft centre where you can watch artists at work, and there's a gift shop and a lovely cafe.'

The woman smiled broadly. 'Did you hear that, Frank? They've got a craft centre! We'll have to call in on the way back.'

'Did you have to tell her? She'll buy half the damn shop.' The man rolled his eyes.

'I love a craft centre,' she said. 'And we need a little memento of our holiday, don't we, Frank?'

'We don't,' Frank sighed, 'but she'll buy one, anyway.'

Mission accomplished, Rocco's attention returned to the scenery. The boat was sailing parallel to the shore, and he was thrilled when he saw several grey shapes sprawled on the rocks. Then he noticed the sleek head of a seal bobbing in the water, gazing at them with huge dark eyes, and his heart melted.

Gradually, the boat moved into deeper water, and soon it was in the middle of the loch. Rocco scanned the surface incessantly, but he couldn't see anything even remotely resembling a fin.

Mack was in the middle of explaining that the conditions weren't ideal for whale spotting when a shout went up from one of the crew. 'Harbour porpoise to starboard!'

'That's to your right, for all you landlubbers,' Mack informed them over the speakers.

Rocco craned his neck. He couldn't see anything for a second, then a stubby grey dorsal fin curved out of the water before disappearing, followed by three more. The animals were about a metre and a half long (according to Mack; Rocco couldn't tell) and had grey backs, with lighter sides and white underbellies.

Mack explained how porpoises differed from dolphins, and that both species used echo location to hunt fish. Rocco was also fascinated to learn they could hold their breath for up to twelve minutes.

The boat kept pace with the animals for a while, until Mack said, 'I think we'll leave them in peace now,' and the boat veered off. The porpoises quickly disappeared, but for Rocco, out of sight didn't mean out of mind.

'That was brilliant. Thank you,' he said to Mack when they were back at the quayside. 'Giselle says hi, by the way.'

Mack gave him a slow nod, his gaze assessing. 'Don't hurt her.'

Surprised, Rocco lifted his chin and gazed steadily back. 'I won't. It's not like that. We're friends, that's all.' And even if they were more than friends, it was none of this guy's business.

Mack's eyes were hooded. 'Let's hope *she* sees it that way.'

'Sees what? There's nothing *to* see.' Last night's almost-kiss flashed across his mind. There would have been something if she'd let it. 'Just friends,' he repeated firmly.

A spark of jealousy lit him from within before subsiding as he remembered that Mack had a girlfriend, a flame-haired potter called Freya. One big family, Giselle had said, so maybe the man was playing the role of a big brother. He clearly had her back, and Rocco realised he was glad she had people looking out for her. And envious, too.

One big family... Giselle was fortunate, indeed.

Two coaches and a car park full of cars and motorhomes greeted Rocco when he returned to the castle, and both the cafe and the gift shop were doing a brisk trade, he was pleased to see. Despite his intention to sell the estate, wages and bills still had to be paid, so any money in the till was welcome. If the craft centre had been making a loss, he'd have no hesitation in winding it up immediately, but since it was paying its way and making a decent profit, it made financial sense to keep it going, and although he wouldn't be there to monitor it, Cal would carry on as the estate's manager until the castle was sold. After that, it would be up to the new owner to decide whether they wanted to keep the staff on.

However, Rocco wasn't popping into the gift shop to check on sales. He was there to make a purchase.

Two staff were working today, Jinny and another woman, and when Jinny saw him, a look of alarm flashed across her face before being swiftly replaced with a polite smile.

'Is there anything I can help you with?' she asked, a note of worry in her voice.

'I'm killing time, waiting for the lunchtime rush to subside,' he said. 'The cafe is full.'

'You'll have a long wait. It's usually busy well into the afternoon.'

'In that case, I'd better join the queue. But since I'm here, I'll have a look around first. I didn't have the opportunity to mooch last time – too focused on trying to orientate myself and get a feel for the place.'

'Mooch away,' Jinny said, adding, 'Shout if you need me,' as she went to serve a customer.

Rocco was relieved to see her go. He didn't want her to guess what he was up to.

Seemingly at random, he dawdled around the shop, picking things up and putting them down again, pausing to admire displays and standing back to study pottery or paintings, until he came to the real reason he was here.

The large sea glass picture of the loch was still for sale. That was all he wanted to know.

Slipping outside, he reached for his mobile, dismayed when he saw the number of notifications pop up. Ignoring them, he phoned Claire.

'Sorry to call you on a Sunday,' he said. 'I'll make it quick. Could you do me a favour? Would you purchase a picture for me if I send you the details?'

'Of course. You know you can phone me any time. I don't mind.'

'Thanks. One other thing,' he added. 'It needs to be done today, and can you be discreet? I don't want my name used. Could you also arrange to have it sent to your place?' It was underhand of him, and Giselle would be furious if she found out, but he didn't like to see her so strapped for cash. Hopefully, this small gesture of his would help a bit.

Claire said, 'No problem, but do you mind me asking, why so cloak and dagger?'

'I'm buying a picture from the castle's gift shop, but I don't want all and sundry to know.'

'I can't wait to see it. Who's the artist?'

'No one you've heard of. Let me know if there are any issues with the purchase. Speak soon.' He ended the call without waiting for a reply and pinged her an email with the details. He'd already taken up enough of Claire's Sunday.

Standing in line for a sandwich and a coffee, Rocco decided to buy it to go. He didn't want to eat on his own, occupying a table a customer could use, so he'd pay Giselle's studio a visit and eat it there, if she'd let him.

'Make that two,' he said, hoping to appease her with an offering of food.

If Giselle was surprised to see him, she didn't show it, although she grabbed her sandwich and drink with enthusiasm.

'I haven't had a minute to myself,' she said, unwrapping the baguette and taking a huge bite. With a hand in front of her mouth, she mumbled, 'I've had people in and out all day, asking questions. I love that they take an interest, but I haven't managed to get much work done.'

'Can I help?' He leant against the counter and tucked into his food.

Her expression was doubtful. 'I'm not sure what you could do.'

'Do you mind if I stay for a while and watch you work? I promise I won't get in your way.'

'If you do, I'll kick you out,' she warned.

Rocco grinned. 'You won't know I'm here.'

'Oh, I think I will.' Her reply was accompanied by a look that sent a wave of desire rippling through him. It quickly receded when she explained, 'I'm always uneasy when someone's in my studio. It's a bit like how I imagine an animal at the zoo feels. I keep waiting for someone to tap the counter to see if I'll move.' She shoved the rest of the baguette into her mouth; from the way she'd devoured it, he wondered whether she'd eaten yet today.

It pained him to think she wasn't looking after herself, which was ridiculous since she'd clearly looked after herself just fine for the past ten years without any help from him.

'How was the boat trip?' she asked, sitting on the stool and picking up a ball of green string.

'I saw harbour porpoises and seals. It was awesome.'

'I thought you might enjoy it. I've been out with Mack a few times, and once, we saw orcas.'

Rocco stiffened. 'I didn't realise you and Mack were...' He ground to a halt. No wonder the guy had warned him off.

'We weren't,' Giselle said. 'When I said "out", I meant out on the boat. With other people. Not just me and him.'

Could a heart sink and soar at the same time? Rocco felt both a fool for thinking – and saying – that Giselle and Mack might have dated, yet relieved to learn they hadn't. Which was even more ridiculous than worrying about whether she was eating properly, because *of course* she'd had boyfriends and been on dates, and she'd probably been in love as well over the last decade.

Rocco was growing concerned; he was having the most absurd notions. And it wasn't as though *he* hadn't had love interests over the years, because he had. Quite a few, and even though none had scratched the surface of his feelings, he'd had fun along the way. There hadn't been much on the dating horizon lately, though, and he blamed that on the pressures of work. All he seemed to do was work and go to the gym, with an increasingly rare evening out with mates thrown in. No wonder he was enjoying this little break so much.

'What are you making?' he asked, after watching Giselle cut the string into varying lengths and arranging them on a sheet of white card.

'A wildflower scene. The string is the stems and the glass will be the buds and flowers. I might put a butterfly in it as well, or a dragonfly.'

He pulled up a chair and peered over her shoulder.

She scowled at him until he moved back, aware he was crowding her.

It amazed him how she could turn a piece of card and some random fragments of frosted glass into something to hang on a wall. He wished he had that kind of talent, but he didn't have a creative bone in his body.

'You don't use a photo or an image to work from,' he observed. 'How do you know what the end result will look like?'

'I have an idea in my head, but I rarely stick to it because a lot depends on the way the glass sits together. Flexibility is the key.'

He watched her select several pale green bits.

'Petals,' she announced, then fished a yellow stone out of a drawer. 'This will be the centre of the flower.'

She played with the arrangement, swapping one piece of glass for another until she was satisfied. Then she started on the next flower, while Rocco marvelled at her patience.

When his phone rang, he considered ignoring it, fearing it was his mother.

It was Claire, however, so he decided to answer in case there was a problem with the purchase. Excusing himself, he went to stand by the door so he could slip outside if there was an issue.

'Hi, Claire,' he said softly. 'What's up?'

'I thought I'd let you know I've bought the picture.'

He lowered his voice. 'Thanks, I appreciate it.'

'If I can do anything, or if you need anything else, give me a call.'

'I will.'

'Beverly tells me you're taking some time off?'

'That's right.'

'Any idea when you'll be back?'

'Wednesday, probably.'

'Don't enjoy yourself too much, will you? We need you here.'

'And you'll have me in a couple of days.'

'Good, because the place isn't the same without you.'

Rocco wasn't sure how to respond to that. 'See you soon,' was all he could come up with. 'Bye, Claire.'

He put his phone on silent and slipped it into his back pocket. 'Sorry about that,' he said to Giselle. 'Where were we?'

'*I* was making a picture. *You* were asking questions.'

'It's the best way to learn,' he quipped.

'The best way to learn is to do something yourself, not watch someone else do it.'

'Are you suggesting I should have a go?'

'Why not?'

'I'm not in the least bit artistic.'

'Give it a go,' she urged, pushing a blank piece of card towards him.

'What should I make?' he asked, pulling up another stool and staring at the card apprehensively.

'You can make the same as me, if you like.'

'OK. What do I do?'

'Cut some lengths of string.'

Obediently, he did as instructed. 'Now what?'

'Lay them on the card, like this.' She leant across, took one of the pieces of string and placed it on the card. She was so close he could smell the magnolia scent of her hair. She was so close that if he moved his head a little, he'd be able to kiss the delicate skin beneath her ear.

Rocco cleared his throat and tucked in his chin, fighting the urge.

She said, 'Try not to make them all the same length. Having the flowers at different heights gives the picture depth and more interest.'

She scooted back and he blew out his cheeks. 'Right.'

'Don't be scared of making a mistake. You won't be gluing anything in place until you're one hundred per cent happy with it.'

It wasn't making a mistake with the picture that worried him. It was his overactive libido.

Trying to keep his mind on the task in front of him, he concentrated on arranging the lengths of string, then selecting various bits of sea glass for the petals. Giselle had finished hers and was watching his progress, making him even more aware of her.

'Try this,' she suggested when he struggled to find a fragment for the centre of the first flower, and she handed him a yellow piece.

Thankfully, she didn't realise the reason he was struggling was because he could feel her warmth on his arm as she peered over his shoulder, and that her nearness unsettled him.

Eventually, under Giselle's tuition, a picture gradually came to life, and even if he said so himself, Rocco was surprisingly pleased with the result, considering his attention had been more on her than on what he was supposed to be doing.

'Can I keep it?' he asked.

'You made it. It's yours. Once it's dry, I'll frame it for you.'

'You must let me pay you for it.'

Giselle burst out laughing. 'Don't be silly. It's your work, not mine.'

'Using your materials,' he pointed out.

'A bit of glue, a length of string, and the sea glass was free.'

'The frame isn't. Let me pay you for that, at least.'

'Absolutely not.' She folded her arms.

Rocco had to smile. Giselle might look as ethereal as mist on a summer morning, but she was as stubborn as a thick fog. He knew when he was beaten. Anyway, little did she know, but he'd had the last laugh today.

'Join me for dinner tonight?' he said.

'Can't. Too much to do. I've got a business to run. These pictures won't make themselves, and if you want me to take you sightseeing tomorrow, I'm going to have to get my skates on. Now go away.' She shooed him towards the door.

Rocco reluctantly left.

He'd have an early dinner and an early night, and try not to dwell on how he would have liked to have shared his table, and his bed, with her this evening.

—

'I wanted to let you know, I've sold your big picture, the one of the loch,' Jinny announced, waltzing into the studio as Giselle was about to lock the door. The rest of the crafters had left for the day, but she still had work to do so she'd be here a while yet.

Giselle felt a surge of relief at the news. It was her most expensive piece and the proceeds would keep the wolf from her door for another week. With a hefty mortgage to service, she was always aware of money: namely the lack of it. It must be nice for some – like Rocco, for instance – not to have to worry about every penny.

'Giselle, did you hear what I said?' Jinny's voice broke through her musing.

'Sorry. Yes, I did. That's fantastic news!'

'I'm going to have to ship it, but Tara's got a doll's house to post, so she said she'll arrange for the courier to collect both items at the same time, if that's OK?'

It most certainly was! Even as Giselle had been making the picture, she'd worried that its size might put people off. After all, it wouldn't fit into the boot of the average tourist's car, not if they had luggage and stuff.

'That's great. I'll thank Tara when I see her. Who bought it, do you know?'

'Some woman. I didn't speak to her; Fiona did.'

Giselle laughed. 'So, when you say *you* sold my picture, it wasn't you exactly; it was your wonderful part-time sales assistant.'

'It's my shop,' Jinny said. 'I run it. Although technically, it's Rocco Moore's now.' She pulled a face. 'For how long, is a question we're all asking. Do I have to start looking for another job, Giselle? You've spent more time with him than anyone, apart from Cal; has Rocco said anything to you?'

'Nothing you don't already know.'

'I suppose I'd better put some feelers out, see what's around. If Mhairi knew, she'd be turning in her grave.'

'I expect she must have guessed.'

Jinny sighed. 'You're probably right. She was a canny one, was Mhairi. It'll be such a shame, though. She'd worked so hard to make the craft centre work – we all have.' She sighed again. 'I'll wait a while and see what happens. You never know; maybe whoever buys it will want to keep it just the way it is.'

Giselle certainly hoped so, but all they could do was cross their fingers.

Chapter 16

Kingsburgh House, home to Flora MacDonald and the man she married after she helped Bonnie Prince Charlie escape, was only eight miles north of Portree, so since today was more about Skye's historical past than its geology, Giselle decided to kick off Rocco's education there. Although, if she was honest, today would be for her benefit too, because she'd always been deeply moved by Flora MacDonald's story, convinced there was more to it than the archives led people to believe.

Unfortunately, there wasn't much to see. Privately owned and in a state of disrepair, the house wasn't the original one that had stood on that spot, but it was enough for Giselle.

'I've heard of Bonnie Prince Charlie, but I don't know the story,' Rocco said, as they walked from the road through a stand of trees towards the dilapidated old house.

'Charles Stuart was the grandson of James VII of Scotland, who was also James II of England – yes, the same James; not two different people – and believed that the British throne was rightfully his. In 1745, he and his followers led a rebellion to overthrow King George II and restore Stuart's claim to the throne. It became known as the Jacobite Uprising and ended at the Battle of Culloden in 1746 when Charles Stuart lost to the British redcoats in a horrifically bloody battle. Two thousand Jacobites were killed, but Bonnie Prince Charlie escaped.' Giselle knew the story off by heart, but it always moved her, and when they reached a metal gate with a view of the old house between the trees, she rested her arms on top of it and carried on.

'This is where Flora MacDonald comes in. Charlie had a price on his head – £30,000, equivalent to about £5 million in today's money – and was being hunted the length and breadth of Scotland. Flora was staying in South Uist with her benefactor, Lady Clanranald, who was a Jacobite sympathiser. The story has it that Flora was touched by the prince's desperate situation and agreed to smuggle him to Skye, where he could get a ship to France. Risking her life, she dressed him in women's clothing, and with him disguised as her maidservant, she took him over the sea to Skye.'

'The "Skye Boat Song".'

'Aye, that's the one. I won't sing it for you again.' He didn't need to hear her pathetic warbling.

To her surprise, Rocco sang it instead. 'Carry the lad who was born to be king, over the sea to Skye,' he warbled, in a pleasing baritone.

'You have a hidden talent, Mr Moore,' she teased. 'We'll have you singing in the ceilidh next.'

'The kaylee?' he repeated.

'It's a Scottish social gathering, with dancing and music. You'd enjoy it. There's a big one held every year after the Highland Games in Portree. It's one of the highlights of the year.' He wouldn't be here to see it, though, and her mood plummeted.

Giselle pushed away from the gate, feeling despondent. 'Let's move on,' she said. There was nothing more to see here. The truth be told, she didn't know why she'd brought him here; Kingsburgh House was hardly a tourist attraction.

Their next destination was.

The Fairy Glen (Bail nan Cnoc in Gaelic, which meant Village in the Hills) was one of the most enchanting places Giselle had ever seen. It was like the Quiraing in miniature. Formed over 100,000 years ago, the sandstone bedrock had been sculpted into small conical hills which were covered in grass and stunted twisted rowan trees. Between the hillocks lay tranquil Highland pools.

It was well worth the short hike.

'Are you sure this isn't the set of a *Lord of the Rings* movie?' Rocco asked, agog. 'No wonder it's called the Fairy Glen.' He gave her a sideways look. 'Not fairies, *elves* – like you.'

Giselle touched her silver hair self-consciously. She'd been compared to Galadriel before on account of it. 'Are you suggesting I've got pointy ears?'

'Not at all. You've got cute ears. Like little shells.'

'Oh, purhleese,' she drawled. 'That's so clichéd.' Then, 'Do you *really* think they're cute?' She'd always thought her ears were on the large side, so she tended to cover them with her hair.

Rocco stroked a strand aside and tucked it behind one of her ears. His touch electrified her.

'Yes, I do.'

She bit her lip, and he let his hand fall. Was he flirting with her? Because she was fairly sure that *she* had been flirting with *him*. There was only one problem with flirting: what if he wanted to take it further? The thought of making love to him filled her with such an intense longing, born of remembered emotion and desire, that she knew she wouldn't be able to resist if he did.

'Are there any stories of fairies or magic here?' he asked, his attention on the landscape once more, forcing Giselle to gather her thoughts.

'Not one. But it feels magical, doesn't it? And that basalt tower might look like a castle, but it isn't,' she said, pointing to a rocky pinnacle of bare stone. 'There's a route to the top, if you want to give it a go, but I warn you, it's a scramble.'

'I think I'll soak up the atmosphere from here, instead,' he said. 'I did enough clambering about on Saturday. My poor legs haven't recovered yet.'

'Soft living,' she teased. 'Too many hours sat behind a desk.'

'You're not wrong. Running on a treadmill isn't the same as climbing mountains. I know which I prefer, though,' he added, taking a deep breath of the fresh clean air.

'A man after my own heart,' she said without thinking, then wrinkled her nose. *Stop flirting*, she told herself. *Nothing good will come of it.*

'I haven't seen a single bit of Skye that I don't love,' he murmured. 'Can we sit here for a moment? There's no rush to get to the next place, is there?'

'No rush,' she agreed. 'You're never going to see Skye in a few days, so you may as well savour the bits you *do* get to see.'

Rocco lowered himself onto the grass, then lay back, his hands behind his head, and closed his eyes.

Giselle sat next to him. Picking a long stem of feathery grass, she plucked the seeds one by one and cast them on the breeze. Then she picked another and delicately tickled him on the nose with it, sniggering as he batted it away, his eyes still closed.

She did it again, and this time she couldn't help a snort of laughter.

Hastily, she dropped the stem of grass as he opened his eyes and sat up.

'That wasn't a bee, was it? That was you.'

Her expression innocent, she said, 'What was me?' She was playing with fire, she knew, but the lure of him was greater than the danger of being burnt. He'd be gone soon. It was unlikely they would ever meet again, so why not enjoy her time with him? And she wanted him so very badly.

Their faces were inches apart and he was looking at her with an intensity that stole her breath and made her heart race. The world slowed and stopped.

He brushed the same strand of hair from her face, his fingers lingering on her skin, and Giselle closed her eyes.

Their lips met, delicate, silk soft, weightless, a mere whisper of the tempest surging through her. It didn't last. It couldn't. Not here, not now. But it held a promise…

Giselle ended it, withdrawing slowly, breaking the connection. She was trembling (desire? need? fear?) and the blood was rushing through her veins, her breathing coming shallow and fast.

Rocco's smoke-grey eyes were clouded and deep, and his murmured 'Giselle' sent a shiver through her very bones.

She caught her bottom lip between her teeth, the taste of him on her lips, the shape of him imprinted on her soul, and thought, *Where do we go from here?* She couldn't decide whether to flee or take him to bed.

In the end, she did neither. There was nowhere to run, and she didn't have the courage to suggest they went back to her place.

'Are you OK?' His voice was gentle.

Taking a breath, she let it out in a whoosh. 'Aye. It was unexpected, that's all.'

Lightly, he said, 'It must be the Fairy Glen, working its magic.'

'That must be it,' she agreed, getting to her feet. 'There should be warning signs.' But the warning signs were already there, and the danger was that she might lose her heart.

Flora MacDonald's grave was a short walk away from the Skye Museum of Island Life, so it seemed rude not to pop in, especially since Rocco had enjoyed the fossil museum so much. Or was he all museumed out, Giselle wondered.

Apparently not. He seemed quite keen, especially when she informed him there was a takeaway snack shop onsite. He didn't even argue when she insisted on paying for the brioche and coffee they consumed while sitting on a bench in front of a converted shepherd's hut, with views of green fields and turquoise sea.

The museum itself comprised seven stone and thatched former crofter cottages depicting everyday life on the island one hundred years ago. One had even been inhabited up to 1957. Each croft depicted something different: one was kitted out as an actual house, and a mangle and spinning wheel made a reappearance, much to Rocco's amusement. There was also a weaver's house, a smithy and a local shop, and everything was set out as though it were an actual village, and was surrounded by farm implements, small boats and carts.

Giselle and Rocco spent a considerable amount of time in each of the crofts, reading the information boards and learning about the tough lives the people lived and the hardships they endured in a demanding landscape.

'There's one thing that stands out above all others,' Rocco said thoughtfully, as they entered the small gift shop full of books and guides, tartan, tweed and knitted gifts. 'The sense of community. Everyone had to muck in and help the others.'

'It's a theme amongst islanders,' Giselle replied.

'One big family?'

'Kind of.'

'I'm beginning to get it,' he said. 'I think I'm beginning to get Skye.'

'But you're still going to sell the castle.' It was a statement, not a question.

He shrugged helplessly. 'Skye isn't my home.'

Not wanting to talk about it anymore, she cast around for something else and caught sight of the cemetery. 'Shall we go visit Flora MacDonald's grave now?' she suggested and pointed to the white spire-like monument visible in the distance.

Rocco readily agreed, and they set off up the hill. The gradient wasn't steep, but even so, the elevation still gave them a glorious view. The cemetery was surrounded by a rough stone wall and they walked through the gate towards Flora's grave.

'Pretty nice for a final resting place,' Rocco said. 'So, she brought Bonnie Prince Charlie to Skye. Then what?'

'Charles Stuart hid on Skye for several weeks before eventually boarding a ship to France. They never saw each other again. She was captured and imprisoned in London but released soon after. She married a MacDonald and lived in Kingsburgh House, and when she died, she was buried here.'

Her gravestone was a narrow white monolith, topped by a Celtic cross. Stone edging surrounded both it and a chunky stone casket. Whether she was interred inside it or buried beneath it, Giselle didn't know. A plaque on the front of the monument read, 'Preserver of Prince Charles Edward Stuart'.

'She was a real heroine,' Rocco said. 'Is it her bravery that appeals to you, or her audacity in smuggling her prince to safety?'

'Her prince,' Giselle echoed softly. 'I think she was in love.'

'With Charles?'

'If she did do it for love – and I don't mean love of her country or her king, but love for him as a man – then it's up there with the other great love stories like Anthony and Cleopatra, and Romeo and Juliet. She loved him so much that she helped him escape, even though she probably knew she'd never see him again, and that it might even cost her her life.'

'Do you think she was happy in the end? That she found love again?'

'In those days, love and marriage didn't necessarily go hand in hand,' Giselle replied wryly. 'She mightn't have had any say in the matter. Single women, even ones of Flora's fame, didn't have it easy in the eighteenth century. She lived in North Carolina in the Americas for a time, with her husband and sons, but at some point she left him and returned to Skye, where she died. So maybe she didn't find love again. Maybe she couldn't forget her prince and came back to the place she felt closest to him. They say she was buried in a shroud made out of a bedsheet that Bonnie Prince Charlie had slept in.' Giselle felt tears pricking the back of her eyes and she blinked them away, feeling foolish.

'That's beautiful, and sad,' Rocco said. 'I feel honoured to be here.'

'As far as I know, there's nothing in the archives to suggest she was in love with him. The consensus is that she was simply a staunch Jacobite supporter, which was why she acted the way she did.'

'But you don't believe that?'

Mutely, Giselle shook her head. She hoped Charles had felt the same way about Flora. Giselle wanted to believe that life had conspired to keep them apart, and not that her love had been unrequited. Giselle hoped one day she would experience the kind of love she believed Flora had felt for Charles Stuart, and she prayed her own personal prince would love her in return.

—

'Claire informs me you're coming back on Wednesday.' Beverly's voice rang out of the speaker on Rocco's phone. 'That's good to know,' she added, and he heard the admonishment.

She was miffed he hadn't kept her updated, that she'd had to hear it from someone else.

'Actually, I've changed my mind. Skye's Highland Games take place on Wednesday and I'd like to be here for them.'

Beverly was silent. Had they been cut off, or had he actually managed to render his mother speechless? If so, it would be a first.

'I wasn't aware you had an interest in sport,' she said eventually.

Rocco didn't, but this was different. After he'd dropped Giselle off earlier (with a chaste peck on the cheek), he'd hurried back to the castle to look up what a Highland Games consisted of. He hadn't told Giselle he was thinking of going to Skye's games, but he hoped she would accompany him.

'Highland Games are more tradition than sport,' he replied.

'So is cricket, but you've yet to show an interest in *that*. This is most unlike you, Rocco.'

'Taking some time for myself? I suppose it is,' he agreed mildly, refusing to let her get to him. His mother was the queen of manipulation.

'Is everything all right?'

'Everything's fine.'

'So why do I feel there's something you're not telling me?'

'I have no idea.'

'Is there a problem with probate?'

'Not that I'm aware of.' He needed to start the ball rolling on that…

'You would tell me, wouldn't you? Don't think that because your inheritance is a personal matter you can't use the firm's resources to deal with it. I still maintain you should let Claire handle it.'

'It's fine, Mother.'

'If you call me Mother, I'll definitely think something is wrong.'

'I wish you'd stop worrying. There's nothing to worry about.'

Beverly's problem – or rather, *his* problem – was that she had a nose like a bloodhound and could sense when someone wasn't being completely truthful with her.

Would Rocco still be on Skye if it wasn't for Giselle? Unlikely.

Would he be planning on going to the Highland Games?

Definitely not. It would never have crossed his mind. But by showing him some of the places she loved on the island, Giselle had made him appreciate it. Skye had got under his skin, and he was beginning to fall under its spell.

Just as Giselle had gotten under his skin. And he feared he might be a little in love with her, too.

Chapter 17

'Who's the hottie?'

Giselle laughed at Izzy's excited voice. 'Good morning to you, too.'

'Well?! Who is he?'

Yesterday evening, Giselle had sent her sister some photos of Lealt Falls, the Quiraing and the other places she'd visited over the past few days. Rocco had featured in a couple of them.

'The castle's new owner,' she replied.

'Flipping heck, Zelle, he's *bellissimo*! Are you two...?'

'No, we're not.' She deliberately didn't think of the kiss at the Fairy Glen, and she'd been deliberately *not thinking* about it ever since it had happened. 'He wanted someone to show him the highlights of Skye, that's all.'

'If you ask me, *he's* one of the highlights,' Izzy shot back. 'Don't take this the wrong way, but why you?'

'Thanks!' She'd been asking herself the same thing.

'What I meant was, why ask you to play tour guide and not Cal? Is it because he fancies you?'

'I doubt it.' She'd been asking herself that too, but the far more likely explanation was that he knew her. They had a shared history, however brief.

'I thought he was selling the place?'

'He is.'

'So why are you getting into bed with the enemy?'

I wish! she nearly said out loud.

Izzy continued, 'Are you hoping you can persuade him to change his mind?'

'He won't.'

'Shame. I can just picture him in a kilt, acting all lord-like.'

So could Giselle. 'I'll be seeing lots of men in kilts today,' she said, changing the subject. 'I'm off to the Highland Games.'

'Och, now I'm feeling homesick. I can't remember the last time I went to the games.'

'You must be due a visit soon,' Giselle pleaded. She missed her sister so badly.

'I'll see what I can do.'

Giselle had to be content with that, because there was no way she could afford to visit Izzy. They chatted for a while longer, Giselle studiously avoiding any further mention of Rocco, then she realised the time. 'Gotta run; I need to get ready. Love you, Izzy.'

'Love you too, Zelle.'

A fizzing excitement partly eclipsed the familiar ache in Giselle's chest from missing Izzy this morning, brought on by the thought of spending the day with Rocco. When he'd told her he was delaying his return home in order to go to the games, her heart had soared. Her fragile, treacherous heart, which was going to get itself broken if she wasn't careful.

A recklessness filled her, despite the certainty that her growing feelings for him would end in tragedy. She'd take whatever she could get, however small, however fleeting, and if she regretted it afterwards, so be it.

The rolling of the drums swiftly followed the call of the pipe major as he brought the band to arms, then the first swelling, uplifting notes of the bagpipes soared into the air. The sound made the hairs on the back of Giselle's neck rise. She loved the bagpipes, and the sight of so many blue-kilted marchers with their pipes and drums filled her with patriotic pride. The band would march from the square in the centre of Portree to the field on the headland above the town, where the games would take place, officially opening the ceremony.

Crowds lined the streets, falling in behind the procession, and Giselle grabbed Rocco's hand to avoid them being separated. The excitement was palpable, and she was thoroughly caught up in it; and when she looked at Rocco's face, he was also wearing a great big smile.

'I can hardly hear myself think!' he shouted, his breath warm on her ear, and she shivered in response.

He was still holding her hand when they reached the tree-lined open space overlooking Loch Portree, and didn't seem in any hurry to let go.

A large central area was cordoned off for the participants, and people were already gathering around it. From experience, Giselle knew that the best place to watch the games was the elevated ground to one side, and she led him towards it to stake a claim. Kilts and tartan abounded (she was wearing a tartan skirt herself), and everywhere was a riot of colour. Vans and stalls selling food and drink were dotted around, and the smell of frying onions and doughnuts hung in the air. A hot dog or a burger wouldn't go amiss later, but for now a coffee and a doughnut would suffice while they watched the marching bands battle it out, followed by the dancing competitions, which would take place on a stage set up to one side.

Giselle, like most Scottish children, had learnt traditional dance in school, and she couldn't help tapping her feet and pointing her toes when the Highland Fling was performed. Her favourite, though, was the Ghillie Callum – known in English as the Sword Dance.

'It originated as a dance of war,' she told Rocco. They were drinking their coffee sitting on a tartan blanket that Giselle had brought with her for this very purpose, and were watching four tartan-skirted girls in long white socks and soft black pumps dance around four swords placed in a cross on the ground. Every time they jumped and spun, Giselle could feel herself wanting to jump and spin with them.

'Can you dance like that?' Rocco asked, as her body swayed next to his.

'I can, but not half as well as these girls.'

'I'd like to see you dance.' His eyes were full of mischief.

'You will later, at the ceilidh. I'm expecting you to dance as well, mind.'

'Me? No chance. I've got two left feet. Anyway, I don't know the steps.'

'Och, it's easy. I'll teach you.'

He pulled a face, and she laughed at his expression. 'You wanted the full Skye experience, so don't complain if that's what you get.'

'Yeah, but *dancing*?'

'It'll be fun,' she assured him.

'We'll see.' His tone implied that it definitely wasn't going to happen, but if she plied him with a wee dram or two of whisky, she thought she might get him on the dance floor.

Along with the dancing, the putting the stone competition (which was similar to the shot put, but involved an eighteen-pound actual stone instead of a steel ball) and the long jump were going ahead at the same time. Each attempt was accompanied by lots of cheering and clapping. The spectators were having as much fun as the participants, and with a crowd a couple of thousand strong, the noise was incredible.

Then an even louder roar went up as the over-the-bar entrants were called onto the field.

'What is over the bar?' Rocco asked.

'See that contraption? The one that looks like the highest high jump in the world? That's the bar. The aim is to stand with your back to it and throw a fifty-six-pound weight over it. Like the high jump or the pole vault, the bar will get higher each time.'

When the ceremonial chieftain (who was overseeing the games) announced that the bar was currently sitting at fifteen feet ten inches, there was a collective gasp and a round of applause.

'Dear God, I don't think I could lift fifty-six pounds, let alone throw it into the air over my shoulder!' Rocco exclaimed. 'That's…' He squinted. 'Four stone, or twenty-five kilos!'

'I'm sure you can lift more than four stone,' she teased. 'I bet you could even pick me up.'

'I expect I could, but I couldn't throw you far.'

'Anyway, if you think that's heavy, wait until you see the caber. It's one hundred and twenty-five pounds and about sixteen feet long.'

'You lot are nuts. Who was the first person who saw a tree and thought, *I know, I'm going to pick that up and toss it*? And then turn it into a sport!'

But Giselle noticed that he cheered and clapped and laughed and groaned along with everyone else, as cabers were lifted and tossed – or *not* lifted, in some cases. One poor chappie actually toppled over backwards when he tried to carry it. And when the current favourite stepped up to the mark, Rocco joined in with the rhythmic clapping.

Giselle found she was having as much fun watching Rocco's delighted face as she was watching the games itself.

'Aren't you glad you stayed for this?' she asked.

'Absolutely! This is so much fun.'

'It's not over yet. Look, they're getting ready for the tug of war.'

With much stamping of feet and digging heels into the ground for purchase, the two teams lined up along a length of rope, their supporters egging them on with lots of shouting and screaming. Rocco was shouting as loudly as anyone.

'Which team are you rooting for?' she yelled above the noise.

'I don't care who wins,' he replied, whistling as one team dragged the other across a line only the umpire could see.

He was hoarse by the time the games drew to a close. 'I need a drink,' he rasped.

'Let's go for something to eat,' Giselle suggested; the hot dog she'd consumed for lunch seemed like an awful long time ago.

'Good idea.'

'Most places will be packed, so I'm up for a fish supper if you are. We'll celebrate your last evening on Skye in style.' She couldn't believe he was leaving tomorrow, and she'd been trying not to think about it all day. The thought of him not being around was poking a hole in her heart.

'About that...' he began. 'Would you mind if I stayed a while longer?'

Would she mind? Hell, no!

Was it wise? Again, hell, no.

Was it delaying the inevitable? It was, but she didn't care. She felt like a prisoner who'd been given a stay of execution.

'I don't mind.' Her voice was hardly above a whisper.

'Good,' he replied. Then he kissed her.

—

Rocco had assumed the ceilidh would be held in a pub, but when Giselle took him to what looked like an old chapel hidden away behind the colourfully painted houses lining Portree's harbour, he was surprised.

'This is the Gathering Hall,' she said. 'I love the name; it makes me think of the gathering of the clans in olden times, when they'd get together for things like the Highland Games. This building is only 150 years old, though.'

'That's olden times, isn't it?'

Giselle presented a pair of tickets at the door. 'Och no. Scottish history, as you well ken, goes back an awful lot further than that. The way we see it, olden times is, like, *hundreds* of years ago.'

The elderly man on the door chuckled. 'It's nice to see a lassie with a genuine sense of history. Local, are you?'

'Skye born and bred,' she replied proudly. 'This guy here—' she jerked her chin at Rocco '—is a redcoat.'

Rocco felt the need to explain. 'She's been teaching me about the Jacobite Uprising.'

'Aye, there's a lot of history on Skye. Enjoy your evening.'

Rocco couldn't help glancing at Giselle as he said, 'Thanks, we will.' He felt giddy with the promise of what the night might hold. Was the kiss just now only the start of it? He hoped so. Rocco had wanted to say, 'Sod the fish supper,' and take her to bed, but he hadn't dared. He hadn't wanted to spoil such a perfect day, and he wasn't entirely sure whether she'd welcome it. Her kiss had tasted of sunshine and sea, and she'd melted into his arms for the briefest of seconds before someone had stood on their blanket and brought him back to the present. However, kissing him didn't mean she'd want to make love to him, especially since he'd love her and leave her. They'd been lovers before, one wonderful night together, after which they'd gone their separate ways, but they'd been young, and possibly foolish. This older and wiser Giselle mightn't want a one-night stand. Neither did he. Rocco wanted more, but more was impossible. So he'd settle for what he could get, and if that meant a few stolen kisses and the rest of the evening by her side, he'd take it and be grateful.

The hall was a rectangular space with a wooden floor and a vaulted, black-beamed ceiling. A stage was at the far end, where a group of musicians sat, and tables with benches were arranged around the edges of the room, leaving the centre clear for dancing. Fairy lights were strung across the beams, giving it a festive air.

Most of the tables were occupied, but Giselle found one with a couple of chairs free and she commandeered them. A guy on the stage introduced the band, and immediately the dance area began to fill as people got to their feet.

When the music started, Rocco found himself tapping his toes. The tune was upbeat and catchy, and he was mesmerised by people linking arms and twirling around with one arm in the air. The dance didn't seem particularly difficult, and although he felt self-conscious, the urge to hold Giselle in his arms was greater than any embarrassment he suspected he might feel. Which was why he stood up and offered her his hand.

'Would you like to dance?'

The dazzling smile she bestowed on him lit up the room and turned his heart to mush.

She leapt to her feet. 'I'll be gentle with you,' she promised.

His breath hitched. 'I don't mind it rough,' he said, and led her onto the floor.

When he turned around, it was to find her studying him. She offered him an elbow. 'Rough, eh?'

He linked his arm through it. 'Not too rough,' he amended, hoping he wasn't coming on too strong.

She spun him around, and he stumbled for a moment until he found his feet. 'Too rough for you?' she teased. Her smile was wry, her eyes full of laughter.

'This is fine.'

She released him and kind of hopped on the spot. Others were doing the same, their partners clapping. Rocco clapped, too. Then she was gone, dancing over to someone else, leaving him wondering what to do, before a middle-aged woman offered him an elbow. He took it, spun around, and she let go, and he was left alone once more to clap and wait for Giselle to rotate back to him.

When he'd asked her to dance, this wasn't what he'd had in mind. He'd imagined a kind of waltz thing, with a hand on her waist and their palms clasped together – not sharing her with all and sundry.

She was back, her arm in his for another spin, before disengaging and grabbing his hand.

This is more like it, he thought, until his other hand was grabbed by someone on his right, and a circle was formed.

Rocco had no idea what he was supposed to be doing, but with a resigned laugh he threw himself into the moment. And ended up thoroughly enjoying himself.

Several dances later, he begged to be allowed to sit down. 'I'm parched,' he said. 'Fancy a top-up?'

He was on soft drinks because he was driving. Giselle had suggested he might like to leave the car in Portree so he could have a drink, and Cal could bring him into town early tomorrow morning to collect it. He'd been tempted because a glass of something alcoholic might have given him Dutch courage in the dancing department. He hadn't needed it, though. Wanting to dance with Giselle had been courage enough. But as the evening drew to a close and it was time to make the journey back to Duncoorie, Rocco wondered whether he'd have the courage to kiss her again.

—

It had been a long and busy day, exciting too, but Giselle wasn't tired. She was too nervous to be tired. She was going to invite Rocco in when he dropped her off. And she was pretty sure what that would lead to. The issue was, she both feared he might turn her down and feared he *might not*.

The journey was undertaken in silence, and the atmosphere felt strained. Or was that her imagination? Could she be reading too much into it? Was it only her who thought it strained?

The car bumped up the rough road to the bothy, the headlights piercing the dark. As soon as it drew to a stop, she turned to him and the question she'd been about to ask died on her lips.

The hunger in his eyes was intense and she swallowed hard, a fizz of exhilaration rushing through her. When he leant towards her, she met him halfway, as eager for this as him. Her own hunger was devouring her, eating her from the inside out, turning her to liquid. Her bones were jelly and she sank into him, savouring his solidity, his scent, his maleness, the sheer bulk of him as he caged her in his arms, his mouth capturing hers. She couldn't think, could only feel, and what she was feeling was a desire so strong it robbed her of breath. There wasn't enough air.

His hand was on the back of her head, his fingers in her hair; the other was on her waist, and her skin flamed at his touch as his mouth explored hers.

She made a small noise, part pleasure, part frustration, and he drew back, concern in his eyes.

The concern changed into something else entirely when she led him inside and took him to bed…

Chapter 18

'I'd better get back,' Rocco said, making absolutely no attempt whatsoever to get up. It was mid-afternoon and he was lying in Giselle's bed, where they'd spent most of the previous four days since the games. He was far too comfy to move – and horny.

Her head was on his chest, her arm lying across his stomach, one leg hooked over his, but it wasn't enough. He wanted to feel every inch of her again. And again, and…

'I'd better create some pictures,' Giselle said, although she didn't make any move to get up either. Or rather, she *did*, but not the kind of move that lent itself to getting out of bed.

There was a sort of up involved, though, as she climbed on top of him, smiling wickedly.

'Not just yet,' she added, her lips hovering above his. 'Kiss me.'

His breathing was ragged, his voice hoarse. He couldn't get enough of her. With a groan, he buried his fingers in her hair, pulling her head down—

And then his phone rang.

Rocco groaned again, but this time with frustration.

'Do you need to answer that?' Giselle asked.

'No, what I need is *you*,' he replied, waiting for it to stop. 'Where were we?'

'Here, I believe,' she said, nibbling his neck. 'And here.'

It rang again.

'For goodness' sake!' he cried. 'Can't a man have five minutes' peace?'

'I think you'll find you've had more than five minutes,' Giselle giggled.

'Let me get rid of them.' He eased himself out of bed and down the ladder, wishing he'd put the damned thing on silent, or had turned it off completely. He'd left it in the pocket of his jeans, which were currently on the floor near the sofa, along with the rest of his hastily discarded clothing.

'Nice view,' she called, and he glanced over his shoulder to find her leaning over the balustrade, her chin resting on her folded arms as she ogled his bare backside.

Rocco blew her a cheeky kiss.

His phone stopped as he got to it, but began ringing again almost immediately. 'It's Cal,' he said, filled with sudden worry. 'Hi, what's wrong?'

'Your mother is asking for you. She's—' Cal paused, lowering his voice '—quite insistent.'

'Tell her I'll call her later. It's not really convenient right now.' Then he added hastily, 'No need to mention that last bit.'

'There most definitely isn't,' his mother said frostily, 'because she can hear you.'

Rocco froze. 'Beverly?'

'The very same.'

'What—? Why are you on Cal's phone?' The penny dropped. She was *here*, wasn't she? On Skye. In Duncoorie. In the castle.

'Because,' she replied, '*he* seems to be able to get through to you when no one else can.'

Rocco was lost for words.

Unfortunately, Giselle wasn't. 'Is everything OK, Rocco?' she called.

'Who's that?' Beverly demanded.

'No one important.' Not to *her* at least; if it wasn't business, Beverly wasn't interested. He put a finger to his lips and shook his head at Giselle. His instinct, whether or not it was right, was to keep his mother as far away from Giselle as possible. Beverly would eat her alive. 'I'll be there in ten minutes,' he said to his mother. 'Can you put Cal back on?'

'Sorry,' Cal muttered. 'She grabbed it out of my hand.'

Rocco said, 'Not your fault. Could you arrange for some refreshments for her? I'll be there as quick as I can.'

'Problems?' Giselle asked.

She was standing at the foot of the ladder wrapped in a silky satin robe, her hair tousled, her lips full and pink, her alabaster legs bare. The robe left little to the imagination and Rocco wanted nothing more than to take her to bed again.

'Beverly is here.'

'By "here" you mean…?'

'At the castle. I'd better go.' He ran a hand through his hair.

'Were you expecting her?'

'No.'

Giselle bit her lip. Rocco felt like doing the same. Why was his mother here? What was going on?

'Do you mind giving me a lift to the studio?' Giselle asked. Her tone was formal, and when he opened his arms, she hesitated before stepping into them.

Rocco held her close, revelling in the feel of her body pressed against his, even if there was a layer of green satin between them.

'I'm sorry,' he whispered into her hair.

'So am I.' She pulled back. 'Have I got time for a shower?'

'Only if I can join you in it,' he murmured huskily. 'My mother can wait five more minutes.'

'Five minutes won't be long enough.'

'No,' he replied thoughtfully. 'I doubt it will be.'

Thirty-five minutes later, Rocco's car pulled into one of the castle's reserved parking spaces, and he cut the engine with a resigned sigh. He couldn't put this off any longer. It was time to find out why his mother was here, then pack her off back to London.

'I'll speak to you later,' he promised Giselle, and as she leant across to kiss him, he hesitated, but only for a fraction. Beverly was unlikely to be watching, especially if Cal had secreted her in the lounge.

Giselle's mouth was warm and soft, and he had to drag himself away.

'Hope everything's OK,' she said, getting out of the car.

So did he. Rocco knew Beverly had expected him home before now, but surely he was entitled to a few days of R&R.

Resolutely, he entered the castle, smiled a greeting to Avril, who was staring at him with wide eyes (his mother often had that effect on people), and straightened his shoulders as he walked into the lounge.

Beverly was seated near one of the windows with a view over the loch, but either she'd had her fill of the scenery or it didn't impress her, because she had a slim electronic notebook open on her lap and was staring at the screen. He was pleased to see she'd had a coffee, but the presence of a second cup was a silent admonishment that he'd kept her waiting long enough for her to have drunk another.

As he headed towards her, he signalled to one of the staff to bring a couple more coffees, although he had a feeling he'd need something stronger than Jamaica's finest Blue Mountain blend.

'Beverly, hi.' He sat opposite on one of the low-slung leather sofas and cocked an ankle across his knee, the epitome of relaxed despite feeling distinctly *un*relaxed.

His mother took a moment to finish typing and close the notebook before she acknowledged his presence. 'I was beginning to think you'd been eaten by the Loch Ness Monster.'

'Wrong loch. Sorry I wasn't here when you arrived. I would have been, if I'd known you were coming. I'll have a word with Nora.'

Beverly's eyes were wide with fake innocence. 'I must have forgotten to tell her.'

His mother had her own PA, so she hadn't needed Nora to make the travel arrangements, but the PAs did talk so he could only assume Nora had been deliberately kept out of the loop.

'Do we have a problem?' he asked.

'I'm not sure. Do we? Do *you*?'

'Not at all.'

'You see, I thought you might be floundering, in over your head. Otherwise, why the delay? You've been here two weeks, Rocco.'

'I needed a break.'

'Hmm.' She wasn't convinced, he could tell.

She was about to say more when he sensed someone approach from behind. Expecting it to be a waiter with their drinks, he glanced up and inhaled sharply when he saw who it was. 'Claire!'

Claire placed a red-nailed hand on his shoulder and bent to kiss him, her scarlet lips landing just to the right of his mouth. 'Mmm,' she said, sotto voce, 'You smell as though you've just come out of the shower.'

He blew out his cheeks. 'I didn't expect to see you here.'

'Beverly thought you might benefit from my expertise.'

His mother smiled sweetly at him as Claire sat down, smoothing her tight-fitting skirt. Claire favoured slimline skirts, smart tailored jackets and power heels. And red. She liked red when it came to lips, nails and the soles of her shoes. Today's suit was navy, the blouse cream and silky. Claire was attractive, efficient, highly intelligent and ambitious, and Beverly had employed her for those very qualities. And, Rocco suspected, for one or two that weren't so obvious. But although Beverly held a certain sway over him because she was his CEO, he drew the line at his mother trying to organise his private life. Arranged marriages weren't his cup of tea, even if it would be good for the business.

'We'll talk over dinner,' Beverly said. 'See how Claire can help. I'd like to freshen up first. That drive was interminably long.'

Rocco closed his eyes, drew in a deep breath, then opened them again. 'Wait here.'

He headed back out to the foyer and approached the front desk. Even before he asked Avril the question, he knew what her answer would be. 'We have just the one double room available,' she told him.

'Not a twin?'

'Sorry, it's a double.'

'No room at the inn?' Claire's breath tickled his ear, making him jump.

Rocco scowled. Thinking aloud, he said, 'I suppose you could have that, and my mother could have my room. I can sleep on the sofa in the sitting room.'

'Beverly won't like that.'

'She hasn't got any choice. If she'd discussed her visit with me first, I'd have told her the castle is almost at full capacity.'

Claire wound her arm through his. 'Let your mother have the double. I can share with you.'

Aware that Avril was hanging on every word, he said to the receptionist, 'Can you ensure the double room is ready and see if housekeeping can put fresh sheets on my bed, please?'

He'd get his mother and Claire settled, then he really needed to speak to Cal.

—

Giselle was startled when Avril barrelled into the studio. 'I was going to phone across, then I saw your light on,' she puffed.

She looked odd and Giselle got to her feet, concerned. 'Are you all right?'

'I've, um, got some news. About Rocco. His mother is here.'

Was that all? Giselle breathed a sigh of relief. 'I know. Let me lock the door and you can tell me what she's like.'

It was a bit early to close, because the gift shop and cafe were still open and most of the other studios were too, but she turned the key in the lock and flipped the sign on the door to 'Closed', anyway.

'I was with Rocco when Cal phoned him with the news,' she said, hoping she wasn't blushing as much as she feared she might be.

'She isn't on her own. She's brought someone with her.'

From the tone of Avril's voice and her expression, Giselle had an awful feeling she wasn't going to like what she was about to hear. 'Who?' she asked.

'Her name's Claire, and I think she's going to be staying with Rocco. *In his room.*'

'*What?*' Giselle slumped against the counter.

Avril hurriedly continued, 'It might be perfectly innocent because we're fully booked, apart from one room, and his mother is having that, so Claire suggested she share his.'

'And he *agreed*?'

Avril hung her head and nodded. 'The woman was all over him.'

Claire. It was a name Giselle had heard before. He'd told her she was a colleague. Ha bloody ha!

She gasped, sucker punched, as her chest filled with a pain she'd never experienced before. Hurt and betrayed, she wanted to bawl her eyes out, but another emotion simmered underneath. Jealousy. Make that two emotions, as anger joined in. She went with anger, closely followed by the green-eyed monster, as the better option. She would allow the heartache free rein later, when she was alone.

The bastard!

'What does she look like?' she demanded savagely.

Avril's face was full of sympathy. 'Don't do this, Giselle,' she advised. 'He's not worth it.'

'You may as well tell me. It's not as though he'll be able to hide her away in his flaming turret, so I'll see for myself soon enough. I'm asking so I know to avoid her.'

'Tall, slim, corporate.' Avril spat out the last word as though it were an insult. 'All glossy dark hair and long red talons. She wore a power suit and lots of make-up.'

Giselle seethed. It was preferable to bursting into tears.

Avril continued, 'He didn't look happy. He told her off for not telling him she was coming.'

Giselle wasn't surprised. No man wanted his girlfriend and his bit on the side to meet. No wonder he'd been reluctant to kiss her in the car just now. He'd clearly been worried Claire would see them.

Giselle pressed her lips together to stop her chin wobbling, conscious of Avril's pity.

When she'd wrested control, she said, 'Thanks for letting me know.'

'Will you be all right?'

She most definitely wouldn't be. 'Of course I will. It was just a bit of fun, although I would never have had any fun at all if I'd realised he was already taken. I feel sorry for his girlfriend. The poor cow doesn't know what she's letting herself in for.'

'Do you want me to stay with you for a bit? I've just clocked off, so...'

Giselle shook her head. 'I'm fine, honestly. I've got lots of work to do.' That bit was true, as she hated being short of stock to sell in the gift shop, but the 'I'm fine' bit was an outright lie.

How could she be fine, when she was in love with a two-timing shit like Rocco?

Chapter 19

The text said:

> Wish I could see you later, but Beverly... :(

If Giselle could have afforded to replace her phone, she would have thrown it at the damned wall. Anger was still at the forefront of her mind, but desolation was hot on its heels. She was frantically trying to stoke the fires of her temper to keep the deluge of her grief at bay, but she could already feel heartache lapping at her feet, and if she let it in, she feared she might drown.

Instead of throwing the phone, she placed it firmly screen-side down on the workbench. Then picked it up again and turned it off, before returning to the Highland cow she was working on. Anything with a shaggy ginger and brown cow on it did well in the gift shop, and they rarely took her long to do. However, she'd been working on this one since before Avril had arrived with the news that Rocco was a sneaky, two-timing ratbag, and she hadn't managed to do much more on it.

Horns. It needed horns. And a nose. Maybe even a hint of a black eye peeping out from behind a shaggy fringe.

Giselle opened the drawer of white sea glass and sifted through some of the longer pieces, searching for two of a similar length and colour. Of course, they weren't bright white: they were milky shades of bone, stone, linen and alabaster.

She'd already arranged the cow's hair, using various shades of brown, which was one of the most common colours. It came mostly from old beer and whisky bottles, and in terms of findability was abundant on Scottish beaches, compared to the rarer colours such as teal and amethyst.

What was Rocco doing now, she wondered, as she searched through the drawer for a second time, without really noticing what was in it. Getting ready for dinner? And would that involve some more shower sex? Her stomach churned at the thought, and she felt sick. Physically sick and *heart* sick.

She only had herself to blame; she should never have become involved with him again. They were from different worlds, and she'd known it couldn't last. What she hadn't known was that she would fall in love with him.

'Stupid,' she muttered, picking up a fragment of sea glass at random, then putting it back again immediately.

It was no good; she couldn't concentrate. She had to get out of here, get as far away from the castle as she could.

Grabbing her phone and her bag, she locked the studio and headed out, determined to go home and expunge all trace of Rocco from the bothy. And if that meant burning the bedsheets, then that's what she'd do.

In the end, she didn't burn them – she washed them. Twice. But although the scent of him had gone, replaced by lavender and patchouli, she could still feel his hands on her body, his breath on her face, and he was hiding behind her eyes every time she closed them.

Ridding Rocco Moore from her heart and her mind was going to be considerably harder than a rinse and spin.

—

'It's very old fashioned,' had been Beverly's reaction when Rocco had shown her into the suite in the turret.

'I thought that was its charm,' he retorted when she repeated the comment again, this time for Claire's benefit.

They were having dinner in the dining room and Claire's face was wooden, her lips pressed into a straight line.

'How is your room?' he asked her, sounding like a concierge.

'Fine.'

'Shall we order?' He flicked open the napkin and draped it across his lap. 'I expect you're hungry after such a long journey. You really needn't have come all this way, either of you.'

Beverly's gaze was piercing. 'I wanted to see what all the fuss was about.'

'What fuss? There isn't any fuss.'

'There's something, otherwise you'd be home. Is there a problem?'

'No.'

'Have you spoken to Jermyns yet?'

'Not yet.'

'What's the holdup? I thought you wanted to get rid of this place ASAP?'

'It's got to go through probate first.'

'And that's where I come in,' Claire interjected smoothly. 'Beverly thought my expertise would come in handy. After all, figures are my speciality. I'll take a look at the books for you.'

'I already have.'

'A *proper* look. I'm a qualified accountant, remember?'

'I haven't forgotten.' Rocco couldn't work out why he was being so reticent. Claire was the ideal person to go over the accounts and prepare a valuation for probate. He was planning on using her anyway, so...

'That's settled,' Beverly announced, even though it wasn't. 'She can help you sort this out. How long do you think it'll take, Claire?'

Claire lifted a shoulder in a delicate shrug. 'It depends how much progress Rocco has made. A day, two at the most if things get complicated.'

Beverly pursed her lips. 'Let's say one.' She turned to Rocco. 'We'll spend tomorrow going over the Oaklands contract while Claire does what she needs to do. We can all travel back together on Wednesday.'

Rocco was aghast, but he concealed it, merely showing mild surprise.

Claire showed no surprise at all. She was obviously already aware of the travel arrangements, and he realised he was being tag teamed. Rocco wasn't ready to leave his castle yet. He wasn't ready to leave Giselle. And he was beginning to wonder whether he ever would be.

Rocco climbed into his car and rested his head wearily on the back of the seat. He was bushed. It was ten to eleven, and only now had his mother called it a day. After a dinner he'd had no appetite for, she'd insisted on catching up on work since she'd 'wasted a whole day' getting to Duncoorie and would be wasting another day travelling home.

At one point, she'd mentioned a small airfield in Broadford, until Rocco had pointed out that it was no longer in use except for the air ambulance. It had been one of the things he'd checked out when he'd first discovered he owned a castle on Skye. Or, to be more precise, *Nora* had checked it out for him when he'd asked her to find the quickest way to the island.

Finally, Beverly had retired to bed, and although Claire had suggested a nightcap in the lounge, Rocco had feigned tiredness. It wasn't a lie. He *was* tired. But he also wanted to see Giselle.

He'd sent her several messages, but except for the first, which she'd read but hadn't replied to, none of the others had even been delivered and his calls were going to voicemail. He was beginning to get worried.

Driving up to the bothy was the only thing he could think of doing, so despite it being late, that's what he did.

The little cottage was in darkness when he got there and there was no answer to his knock. He even tried the door handle on the off chance she'd left it unlocked.

She hadn't.

Feeling like a criminal, he peered through the window but couldn't see a great deal. He certainly couldn't see *her*.

Rocco walked back to the car and stood for a moment without getting in, tapping his fingers on the roof. He was tempted to call Cal and ask him if he knew where she might be, but he didn't. Cal managed the estate; he didn't manage the crafters' social lives.

Should he wait, he wondered, then decided against it. He'd return to the castle and check whether she was in her studio.

To his intense disappointment, she wasn't. Not knowing where to look next, he walked down the lane to the loch.

The water was a black stain beyond the paler sliver of beach and the neat oblong of the former boathouse. Feeling for the key in his pocket, Rocco took it out, unlocked the door and went inside.

When he'd been shown around the estate on the day of Mhairi's funeral, he'd taken little notice of the boathouse, apart from acknowledging its existence, but now he was curious.

A tiny entrance hall had three doors: one led to a double bedroom, behind an opposite door was a bathroom, but the door directly ahead showed him an open-plan kitchen, living and dining room, with a large picture window overlooking the loch. He had a feeling that come morning, the view would be stupendous.

The boathouse was a proper home, albeit small, and if he'd realised it was this nice, he might have moved into it, rather than stay in Mhairi's suite in the castle. It was considerably more private, he realised, as his thoughts turned to Giselle. But possibly not private enough. It was too close to the castle, for one thing; and for another, Cal's cottage was only a short distance away.

Rocco had flung a few things into his overnight bag, which took him all of thirty seconds to unpack, and he'd also brought his laptop with him, so he set that down on a low table near the picture window. If he was awake early enough, he'd get some work done, which would please Beverly.

After he'd changed into a baggy pair of PJ bottoms and completed his ablutions, he plugged his phone in to charge and checked his messages. Still nothing from Giselle, and neither had she read his latest messages.

His disappointment was acute. Despite having only seen her this afternoon, he found himself missing her badly.

Not good, considering.

Unsettled, Rocco went to bed.

Two hours later, he got up again, having not slept a wink. He should have got up before now, but he'd lain there, tossing and turning, and living in hope. Finally admitting defeat, he padded into the living area and eyed the kettle longingly. If only he'd thought to bring a teabag or two with him.

Settling for a glass of tap water, he switched on a lamp, opened his laptop, and guessed he'd either get a chunk of work done or bore himself to sleep.

However, he did neither, although more working than sleeping took place, but only marginally, as he found his thoughts wandering.

After he'd read the same report three times and had taken none of it in, he gave up, closing his laptop and switching off the lamp. Was there any point in going back to bed since he was wide awake? He thought not. But he couldn't just sit there and stare into space. He wasn't made for idleness. He had to be doing something. Or – looking at it from a different perspective – did he feel that he *should* be doing something? That by doing nothing, he was wasting valuable time? That was the problem with living life in the fast lane: it wasn't easy to slow down.

He'd slowed down in Duncoorie, though. Which was why Beverly was here. She clearly felt he was skiving off and not pulling his weight. Or did she sense something was amiss?

Rocco snorted. It was unlikely. She was just concerned he was taking too long to wrap up his affairs on Skye.

It was only when he jerked awake did Rocco realise he must have drifted off to sleep after all. Chilled and stiff, he got to his feet and stared out of the window.

It was light outside, but only just, the sun not yet having risen over the mountain behind the castle. Mist curled and coiled over the loch, the water unusually calm. A bird called, the sound haunting and melancholy.

God, this place was beautiful.

And so was *she*.

Giselle was picking her way across the sand, barefoot, her hair tumbling over her shoulders and her white dress as ephemeral as the mist itself. Sprite, fairy, enchantress… She was as magical and as mystical as the landscape, and his heart ached at the sight of her. He wanted her more than he'd ever wanted anything in his life. Giselle was a contradiction: delicate yet strong, timid yet fierce.

And in that moment, he realised he was in love with her.

Mesmerised, he left the boathouse, the chill air damp on his skin, the sand cold beneath his bare feet, and saw her at the end of the jetty. She had her back to him and was facing out to sea.

When he drew nearer, he knew she was aware of his presence by the tension in her slender shoulders, and he came to an uncertain halt, longing to take her in his arms, but holding back because something wasn't right.

'Giselle? I'm, um, leaving tomorrow. I have to go home.'

'You should have told me you have a girlfriend.' Her voice was wooden.

He wished he could see her face. '*What?*'

'You're up early.'

The abrupt change of subject confused him. 'I fell asleep in the chair,' he replied absently, then said, 'I don't have a girlfriend.' Not true: he'd kind of hoped Giselle was his girlfriend.

'You fell asleep in *the chair*?' She spun on her heel to face him.

'Yeah, I couldn't sleep, so I did some work and— What's this about, Giselle?' He searched her face, looking for clues.

'Claire.'

Rocco blinked. For a second he thought she'd changed the subject again. Then everything slotted into place. 'You think *Claire* is my girlfriend?'

'Isn't she?'

'No!'

'She spent the night in your room,' Giselle said, but her voice lacked conviction.

'She spent the night in her *own* room. *Beverly* was in mine. I stayed at the boathouse.'

Her eyes widened, registering his pyjama-and-T-shirt state, along with his bare feet. 'But... she was all over you.'

Rocco thought back to the kiss Claire had planted on his face in the lounge yesterday and her suggestion that she share his room, and he could see how it might look. 'That's just her way. She's not my girlfriend.' He was disappointed that Giselle thought he was capable of being so underhand and deceitful, and his voice hardened. 'I don't sleep with one woman while dating another.'

Giselle hung her head, her hair falling around her face. Rocco stepped closer to brush a strand away.

'You know me better than that,' he said.

Looking up from under her lashes, she whispered, 'Do I?'

Emboldened, he took her in his arms. 'Yes.'

Then he kissed her, a long, deep satisfying kiss, and when it eventually ended, the sun had crested the mountain and the mist had evaporated. It was going to be a glorious morning.

'I went to the bothy last night; you weren't replying to my texts or answering your phone, and I wanted to see you, to hold you.' He was holding her now, but it wasn't enough. He wanted more.

'I know. I was there, in the garden.'

'Oh, Giselle,' he sighed. They'd wasted an entire night, when they could have spent it together.

He was about to suggest they make up for lost time and ask her into the bothy, but a cheery 'Good morning,' made them both jump. Cal was putting something into a small boat halfway up the beach and grinning at them. 'Going fishing,' he explained.

The mood was broken. Rocco should return to the castle.

'Can I see you later?' he asked, after pretending the estate manager wasn't there and kissing her again.

'You know where to find me.' She was beaming at him.

'And you know where to find *me*,' he countered, gesturing to the boathouse. 'Although your place might be better as there are too many nosey parkers around here.' He shot a meaningful look at Cal.

'Nothing gets past Cal,' she replied, slipping around him, her feet dancing on the dew-covered jetty.

Rocco caught hold of her hand, pulling her back for one more kiss. Then she was away, running across the beach, her laughter floating on the air.

He watched until she disappeared, his heart full, then he tipped his head back and gazed at the sky, the mountain, the castle... *His* castle. For now.

Could he—?

The unformed thought was derailed by movement at one of the turret's windows.

Beverly was gazing out of it. He wondered how long she'd been there and what she might have seen.

Chapter 20

'Cal can show you around the estate,' Rocco told Claire. 'And he can answer most of the questions you might have.' He had to free up some time to spend with Giselle before he left. *He had to*.

'Do you think that's wise?' Claire spooned Greek yoghurt into a miniscule bowl of berries and ate a mouthful.

Rocco was having his customary strong coffee, scrambled egg and sourdough toast. 'Why wouldn't it be? He's got all the facts and figures when it comes to the acreage of woodland, the annual turnover of the gift shop, and so on.'

'Don't *you* have that information?'

'Yes, but I've got other things to do. Anyway, where do you think *I* got it from?'

Claire frowned and dropped her spoon into the bowl with a clatter.

His mother spoke up. 'You can use the parlour, Claire. Rocco and I can work in the little sitting room. He's got a lot to catch up on.'

Rocco's heart sank. There'd be no skiving off for him today; his mother would make sure of that.

Claire dabbed her lips with a napkin, leaving a scarlet imprint on the white linen. 'In that case,' she said, getting to her feet, 'I may as well get started. Tell your estate manager to come to the parlour at ten o'clock.'

Rocco remained silent as she left the dining room, but as soon as she was out of earshot he said, 'You shouldn't have brought her; she's busy enough without this.'

Beverly's eyebrows rose. 'She offered, and I think I was right to bring her, considering.'

'Considering what?' Was his mother implying he wasn't capable of managing his own affairs? That this unexpected inheritance was too much for him?

Then she asked, 'Who's the girl?'

Rocco stilled. Ah, so she *had* seen him with Giselle. He'd suspected as much. 'Her name is Giselle.'

'She's local, I take it?'

'Yes.'

'A member of staff?'

'She doesn't work for me, if that's what you're implying.'

'I'm not implying anything. I'm merely curious. I had a feeling something other than sightseeing was keeping you here. You're not the outdoor type.'

'Actually, I am.'

Another raised eyebrow. His mother's eyebrows could hold a conversation all by themselves. 'You've never shown any interest in the past.'

'Not recently, but the last eight years have been rather hectic.' By 'hectic', he meant that both he and Beverly had worked flat out to keep the business afloat after his father died. And they'd achieved it – the company wasn't just floating, it was positively buoyant.

His mother studied him over the rim of her cup. He met her gaze head on.

Eventually, she said, 'Is that why you've been so tardy about wrapping this up? Because you've discovered a sudden passion for hiking?' She drew out the word 'passion', the double entendre obvious.

Rocco refused to be drawn. His love life was none of her business.

He changed tack. 'Do you begrudge me a holiday?'

'Not at all. But this—' her gaze swept around the dining room '—is hardly a holiday.'

'Think of it as a holiday *home*,' he quipped, rather unwisely, admittedly, but she was starting to annoy him.

It looked like they were about to butt heads. Beverly was a control freak, and she liked things done her way, and Rocco was looking forward to the time when he was running the company and could do things *his* way. Unfortunately, his mother was only in her late fifties and was showing no sign of wanting to take a step back. In some ways, she *was* the business and the business was her, so what she'd find to do with herself when she did eventually retire, he couldn't imagine. At this rate, she'd still be at the helm at eighty. And he'd still be her second-in-command. The thought made him wince.

'Holidays, by their very nature, come to an end,' Beverly pointed out. 'As do holiday flings.'

He was well aware of that, unfortunately, and a sharp pang of misery lanced his heart. He couldn't stay, yet neither did he want to leave. An old song by The Clash drifted into his head. If he stayed, the trouble would most definitely be double.

His mother reached across the table and put a hand over his. 'I understand, truly I do. And I'd love nothing more than for you to remain on Skye and hike to your heart's content. But I need you in London. *The business* needs you. It can't function without you playing your part, and your absence is already having repercussions. You being here is creating more work for everyone, me and Claire especially. Claire has been a godsend these past two weeks, but it's not her business: *it's ours*. *Your* inheritance, everything your father worked for.' She removed her hand. 'Get this wrapped up, Rocco. You've had your holiday; it's time to put it behind you.'

—

The sick feeling in the pit of Giselle's stomach earlier this morning had driven her to seek solace in her favourite place on the shore of the loch, and she'd left her sandals at the edge of the beach and had walked barefoot across the damp sand. The mist rising from the water was otherworldly and beautiful, and it had made her heart ache to see it, but not as much as Rocco's betrayal. That was an ache no amount of morning sunlight could drive away.

Then Rocco had emerged out of the mist to join her on the jetty, and her world had shifted again with the knowledge that he *hadn't* spent the night with Claire, that the woman wasn't his girlfriend.

The panicky sickness and the pain in her chest had evaporated like the mist itself when he'd taken her in his arms and kissed her. But when he'd told her he was leaving tomorrow, she thought her heart might break, and now she was sitting in her studio, misery wrapping her like an old blanket.

Needing to keep busy, but not in the right frame of mind to make any more pictures, Giselle was relieved when a delivery driver poked his head around the door and left a rather large box on the counter. Her latest purchase of frames had arrived.

It didn't take long to frame up a few of the finished pictures, and she was soon ready to carry them over to the gift shop. Giselle always loved visiting the shop, although she tried not to pop in too often because of the temptation to buy something gorgeous. It was a treasure trove of everything the crafters made, and a few more things besides. The most noticeable were Tara's doll's houses. Three of them made an eye-catching display in the centre of the shop, and Giselle always had an urge to sit on the floor and play with them.

Jinny was her usual effervescent self, exclaiming in pleasure when she saw her. 'What have you got for me?'

'Another Highland coo, with three more in the studio when this one is sold; a rock pool scene; a—'

'Ooh, let me see!' Jinny demanded, holding her hands out as Giselle placed the pictures on the counter, one at a time. 'It's lovely. Look at the starfish!' She held up the picture, turning it to the light. 'Are you going to make another large picture? I know it took a while to sell the last one, but it was such a great central piece. It always received loads of lovely comments.'

'I might.' The large loch scene had been one of her favourite pictures. No two sea glass pictures were ever the same, although some might be very similar, like the seagulls or the shaggy cows, for instance. And she only ever had one of each design on sale in the shop at any one time because she didn't want her work to look as though it was mass produced.

'I've put the island one in its place,' Jinny pointed out.

'So you have. It looks lovely.' Jinny had rearranged the wall to show it off to the best advantage. Bless her, Jinny was always having to move things around because business was brisk. Few people could resist taking home a little handmade souvenir of their time on Skye.

As Jinny priced up Giselle's newest stock, she said, 'I hear Rocco's got a couple of visitors.'

'Um, yeah. His mother, who's also his boss, and one of his colleagues.'

'I'm not sure I could work with *my* mother.' Jinny shuddered. 'And it would be even worse if she was my boss. Can you imagine? I wouldn't get a minute's peace. No wonder he hasn't been in any hurry to go home.'

'I know what you mean. I love my mum to the moon and back, but we'd soon get on each other's nerves,' Giselle joked feebly, trying not to show how badly she was hurting at the thought of Rocco leaving.

She kept hoping he'd call or message her, and she checked her phone yet again, but nothing. Maybe he wouldn't call first, but would come looking for her in the studio? She should get back. He might be there now, wondering where she was.

Panicked, she was about to dash for the door when common sense held her back. If he couldn't find her, he'd call or message.

'I heard Avril got the wrong end of the stick and thought that Rocco had a girlfriend,' Jinny said casually, not looking at her.

Giselle took a steadying breath. 'Nothing gets past you, does it?'

'Not a lot.'

'She was mortified.' Giselle thought back to Avril's apology when Giselle had phoned her earlier to tell her where Cal had really spent the night. 'She wanted to make it up to me by buying me lunch.'

'Aw, that'll be nice. I happen to know they've got your favourite on the menu today.'

Giselle's stomach turned over, and she pulled a face. She hadn't had much appetite since yesterday, and the subsequent news that Rocco was leaving tomorrow had killed it completely. The blissful bubble she'd been living in had well and truly burst, with his mother's arrival signalling the end of their relationship and probably that of the craft centre.

Wheels were being set in motion, the sale was going ahead and Rocco would return to his life down south, and there was nothing Giselle could say or do to alter it.

'Who's that with Cal?' Jinny was staring out of the window with narrowed eyes, and Giselle followed her gaze.

Despite never having set eyes on the woman, Giselle knew without a shadow of a doubt that it was Claire. And she was stunning. She was also heading this way.

When the door opened and the woman stepped inside, Giselle could hear Cal talking about cold facts and figures that had nothing in common with any of the wonderful things in the shop. She understood it was a business, but did it have to sound so dry? Hard work, talent and dedication had been reduced to little more than markups and percentages.

Claire's face gave nothing away, but her eyes were everywhere, taking it all in.

Cal said, 'Hi, Jinny. This is Claire Wallace. She's doing an initial assessment and valuation of the castle. Jinny is our gift shop's very successful manager.'

Claire gave Jinny a nod and a professional smile, but that was the sum of her attention because she was too busy assessing the contents of the shop. She hadn't noticed

Giselle, or if she had, she didn't think her important enough to acknowledge, so Giselle took the opportunity to do some noticing of her own.

High heels, smart suit, glowing skin, brown eyes, glossy dark hair, red lips – Claire was the polar opposite to Giselle in appearance. She also reeked of expensive perfume, confidence and money.

An image of Rocco at Mhairi's funeral flashed into Giselle's mind, and abruptly she envisaged Rocco and Claire together, birds of the same feather, flying in the same lofty airspace. They'd make a perfect couple. No wonder Avril had thought Claire was his girlfriend! She was far more suited to him than Giselle could ever be. And they spoke the same corporate language and worked for the same company.

Once again, a sick feeling rose from her stomach to lodge in her chest, and Giselle feared she might throw up. Screwing her eyes shut, she fought the nausea, swallowing hard and concentrating on her breathing.

When she opened them again, it was to find Claire standing in front of the sea glass island picture, her head tilted to the side, her expression thoughtful.

'It's lovely, isn't it?' Jinny gushed. 'Made by this extremely talented lady right here.'

Claire's head swivelled towards Giselle like a raptor sensing prey, and Giselle found herself the focus of a sweeping, yet comprehensive, assessment.

'*You* made this?' Claire's voice was sharp, her words clipped, disbelieving almost.

Giselle lifted her chin, her hackles rising. She was proud of her work. 'Yes, I did.'

The woman held her gaze for a fraction longer than necessary before turning away and speaking to Cal. 'Let's move on. I think Rocco will agree that there's little of any significant value here.'

Cal looked nonplussed. 'Well, no, I suppose not, since the stock is owned by the artists themselves. The shop takes a commission from each sale.'

For some reason, Giselle didn't think Claire had been referring to the stock.

Did the woman know that she and Rocco were... Actually, what were they? Lovers, certainly, but did their relationship go any deeper than that? For Giselle it did, but she couldn't say the same for Rocco: she had no idea how he felt about her. He enjoyed making love with her, that much was obvious, but was that all there was?

Giselle watched Claire leave, Cal trailing behind her after throwing an apologetic look in her direction.

'Blimey, she's a piece of work, isn't she?' Jinny huffed. 'I wouldn't like to have her for a boss. What is she? Some kind of hatchet woman? *Little of value*, indeed. Huh!'

'She's right. There isn't anything of value to the estate.'

'I know, but it was the way she said it. All scornful, like.'

'She's just doing her job.' Giselle didn't know why she was defending the woman, considering she'd taken an instant dislike to her. Or maybe she did know. It wasn't Claire's fault that jealousy had risen its head again.

Claire knew Rocco better than she did. Not physically, but physical was only skin deep. Those two had a connection that was outside Giselle's experience.

Jinny sighed. 'It's the uncertainty I can't handle. Is the craft centre going to close or not? Will Rocco sell it?'

Oh, he was going to sell it all right; Giselle didn't doubt that for a second. And she wasn't entirely sure what would hurt the most: saying goodbye to her studio and everything she'd worked so hard for, or saying goodbye to the man she'd fallen in love with.

—

Rocco checked the time yet again. He thought he was being discreet, but his mother clocked him doing it.

'Am I keeping you from something?' she asked archly.

'There are a few things I'd like to wrap up before we leave.'

'Would it have anything to do with that girl?'

'As a matter of fact, it does.'

'Surely you don't expect to carry on with this relationship once you return to London. It's hardly feasible.'

Rocco ran his hand through his hair, exasperated. Until his mother's arrival, he'd been trying hard not to think about going home, stupidly pretending that things could carry on as they were. But now Beverly was forcing him to make a decision.

However, the problem with her not-so-subtle manipulation was that he might make a decision she didn't like.

His mother pressed on. 'You've known her, how long? A week? Two?'

'I've known her longer than that. I met her when I went to Venice the summer I dossed around Europe.'

'That was just after you'd finished university!' It surprised her, and he felt a momentary satisfaction. The feeling swiftly disappeared when she added, 'You couldn't have kept in touch, otherwise you wouldn't only be taking an interest in Skye now. Therefore, I say again, you've known her for two weeks. People change. Take you, for example: would you say you're the same person now that you were when you were twenty?'

He'd been twenty-one, nearly twenty-two, but she had a point. He didn't know Giselle as well as he wanted, but he was thoroughly enjoying getting to know her. Or he had been, until his mother had brought him down to earth.

He had to face facts: staying on Skye wasn't an option. It was simply too difficult to travel to and from London. He needed to be there, not all the time, but a lot of the time. Distance working was possible, but much of what he did was networking and making contacts. Moore Asset Management's clients liked the personal touch, not a face on a screen.

His life was there. Giselle's was here. And tonight would be the last time he'd hold her. When he left tomorrow, it would be for good, because it would be too painful to leave her for a second time.

Chapter 21

Rocco slammed the lid of his laptop shut and got to his feet. Beverly blinked over the top of her glasses.

'Where are you going?'

'I'll see you in the morning.'

'Rocco!' his mother called after him, but he didn't stop. 'What about dinner? *Rocco!*'

Taking the stairs two at a time, he was in the castle's impressive hallway and out the door in seconds, speeding across the car park to Giselle's studio, praying she was still there.

She was.

Startled, she leapt to her feet when he barrelled inside. 'Come on,' he said, holding out his hand.

'Where are we going?'

'Anywhere, as long as it's not here. I'm not wasting another second of our last day together.'

'We'll go to my place.'

'I was hoping you'd say that,' he replied, heading towards his car. 'But to be honest, I don't care where we go, as long as we're together.' It was corny, but true. He didn't want to think about tomorrow; tomorrow was another day. It was *this* day that counted.

He didn't want a hurried goodbye. He wanted a long-drawn-out farewell, even though it would hurt. More fool him for falling in love, and he was being even more foolish by torturing himself like this, but he had to hold her, had to kiss her, had to make love to her until the very last second.

When he brought the car to a stop outside the bothy and cut the engine, he blurted into the ensuing silence, 'I don't want to return to London.'

Giselle gazed at him, but said nothing, her expression unreadable.

Rocco tensed in dismay. She didn't feel the same way. He could have sworn... But she'd known all along that theirs was a transient relationship, so why would she feel more for him? It was only him who was hoping for more and it was only him who'd committed the cardinal sin of falling in love.

So he hastily added, 'It's so beautiful here. You're incredibly lucky having all this on your doorstep. I'm going to miss it.' *I'm going to miss you.*

'Everyone feels like that after a few days away.' Her tone was flat, then she seemed to shake herself. 'Why are we sitting in the car when we would be much more comfortable in bed?'

With a sad smile he followed her into the bothy, and no sooner had the door closed behind him than she was in his arms and his mouth was on hers. And as he kissed her, he prayed she couldn't see the pain in his eyes.

—

It was dark. The only illumination came from the smattering of stars visible through the skylight.

How many nights had she lain here staring up at them, Giselle wondered.

Rocco lay on his side next to her, his eyes closed. She assumed from his regular breathing that he was asleep, worn out from their lovemaking. She was weary too, but sleep eluded her. And in a way, she was glad, wanting to relish every second of the time remaining with him. Soon it would be morning and he'd be gone, but for now she could pretend.

If you stare at them for long enough, you can almost see the stars moving, she thought absently, a physical passing of time far more ancient than any clock, but just as implacable. There was no arguing with time; no amount of pleading or bargaining could slow its progress. It would move on, and what was the present would all too soon become the past. And she'd be living in a future without Rocco.

She badly wanted to beg him to stay, but she knew it was pointless. By rights, he shouldn't have stayed as long as he had, but Skye had worked its magic, as the island often did.

Or was the reason simply that he'd wanted to enjoy owning the castle for a while before he put it on the market?

What had Claire made of it, she wondered. Had she arrived at a figure yet? Had she seen enough to be able to put a value on something that should be priceless?

Rocco needed someone like Claire: a woman who understood his world, who was at home in it. A woman who spoke spreadsheets and pivot tables, not sea glass and shells. A woman who could accompany him to expensive restaurants, not one who preferred picnics on the grass or fish and chips out of paper.

The stars had definitely moved; the three glittering ice chips of Orion's Belt were now two, as the world wheeled beneath them. Soon they would fade, replaced by the harsh reality of the morning sun.

If she could stay here forever, hold this moment forever, she wouldn't hesitate.

Slowly, Giselle turned her head and found Rocco gazing at her, and when he reached for her again, she went to him with a heart full of love – and sorrow.

'Just coffee,' Rocco said.

Giselle poured him a cup of the instant stuff. It was all she had.

Despair encompassed her. She handed it to him as he sat on her sofa.

That plain blue mug of cheap black liquid was a symbol of the differences between them. No coffee maker for her. No ground beans, no filters, no fancy cup. Hers was a simple life. His wasn't. She lived hand to mouth. He owned a sodding castle. And he was about to leave it – and her – for good.

'What time is your flight?' she asked.

'One p.m.'

'It's five thirty now.'

'Yes.' The word trickled out of his mouth on a sigh, and she knew what the next ones would be. 'I'd better go after I drink this.'

Giselle bit her lip. So he had.

The coffee was drunk far too quickly, and she watched him put the mug down and get to his feet. She rose, feeling awkward and uncertain, and praying she wouldn't cry. Not until he'd gone, at least. After that, she'd howl the house down.

'I know it's early, but do you want a lift to the studio?' His eyes were on hers and she looked away.

'I think it's best if we say goodbye here.' She even managed to say it without her voice breaking.

'Come here.' He opened his arms wide, and she stepped into them.

Sliding her hands around his waist, she held him tight, burying her face in his neck, breathing in the scent of him one last time.

Giselle pulled away first. She had to. She needed him to leave *now*, before she broke down completely. She was barely managing to hold it together.

'I'll—' he started.

'Shh.' She put a finger to her lips, and when he opened his mouth to speak again, she pushed him towards the door. 'Go,' she urged.

His eyes boring into hers, he nodded, gave her a small smile, then was gone.

Giselle heard him walk towards his car, hesitate, then carry on. The engine fired, idled for a moment, and then he drove off.

She strained to listen as the sound grew fainter and fainter, until it faded completely. Then she sank onto the sofa, put her face in her hands and let the tears come. Sobbing, she rocked back and forth, sharp talons savaging her heart with a pain that was physical. It hurt so much she couldn't breathe, and she gasped as wave after wave of desolation engulfed her. She wished he'd never come back into her life. She wished Mhairi had left the castle to anyone other than him. She wished, she wished, *she wished*...

Giselle leapt to her feet. The walls were closing in. She had to get out of here.

Her instinct to head to the loch was out of the question. Not today. She couldn't take the risk of bumping into him.

Instead, she headed away from Duncoorie, its castle and Rocco.

There was a standing stone high on the mountain above the bothy. Grey, weathered and ancient, she craved its promise of solitude. She'd not taken Rocco there, and few people knew of it, which was what she loved about it. She'd been planning on showing it to him, but…

Oh God, he was gone. *Really gone*. And she didn't know how she was going to go on without him. In a far too short a time, he'd stolen her heart and left her empty and bereft. Apart from the pain.

The steep gradient levelled off, and the stone came into view. As monoliths went, it wasn't large, but it was old, and it might seem silly, but she could sense its power. Why it had been driven deep into the mountain to stand sentry wasn't known, and right now Giselle didn't care as she sat, breathless, at its base.

Her fingers dug into the springy grass, and she could feel the warmth of the rough rock against her back. Automatically, her gaze sought her little bothy, then travelled over the landscape, picking out the kirk where darling Mhairi lay, then moved across the waters of the loch before coming to rest on the castle.

Her heart squeezed and she suddenly felt incredibly weary with a tiredness she'd never experienced before. It was more than bone deep – it was *soul* deep.

What was the time?

Giselle wished she'd thought to bring her phone with her, but she'd rushed out of the house so fast she'd forgotten it.

Would he have left yet?

She tried to guesstimate the time and concluded that it was unlikely to be more than seven thirty, but she wasn't sure how long she'd been lost in her misery. It already felt like days.

She would stay here a while longer, then she supposed she'd have to return to her house and later to her studio, when she was sure he'd left, and begin to live the rest of her life without him.

Rocco's car wasn't in its customary place in the castle's car park, but Giselle didn't expect it to be. He had long gone by the time she hesitantly slipped into the studio, locking the door behind her. She didn't switch the lights on because she couldn't face talking to anyone right now. In fact, she wasn't sure why she was here; she certainly wasn't in the mood to do any work. But she felt she had to try to return to some semblance of normality, and being in her studio was a start.

Feeling shaky and weak, she perched on a stool and massaged her temples. She really should try to eat, having had nothing more than the coffee she'd half-drunk with Rocco this morning, but the thought of food turned her stomach.

A hot drink, then. She had a kettle in the studio, so she made a coffee with plenty of milk. At least she'd have something in her tummy, and the caffeine might perk her up a bit.

It kind of did, because after she'd swallowed the last mouthful, she felt jittery and restless, unable to settle, so she did what she always did when she was crabby – she went to the beach to search for sea glass. Even if she failed to find any (and there were times she didn't), the very act of scouring the seashore would be soothing.

Hoping no one would see her and want to speak to her – Avril and Jinny in particular, because she didn't want to have to answer any questions or see their sympathy – Giselle took the longer route to the loch around the rear of the craft centre. Skirting the cafe's outside seating area, she scooted past the duck pond and took a lesser-known path to the beach.

The tide was still quite high, but was receding, the waves sucking at the bank of pebbles, the familiar music filling her ears and the smell of brine filling her nose. The wind had picked up, clouds scudding across the sky, obscuring the sun. Rain was on its way, she guessed. It would be another damp walk home, but she kept a foldable rain jacket in her bag, so hopefully she wouldn't get totally soaked. But even if she did, she didn't care. It would be a fitting end to a shitty day and would reflect her mood perfectly. Anyway, she was used to hunting for sea glass in all weathers, so a bit of rain didn't bother her.

She wasn't doing much foraging now, though. She was too busy feeling sorry for herself.

The jetty caught her eye, and she made her way towards it, dragging her feet. As she stepped onto it, her mind took her back to yesterday morning, and she swallowed hard.

When she reached the end, the waves lapping around the wooden struts below, she could almost feel Rocco's breath on her neck, and she turned, half-expecting him to be there.

But it was empty, just like the future which stretched ahead of her, a line of loneliness disappearing into the distance.

Chapter 22

A knuckle rap on his office door jerked Rocco out of his reverie, and he dragged his eyes away from the sea glass picture of the loch on the wall opposite his desk. The sun was streaming in through the window, illuminating the artwork perfectly, and he'd found himself gazing at it. He'd been doing that a lot since his return from Skye. He'd been back less than three weeks; it felt like a lifetime. It had been the longest nineteen days of his life.

'Wakey, wakey,' Claire chirped. She was standing in the open doorway, one hip cocked, her head tilted to the side, a smile playing about her mouth.

'Sorry, I was miles away.' His gaze flickered to the picture, then away again. 'What can I do for you?'

'The Robinson report: have you finished it?'

Guiltily, he replied, 'Almost done.'

'I need it today.'

'I'm aware of that. You'll have it by three p.m.'

She pursed her red-painted lips. 'I suppose that'll have to do, but if you can get it to me sooner, I'd appreciate it. I'm out of the office tomorrow and the day after, so I need to look at it today.'

'I said you'll have it, and you will.'

She did the head-tilt thing again. 'Are you OK, Rocco? You seem a bit distracted.'

'Distracted' could hardly describe the abject misery he felt. He wished he'd never set eyes on that damned castle. He should have listened to Beverly and instructed Jermyns and his solicitor to deal with it. But oh no, he'd just had to see it for himself, hadn't he?

And had turned his life upside down as a result.

He'd been perfectly happy, right up to the point he'd locked eyes with Giselle in the graveyard. Now he wasn't sure whether he'd ever be happy again.

'How's probate coming along?' he asked.

'It's getting there, but these things take time. There's a lot to sort out.'

That was a pity. He could do with severing his ties to the castle as quickly as possible because the temptation to go back was intense. But what would that achieve? He'd only be torturing himself. Giselle hadn't exactly been distraught when he'd left, and he wasn't interested in merely carrying on where they'd left off. He wanted more than friends-with-benefits or a casual fling. Besides, leaving her again would be intolerable.

'How about we have dinner this evening and I can bring you up to date?' Claire offered.

Huh? He'd been lost in thought again, and it took him a second to remember what they'd been talking about. 'Um, no thanks. I've got plans. Pop it in an email.'

Claire pressed her lips together and her face tightened. 'As you wish,' she snapped and stalked off on her high heels, her hips swaying in her slimline skirt.

Giselle continued to play on his mind as he completed the report, stopping frequently to lose himself in this memory or that. If he closed his eyes, he could see her, feel her, taste her. And if he tried hard enough, he could imagine being on Coral Beach, or Lealt Falls, or any of the other places that were indelibly imprinted on his memory.

After uploading the report to the firm's shared drive and notifying Claire that it was available, Rocco slumped back in his leather chair, the spring-loaded back bouncing. It was a far cry from the elegant Queen Anne chair in the parlour. And his modern glass and chrome desk couldn't compare to the solidity of the polished wooden one Mhairi had favoured.

He hadn't been able to tell whether either of those pieces of furniture were antiques, or whether anything else in the castle was, but no doubt the expert that Claire would employ would shine some light on the value of its contents.

He missed the sense of history those old things had given him, and as he gazed around his office with its sleek, ergonomic fixtures and fittings, he realised the only thing of beauty in it was Giselle's picture. It was also the only thing that had any real worth to him, despite its inexpensive price tag.

Rocco decided to call it a day. He'd go to the gym and work off some of his restlessness, then he'd have a sauna. The steam usually relaxed him, and he could do with all the relaxation he could get right now. His shoulders and neck ached with tension, and staring at a computer screen for hours on end wasn't helping.

The gym was a private one, and it wasn't cheap. He'd been remiss lately, not having bothered to go since his return from Skye, so maybe that was the problem. He'd become used to a certain amount of exercise, but since he'd been back, all he'd done was mope around, feeling sorry for himself.

He needed to get into a routine again, and although bunking off in the middle of the afternoon to pound some rubber and lift a few weights wasn't part of his usual routine, it might help get him back on track. Twenty kilometres on the treadmill might also tire him out enough to help him sleep because he was sick of lying awake night after night wishing he was back on Skye. Wishing he was in Giselle's bed.

At the gym, Rocco slung his kit bag in a locker, making sure his mobile was in his pocket. Stuffing earbuds in, he found an upbeat playlist and made his way to the bank of running machines. The place was quiet: no yummy mummies, no corporate types (apart from himself), and only a handful of fit retirees, some of whom had retired well before the official age, by the look of them.

That was what he hopefully planned on doing: work hard for thirty years, then pass the business on to the next generation and kick back and relax.

That's what his father had hoped to do, but he hadn't got the chance.

However, with no offspring on the horizon, it would be a while before Rocco could hand over the business to a son or daughter of his own. The way things were going, he'd have to spearhead it until they nailed down his coffin.

Rocco chose a machine, set it to a steady pace to warm up and began to run. And as he ran, he thought.

Mhairi hadn't stepped down, had she? She'd kept going to the very end. From what Cal and Giselle had told him, she hadn't wanted to hand the reins over to anyone. But then again, who would she have handed them to? She'd had no one, which was why *he'd* inherited it.

Ramping up both the speed and the incline until he was breathing hard, he wondered whether she'd realised he would sell her beloved castle, or had she been hoping he'd keep it as a going concern?

He'd never know.

Or would he?

Two weeks ago, fourteen boxes had been delivered by courier and were now sitting in the small fourth bedroom of his four-storey town house, ready to be shoved into the attic when he could be bothered to get around to it. It didn't matter if they stayed in the bedroom for a while, since there was no one to object. The house was far too big for one person, but he'd bought it as an investment, and also because he'd hoped to have a family one day. But even though it was a fraction of the size of the castle, he'd felt more at home in Duncoorie than he'd ever done here. Which might be why he spent so long at the office.

Suddenly, he couldn't wait to go home and begin sorting through those boxes. It was the closest he was going to get to Skye, Coorie Castle and, in an oblique way, to Giselle.

—

Over the years, Giselle had become rather good at calligraphy. She didn't always write on the pictures she created, but sometimes words were needed, and this picture needed the word 'cheers'.

She was making a row of hand-drawn glasses in various shapes and sizes, and in the receptacle part of each glass lay a piece of sea glass depicting a cocktail. She'd even drawn a little swizzle stick coming out of every glass and was intending to put a tiny fragment at the end of each of them for decoration. For the contents, she was using a selection of blue, green and amber sea glass. And the inscription above said 'Cheers' in flowing, elegant cursive.

She was in the middle of choosing the final piece of sea glass and debating whether to push the boat out and use one of the rarer colours, when the studio door opened. Expecting it to be one of the many visitors onsite this afternoon, she didn't look up. People often popped in briefly to watch an artist at work, and popped out again after a minute, therefore she'd finish picking the right piece, then she'd smile and say hello.

When a voice said, 'I was expecting *some kind* of welcome, since I've come all this way,' Giselle jumped, and dropped the sea glass she was holding.

It fell to the floor, but she ignored it.

'*Izzy?* Oh my God! What are you doing here?' she squealed, leaping from her stool and knocking it over in her excitement. She launched herself towards her twin in disbelief.

The pair hugged, Giselle squeezing her sister so hard Izzy had to beg her to stop. When Giselle finally released her and stepped back, her cheeks were damp. 'I've missed you so much!' she cried.

'And I've missed you.' Izzy studied her critically. 'Are you OK?'

'I'm fine, honestly,' Giselle assured her.

Izzy gave her The Look. The one that said *you can't fool me*. 'You're not, I can tell. You look awful, Zelle.'

'Gee, thanks. You sure know how to make a girl feel better,' Giselle replied dryly. But Izzy was right; whenever she looked in the mirror she flinched at the drawn, pinched face staring back at her. It didn't help that Izzy looked the picture of health and vitality.

'You should have told me you were coming. I might have been away, on holiday or something.'

'I didn't know I was going to be here until yesterday. Anyway, I wanted to surprise you. The look on your face was priceless. Plus, you and I both know you *never* go anywhere.'

'I do, too!'

'When was the last time you left Skye?'

'Christmas, to Mum and Dad's, I think…?'

'I rest my case. I'll be calling in to see them on the way back if you want to come with me,' Izzy said. 'But I wanted to see you first. I was worried about you.'

Giselle had told her about Rocco, but she'd done her best not to let her pain show when she'd spoken to her sister, trying to sound upbeat and unconcerned; clearly, she hadn't succeeded.

'Let me close up the studio,' Giselle said, after giving her another hug, and very shortly they were on the way to the bothy, with a quick stop off at the shop for some supplies because Giselle didn't have much in. With her appetite having deserted her, she'd been relying on the occasional meal in the cafe to keep her going, so the cupboards were looking rather bare.

Izzy insisted on trawling through the limited selection of fresh fruit and vegetables, saying that she wanted to cook something from scratch. And she also bought smoked salmon, shortbread, a bottle of wine and the sweet and creamy tablet that was similar to fudge and which she claimed she'd been craving for ages.

'You can't beat a piece of tablet,' she stated, unpacking the groceries in Giselle's tiny but perfectly serviceable kitchen, and popping some in her mouth. 'Mmm.' She closed her eyes in bliss.

'You should have said,' Giselle told her. 'I could have sent some in the post. Surely it doesn't beat *cantucci* or *panettone*?'

'It reminds me of home,' Izzy replied simply. She ran a critical eye over Giselle, who squirmed uncomfortably. 'You could do with getting some tablet inside you. It'll put a bit of colour in your cheeks.' Her voice softened. 'Would you like to talk about it?'

Wordlessly, Giselle nodded, not wanting to speak for a moment in case she broke down. She'd cried so much lately she was surprised she had any tears left in her, but they leaked out of her eyes every time she thought of him, which was more times a day than she could count.

And as Izzy washed and chopped a load of tomatoes, Giselle began, 'I met Rocco in Venice.'

'*Venice?* That was years ago, or have you been back there since and not told me?'

'I only went the once.'

'And you met him *there*? You stayed overnight, if I remem—' Izzy gasped. '*You didn't?*'

'I did.'

'I *thought* there was something different about you, but when you showed me the sea glass you'd found and said you knew what you wanted to do with your life, I assumed that's what had made you all sparkly eyed.'

'It was Rocco who found the red heart.'

Izzy's eyes widened. 'Were you in love with him?'

'No, but that time in Venice was special. Romantic. Prophetic, almost. I never told you about Rocco because...' She floundered, unable to verbalise exactly *why* she hadn't confided in her sister.

'It's OK. I understand; I haven't told you everything, either. A girl's got to have some secrets.'

'Like what?' Giselle was intrigued.

'You first; I want to hear the rest of this story.'

Giselle continued, 'No one was more surprised than me when I discovered it was Rocco who'd inherited Coorie Castle. I never expected to see him again, but there he was, telling me he was going to sell up.' She fell silent for several seconds. Then she said, 'I hated him at first. Well, not *hated* exactly, but I had trouble reconciling the man I'd met in Venice with the man who didn't give a rat's arse about the castle or the craft centre. Then I spoke to you, and you made me realise I would do the same thing if I'd inherited a property in London. He didn't seem so bad after that, especially when he asked me to show him around Skye. And that's when I realised I really liked him. Unfortunately, I hadn't stopped fancying him, and as you know we ended up sleeping together.'

Izzy had ceased chopping, engrossed in the story, her face full of sympathy. 'And you fell in love,' she said quietly.

'And I fell in love,' Giselle confirmed.

'Does Rocco know how you feel?'

'God, no!'

'How does he feel about you, do you think?'

She shrugged and pulled a face. 'That it was fun while it lasted.'

'What happens now?'

'The castle will be sold, and I'll never set eyes on him again.'

'Do you still think the craft centre will close?'

'Probably.'

'What will you do if it does?'

'I don't know. Get a job or three, I suppose.' She'd done it in the past, before the craft centre had become established, and before selling her art in the gift shop had provided her with enough income to live on. Therefore, she could do it again.

Her best bet at finding employment would be in Portree, but it was going to be a bugger getting there and back on the bus.

'Do you regret it?' Izzy asked.

She regretted not taking Rocco up on his offer to get her push bike fixed. But as for the man himself… 'No, I don't. I'd do it again in a heartbeat.'

Chapter 23

At first glance, the contents of box number six didn't appear to be any different from the five boxes Rocco had already waded through. He wished he'd taken the time when he'd been at Coorie Castle to put Mhairi's photos, letters, ledgers and other assorted papers into some semblance of order, but he hadn't. He'd simply filled box after box.

It was now ten fifteen and he'd been at it all evening, sitting on the floor in the smallest bedroom, telling himself just five more minutes and he'd stop. But he'd kept going, lured into Mhairi's world and that of the castle by an endless supply of hoarded history. Most of it was only mildly interesting, such as how much was paid for restoration works to the jetty due to storm damage in 1953 (the invoice had been made out to Tandy Gray, Rocco's great-great-grandfather).

Those kinds of things should return to the castle, he resolved, since they made up part of its history, but others, such as Mhairi's birth certificate, should remain in the family. And by that, he meant they should stay with *him*, since he was the only surviving member.

Amongst the contents of box number six was a photo album filled with images of people whose names he didn't know and places he didn't recognise, so he put it to one side to come back to later. Unsure whether the photos had any significance, he didn't know what to do with them, or even where to start finding out who 'Pip and Ken in Cairo' were, for instance.

He didn't know who had taken the photo, when or why, so he was reluctant to dismiss the album out of hand, but he didn't intend spending any more time on it, not when he had so much more to sort through.

Five more minutes and he'd pack it in for tonight. There was no hurry. He could take as long as he needed; it wasn't as though there'd be anything in them which would be pertinent to the valuation or the sale of the castle. He might have to have Mhairi's jewellery valued, though, because he could remember seeing some rather nice pieces. Which box had he put them in…?

Ah, here is something different, he thought, as he removed a pile of letters tied with a length of green ribbon. The top one was addressed to Mhairi at the castle, written in black ink. The handwriting was neat, if rather old fashioned, and he wondered who had sent it.

Feeling as though he was prying, Rocco couldn't resist untying the ribbon.

All twelve letters were addressed to Mhairi, eleven of them written by the same hand. The rogue letter was the last in the pile. Opening the flap of the first, he removed a single sheet of folded paper, smoothed it flat, and began to read.

> *My darling Mhairi,*
> *How I long to hold you in my arms again.*

Rocco stopped. This was too personal. He shouldn't be reading it. It didn't matter that Mhairi was dead; it still felt like an invasion of her privacy. But before he returned the letter to the envelope, he quickly scanned the signature.

Your beloved and ever-adoring, Pip

Rocco knew for a fact that Mhairi had never married, but had Pip been a lover? He thought of the photo and wondered which one was Pip. What had happened for him and Mhairi not to end up together?

With so many unanswered questions, Rocco couldn't prevent himself from going back to the beginning of the letter and reading it. And when he had finished that one, he moved on to the next, and the next.

Gradually, a story unfolded, and Rocco was transfixed.

—

Izzy was sitting on the floor, her back against the sofa, her legs stretched out in front of her, twiddling the stem of her wine glass. 'I knew one bottle wouldn't be enough,' she declared, dropping her head so it rested on the cushion.

'There's a bit left, if you want it,' Giselle offered. She'd drunk enough, and was actually feeling a little queasy. After a week of picky and desultory eating, devouring such a big, though absolutely delicious meal had left her feeling uncomfortably full. And tired. She was so very, very tired. Curled up on the sofa, she was also too comfy to move. The mound of dishes in the sink could wait.

'Don't you think it's ironic,' she observed, 'that you work for a fashion house that designs clothes for skinny women, yet you've turned into the most brilliant cook?'

'Italians love their food, but if you notice, I made the meal with good quality fresh ingredients.'

'Don't tell me you make your own pizzas from scratch?'

'I have been known to. Gosh, I'm tired.' Izzy stifled an enormous yawn.

'Travelling will do that to you.'

'You'd think I'd be used to it by now.'

'Ah, yes. I keep forgetting you're the jet-setting sister.'

Izzy twisted around to look at her. 'And you're the stay-at-home one,' she rejoined with a smile. 'Travelling so much becomes wearing, you know.'

'Aw, diddums. I feel so sorry for you,' Giselle teased.

'You'd hate it,' Izzy pointed out. 'I'm beginning to dislike it, too.'

Giselle's tired eyes widened. 'You are?'

'I've met someone.'

'*Ah.*'

'His name is Edoardo. He's thirty-seven, divorced and he adores cooking.'

'Is he a chef?'

'A plumber. We met when he came to fix a leak in my shower.'

'When was this? And why didn't you tell me?'

'Six months ago, and I didn't say anything because...' Izzy shrugged. 'You know me, easy come, easy go. I didn't think it would last more than a couple of weeks. They rarely do. I wanted to be sure before I said anything.'

'Sure about what?'

'That it's the real thing. I love him, Zelle.'

Giselle cautiously asked, 'Does he feel the same way?'

Eyes sparkling, Izzy nodded. 'He's asked me to marry him!'

Giselle was thrilled for her. That explained her sister's glow. Izzy was in love. Bending forward, Giselle gave her twin a hug. 'That's fantastic news! Congratulations! Can I be your bridesmaid?'

'You'd better be. I'm depending on you.' Izzy's voice was muffled by Giselle's hair. When she pulled away, she was beaming, but her expression quickly sobered. 'Are you OK with this?'

'What do you mean?'

'I'm so happy and you're…'

'Heartbroken?' Giselle supplied. 'Of course I'm OK with it. I'm more than OK; I'm over the moon. You deserve all the happiness in the world, Izzy.'

'So do you. I worry about you up here, alone.'

'I'm not alone. I've got Avril and Jinny, and Tara, and everyone else at Coorie Castle.' Everyone except the castle's owner.

'What happens if the craft centre is forced to close?'

'I don't know.' It made her heart ache to think of the happy band of crafters drifting apart. They'd keep in touch, of course, but it wouldn't be the same. 'Anyway, no more talk of me and my problems. I want to hear all about Edoardo and the wedding. And where's your engagement ring?' Giselle's gaze flashed to her sister's conspicuously naked finger.

'We haven't bought one yet. We're going to choose it together.'

Giselle knew how particular Isadora was, and knew she had excellent taste and a keen eye, but it was hardly romantic, was it? Neither was their meeting; a meet-cute it most definitely wasn't. If Giselle ever received a proposal of marriage, she wanted to be presented with a ring that the man she loved had picked out for her, which would be perfect because *he'd* chosen it, and also because he'd know her so well that he'd know what she'd like.

Then again, Giselle's own meet-cute hadn't worked out too well, despite it happening in one of the most romantic cities in the world and with one of the handsomest guys she'd ever seen. So maybe Izzy's way was better. Romance didn't always lead to happily ever after. In her case, it had led to a broken heart that she despaired would ever be whole again.

—

Rocco examined the ring. It was a ruby, oval in shape, with tiny diamond chips on its built-up shoulders and around the band. Was the metal platinum? He thought it might be. It felt substantial as he weighed it in his palm, and he tried to make out the hallmarks but they were tiny, and he wouldn't know what he was looking for anyway.

It wasn't the most noteworthy of Mhairi's jewellery – a diamond necklace had that honour – but it was the most poignant since it was the only one with a story. A love story, one with the saddest of endings. It explained why Mhairi never married, because Pip, the man she loved, the man she'd been engaged to, the writer of eleven of those letters tied up with green ribbon, had died before they'd had a chance.

The last letter had been written by his brother Ken, the other man in the photo, informing Mhairi of Pip's demise. It had been heartbreaking to read, and Rocco had had tears in his eyes at the end. Pip's last words had been for Mhairi, his final thoughts for the woman he'd hoped to marry.

The ring had been in the twelfth envelope, wrapped in a scrap of ivory silk. *Cut from a wedding dress?* Rocco wondered. He'd never know.

There had been something else in the envelope too: a half-written letter in Mhairi's own handwriting. It was an outpouring of grief and desolation, and Rocco wasn't sure whether she'd intended to send it but hadn't been able to, or whether she'd been trying to express her overwhelming emotions by putting them down on paper and hadn't had any intention of posting it. Another thing he'd never know.

And although he felt as though he'd intruded on something incredibly private, he was glad he'd read them. Mhairi was no longer a distant relative who'd bequeathed him a castle because she'd had no one else to leave it to. She'd become a real person, and his heart ached for her. Whether his feelings would have run as deep if his own heart hadn't recently been broken, he couldn't tell, but it didn't lessen his pity for her.

Stiff and uncomfortable after sitting on the floor for so long, Rocco clambered slowly to his feet, groaning at the ache in his back. It was very late, and he was shattered.

But even though he was dog tired, when he crawled into bed his brain refused to shut off. He kept thinking about Mhairi and her lost love, and her regret that she hadn't left her Scottish castle to be with the man she'd loved. She'd assumed she'd have a lifetime to be with him, years and years, so when he'd gone to Egypt to work on a newly unearthed antiquity, she hadn't felt the need to accompany him. Besides, the heat didn't agree with her, so she'd remained on Skye.

She'd missed him, obviously, and had been counting the days until his return, but not for one moment had she doubted he wouldn't come back. Then he'd fallen ill…

Pip had returned to Skye, but not to marry her. He'd come back in a coffin, and he'd been buried in the very churchyard where Mhairi had been laid to rest, in a plot next to his. She'd bought it the day after his funeral, when she'd thought her broken heart would kill her.

However, she'd lived a further sixty years, and in all that time she hadn't found another man to live up to her Pip. She hadn't found another man she'd loved as much as she'd loved him.

Rocco turned his pillow over yet again, searching for the cooler side, sleep continuing to elude him. What if *he* didn't find a woman who lived up to Giselle? What if he couldn't find anyone he loved as much as her? Would *he* be destined to spend his life alone, or would he settle for second best?

He didn't relish the thought of doing either.

Mhairi had written:

> *Life is so short. If I'd known just how little time we would have together, I would have grabbed it with both hands and wrung every last drop of love from it, my darling. Please forgive me. I don't regret loving you. How could I ever regret that? But I do regret not being by your side every minute of every day when I had the chance.*

Mhairi was right. Life *was* short. Was he going to live the rest of his, regretting not giving love his best shot?

Skye was calling him, and it was time he heeded her voice.

Rocco mightn't be able to persuade Giselle to fall in love with him, but he had to try, and he couldn't do it while he was here and she was there. He owed it to himself. He owed it to Coorie Castle. And he owed it to Mhairi, because he was praying that if he sold his house and his shares, and cashed in his investments, he just *might* be able to keep the castle after all.

Chapter 24

Giselle scuttled down the ladder and headed for the bathroom, trying to be quiet and not disturb Izzy, who was sound asleep. Sharing a bed with her sister had reminded Giselle of when they were kids. They'd had single beds with a nightstand separating them, but invariably Giselle would wake up in the same one as Izzy; either she'd climbed in with her twin in the middle of the night, or Izzy had crept into hers. They may have gone their separate ways during the day, but at night they'd sought each other out.

Giselle suspected that even if Izzy had begun last night on the sofa, she would have ended up in Giselle's bed with her.

Wearily, she slumped on the loo, feeling dreadful. Not only was she exhausted, but her eyes were gritty, and she felt sick. Thankfully, she didn't have a headache, but that small mercy didn't prevent her from wishing she hadn't drunk so much wine last night. Had it only been the one bottle between them? It felt like she'd guzzled the whole thing on her own. And to top it all off, her period was due. Great. That was all she needed: sore boobs, bloating and irritability.

She was a right bundle of laughs, wasn't she? Hopefully, a cup of coffee and some breakfast would sort her out. Actually, scrap that; she'd have tea. Coffee was just too bleh right now. And she needed to rehydrate before she could face food.

But when she saw last night's dishes in the sink, with the remains of the tomato-covered pasta sauce smeared on them, she had to dash to the bathroom.

I'm never drinking again, she vowed, after dry heaving with her head hanging over the toilet bowl. She hoped Izzy didn't want to do anything energetic today, such as *speaking*, for instance. Giselle might manage a grunt or two, but that would be it.

After rinsing her mouth and brushing her teeth, she felt marginally better, so she made some tea and went outside to sit and drink it.

The grass was still wet with dew, and the air was cool and fragrant with the wildflowers that had self-seeded in the garden. A cheeky blackbird eyed her as it scurried through the stems looking for grubs, and bees cruised from bloom to bloom.

Gradually, Giselle's hangover receded and she began to feel more human, and as she slowly came back to life, her brain kicked into gear as she thought about yesterday.

Izzy's arrival had been a lovely welcome surprise, and so had her news. Her sister was engaged, and to a plumber! Giselle, if she'd imagined Izzy falling in love, would have assumed it would be with someone from the fashion industry, and in a way, she was relieved it wasn't. Izzy needed someone to ground her, and from what she'd told Giselle, Edoardo sounded perfect. She couldn't wait to meet him, but when that would be was anyone's guess. Before the wedding, she hoped, but with the state of her finances and the uncertainty of the craft centre's future, she mightn't meet the guy until he said, 'I do.'

'You should have brought him with you,' Giselle had said, then felt guilty when Izzy had told her she'd sensed Giselle needed her. She'd felt even more guilty when Izzy had confided, 'I debated whether to tell you about me and Edoardo, because of Rocco.'

'Did you honestly think I'd begrudge you your happiness because I'm feeling so miserable? This is the best news ever!' she'd cried.

And it was. Giselle couldn't have been happier for her sister. She just wished she could be equally happy for herself. There are other fish in the sea, she'd said, but she wasn't convinced. She didn't want anyone else. She wanted Rocco.

'Morning.' Izzy yawned sleepily, coming outside to join her. 'How long have you been up?'

'An hour.'

'I'd forgotten how quiet it is here. I slept like the dead, and your bed is so comfy.' She stretched, then curled up in the chair next to Giselle, tucking her feet underneath her.

Giselle envied her twin. She wished she'd slept as well. 'Why haven't you got a hangover?' she grumbled, noting how fresh and rested her sister looked.

'We only had a couple of glasses,' Izzy replied. 'Then again, I probably drink more than you, so I've got a higher tolerance. Wine with dinner seems to be a given in Italy. I draw the line at wine with lunch, though, otherwise I wouldn't get any work done. Speaking of work, are you going to the studio today?'

'No chance! I'm not slaving away over a hot glue gun while you're swanning about enjoying yourself.'

'In that case, could we go to a mill? I have an urge to buy some Skye tweed. And then I want to visit the loch, and pop into the craft centre to see what you've been working on. And we could—' She stopped, and Giselle laughed, the first laugh she'd uttered since Rocco left. 'What's so funny?' Izzy demanded.

'You. You're like a whirlwind.'

'I'm only going to be here for a couple of days,' Izzy protested. 'I don't want to waste a minute.'

That was how Rocco had felt, Giselle remembered. He hadn't wanted to waste any time, either. It struck her that Izzy and Rocco were so much alike in their spontaneity and their zest for life. Unlike her own boring, predictable, introverted self. No wonder she'd fallen in love with him, and no wonder he hadn't felt the same way about her.

An Aston Martin DB9 isn't the roomiest of cars if you have a lot of luggage, Rocco mused, as he pulled into Tebay services on the M6. He'd been on the road for around six hours and had reached the halfway point in the journey, so it was time for a break. It would have been far quicker to fly to Inverness, as he'd done previously, but this wouldn't be a flying visit. This time he intended to stay for good. Which was why the car was jam packed with everything he thought he might need. Including a couple of suits, because one never knew when a suit might come in handy – when he had to beg a local council for something, perhaps?

His stomach rumbled as he entered the restaurant area and smelt coffee and bacon. He was starving, having not eaten much yesterday evening as he'd been too busy sifting through the boxes from the castle. He'd have to arrange for those to be sent back at some point, along with the rest of the things that he hadn't been able to fit in the car. And at some juncture, he'd have to decide what, if any, of his possessions he wanted to bring to Skye with him. There was a lot to consider and a lot to sort out. And there was also his mother; she wouldn't be pleased, but this was his life, not hers, and he had to live it his way.

While he waited in the queue for food, he checked his phone. No messages and no emails of note. He'd shot off an email to Nora before he'd left London, informing her that something had come up and he wouldn't be in the office today, so that if anyone asked, she wouldn't be put in an awkward position. He'd speak to her later today, or first thing tomorrow, and explain, *after* he'd spoken to his mother. He wasn't looking forward to *that* conversation. Not wanting to risk having to speak to his mother before he was ready, he put his phone in airplane mode and concentrated on choosing the items he wanted for his breakfast: bacon obviously, eggs, grilled tomato, a sausage. This meal would have to sustain him until dinner because he had another seven hours to go, longer if he hit roadworks or traffic. He wouldn't arrive in Duncoorie until three thirty at the earliest and he wasn't going to be thinking of food at that point. His mind would be on Giselle, as it had been ever since he'd set eyes on her at the kirk.

He hoped she'd be pleased to see him. If he was honest, he hoped she'd be more than just pleased, but what if she wasn't? She might want nothing more than the brief fling they'd had. It was a fear he'd been grappling with ever since he'd made the impulsive decision to return to Skye last night.

However, the fear hadn't held him back. Mhairi's words had continued to play on his mind: *I don't regret loving you.*

How could I ever regret that? But I do regret not being by your side every minute of every day when I had the chance.

He had to try to make Giselle fall in love with him, because he would regret it for the rest of his life if he didn't. His future happiness depended on it.

—

The mill was a small one, run and owned by the same family for several generations, and a forty-minute drive from Duncoorie. Against a backdrop of green hills, it nestled between a rocky outcrop and grazing land dotted with sheep. Built of weathered grey stone, with a roof studded with moss, and ivy completely covering one side, it had a permanence about it, as though it had grown out of the landscape.

A wooden sign saying 'Viewing Platform' hung above a door, and Giselle followed Izzy inside.

She was immediately struck by the noise. Gosh, it was loud, with several enormous machines clattering away, the shuttles snapping back and forth with dizzying speed. A barrier separated the working area from the long viewing gallery, and at several points along it, information boards described the looms and the weaving process.

A pile of raw wool was in a box near the entrance, and Giselle gently stroked the fibres as she read about how the fleeces were graded, carded, then spun into yarn.

She was fascinated as she watched a length of cloth slowly grow before her very eyes, but although she enjoyed finding out about woollen cloth production, she was far more interested in the finished products in the onsite shop. Cushions, blankets and even curtains were on display, as well as scarves, shawls, bags and hats. The colours were fabulous, reflecting those of the natural world outside, and there were also the most wonderful tartans.

At one point, Giselle leant close to her twin and whispered, 'This is lovely! I can imagine most of these being sold in Coorie Castle's gift shop. I'll mention it to Mhairi…' Then she trailed off. She'd been about to say, 'the next time I have tea with her', but there wouldn't be a next time. And neither would there be any point in mentioning it to Cal, since the future of the castle and its craft centre was so uncertain.

Giselle's mood plummeted, and once again she had a sick feeling in her tummy.

Izzy was busy choosing a throw, and didn't notice, so Giselle had time to gather herself. She didn't want to spoil her sister's day with her glum mood. There would be time enough to be miserable after Izzy left.

Purchase made, Izzy linked arms with Giselle as they wandered back to the car. 'Where shall we go for lunch? My treat.'

'No, Izzy—'

'Don't argue.' Izzy pouted, so Giselle didn't, despite not feeling particularly hungry.

She could do with a sit down and a cup of tea, though. The hangover she thought she'd vanquished was back in the form of a sudden depletion in energy. Hoping food might help perk her up, she suggested the pub she'd been to with Rocco. It was halfway between the mill and home, and she knew the food was good and plentiful. And it was better than attempting to cook at the bothy. She wasn't the most domesticated person in the kitchen, and it wasn't fair on Izzy to have to cook for them. She was here to keep Giselle company, not to slave over a hot stove, even if she was good at cooking and professed to really enjoy it.

After lunch, during which Giselle suddenly found she was absolutely ravenous and hoovered up every last crumb of her Jamaican jerk chicken with salad and chips, Izzy drove them back to Duncoorie.

'It's a lovely afternoon,' Izzy observed, as they approached the outskirts of the village. 'How about we walk off that rather fabulous lunch and go for a stroll by the loch?'

'I'm game, if you are. You can help me look for sea glass.'

'Only if you let me make a picture.'

Giselle chuckled. 'You don't need my permission.'

'I'll need some paper and glue,' Izzy pointed out. 'And I did say I wanted to see what you're working on.'

'You said you wanted to go to the gift shop. Not the same thing.'

'It had some lovely stuff last time I was here,' Izzy argued. 'Anyway, I need to say hi to Jinny.'

'You'd better. If you don't and she finds out you've been to Duncoorie, I'll be toast,' Giselle said. Izzy had met Jinny not long after Giselle had taken up residence in the studio, and the two women had hit it off immediately. Jinny was another live wire, like Izzy.

When Giselle realised how busy the craft centre was today, she felt a little guilty for not being in the studio, but the feeling soon disappeared when she reached the beach and saw the pleasure on Izzy's face.

'I forget how beautiful it is,' her sister said as she gazed around. 'No wonder you don't want to leave. My offer still stands, though: come live with me in Milan.'

'And be a third wheel? No thanks! Anyway, what would Edoardo say? I doubt he'll be happy sharing you with your sister.'

'He'll be fine. Family is a big thing in Italy, and Edoardo's got a very big family indeed!'

'All the more reason for me not to add to it. Besides, I wouldn't feel comfortable knowing I was cramping your newly engaged style.'

'I'm sure we could work something out. Seriously, if you need to get away for a while, let me know.'

'I will,' Giselle promised, having no intention of doing any such thing. If she had to give up her bothy for whatever reason, she'd move back in with Mum and Dad. They didn't have any style for her to cramp.

While Giselle looked half-heartedly for sea glass (she wasn't really in the mood), Izzy poked around in the rock pools exposed by the retreating tide.

'I've found a crab!' she announced excitedly, beckoning Giselle over to take a look. Then she laughed at herself. 'I bet you see these all the time, don't you?'

'Now and again,' Giselle admitted with an indulgent smile.

'Remember how we used to go rock pooling when we were kids? We could do with a net and a bucket right now,' Izzy declared, crouching down to peer into the pool.

Giselle stared at her sceptically. 'Can't you just be content with looking?'

'I suppose I'll have to, but half the fun is trying to net the wee fishes and shrimp things, then seeing how many you get in your bucket. I used to hate it if you got more than me.'

'You always were competitive.'

'So were you! Remember when you fell in when you saw a starfish? You had to have it because then you'd be the one who had the best wee critter.' Izzy was laughing.

'I'd forgotten that. I bawled my eyes out because I got my favourite shorts wet.'

'You loved those shorts. And how about me with that purple dress with the embroidered heart on the front? It was all I'd wear at one point.'

Giselle perched her bottom gingerly on a rock. 'Fast forward twenty years and I'm still mucking about on the seashore, and you're still obsessing about clothes.'

They smiled at each other; they were both doing what they loved. Except…

'Will you ever give it up, do you think?' Giselle asked. 'Now that you have Edoardo?'

'I don't want to be away from him. Ever.'

'Yet you're here,' Giselle pointed out.

'I had to come see you. You're hurting. I could feel it here.' Izzy put a hand on her chest above her heart. 'I know I can't take that away, but I wanted to give you a hug.'

Giselle's eyes filled with tears. She'd missed her sister so much.

'I'll be OK,' she said, not wanting Izzy to worry about her.

'I know you will. You're the brave one.'

'You're brave, too.'

'Och, no I'm not,' Izzy said, sounding the most Scottish Giselle had heard her sound since she'd arrived. 'I'm the reckless one. I dive in without thinking. You think about things, weigh up the risks, then dive in despite the danger. That's bravery.'

Giselle didn't feel brave right now. She felt stupid. She'd fallen in love with a ghost from her past, when there was no hope of him being in her present.

Izzy, sensing that Giselle's spirits had taken another nose-dive, said, 'Can we go to the gift shop now, and stop at the cafe on the way? I fancy a coffee and a slice of cake.'

'You can't be hungry already!'

'I'm bloody ravenous,' Izzy declared. 'It's all this fresh air; I'm not used to it.'

Giselle couldn't eat another bite, but she'd have a cup of tea to keep her sister company.

They made their way back to the crescent of beach, Giselle avoiding looking at the jetty where Rocco had kissed her in the early morning mist, and onto the lane leading from Cal's cottage and the boathouse to the castle.

Rounding the corner, she waved to Fergus, the glass-blower, who was in his oven of a studio (with three furnaces, it was always roasting inside), and lingered for a moment outside Tara's because Izzy wanted to examine the exquisite doll's houses in the window.

'If I ever have kids, I'll buy them a doll's house,' she said, adding with a laugh, 'I'm not sure I'd let them play with it, though. They're far too lovely for sticky fingers.'

'And expensive,' Giselle told her. 'You wouldn't want it to get broken.'

Whatever Izzy was about to say in response was lost when Giselle heard her name being called.

'Where have you been?' Avril demanded. 'Haven't you seen my message? Hi, Izzy,' she added absently, her attention on Giselle.

'What message?' Giselle asked, realising she'd left her bag containing her phone in Izzy's car.

Avril bit her lip, her eyes wide. She looked nervous. Then she said, 'You'll never guess who's here.'

Chapter 25

Giselle's heart leapt. Was it Rocco? Had he returned? '*Who?*' she squeaked.

'That Claire woman. And she's got a guy with her. An estate agent. A posh one. He seems fairly impressed, and I heard him say he's got someone in mind who is looking for a place exactly like this.'

Staggered, Giselle struggled to remain calm as disappointment swept through her in a flood of misery.

'They arrived a couple of hours ago. How inconsiderate not letting us know in advance. It was pure luck we had any rooms free,' Avril said. 'She insisted on staying in Rocco's suite, but I put him up in one of the smaller rooms. Bloody ironic that we're the busiest we've ever been, yet the castle is about to be sold. I hope whoever buys it doesn't turn it into flats or something.'

'Isn't it a listed building?' Izzy asked.

'It is, but there are ways and means,' Avril replied darkly. 'My uncle is on the council, and you ought to hear the stories he can tell. And don't mention turning it into flats to my dad; he'll throw a fit.'

Right now, Giselle didn't care about listed buildings or planning permission, and she'd already resigned herself to having to look for a job soon, but she couldn't move past the hope she'd felt when she'd thought Rocco was here, which had been swiftly followed by renewed heartache.

He wasn't coming back. Deep down she'd known this, but a part of her had clung on to a smidgen of hope.

'Thanks for the heads-up,' she managed.

'I didn't want you to bump into them without some warning, in case you thought—'

'Rocco was with them?'

'Yes,' Avril said with a small sympathetic smile. 'If I've got any more news, I'll let you know.' She shot an anxious glance at the castle's main entrance. 'I'd better get back before I'm missed.'

'Do you want to go home?' Izzy asked Giselle as Avril hurried away.

'Definitely not.' Giselle was firm on that score. She wasn't going to let Rocco's henchwoman drive her out of the studio she paid good money to rent. In fact, she had a feeling she'd need to create as many pictures as she could with the materials in her possession. She should sell as much as possible while the craft centre was still open. It would take time to search out new shops who'd be willing to stock her pictures. And that was if she actually wanted to keep making them, because her heart wasn't in it anymore.

'We'll grab that coffee and cake, then you can have a play with card and glue while I do some work,' Giselle said.

'That's my girl!' Izzy linked an arm through hers and gave it a squeeze. 'But seriously, Zelle, if you're not up to it... You look washed out.'

'I feel it,' Giselle admitted. *But perhaps it is normal to feel meh when you've got a broken heart*, she pondered miserably.

The cafe was busy as usual, but there was a table free and no sign of Claire, so Giselle grabbed it while her sister went to the counter to drool over the selection of freshly made cakes.

'I couldn't decide whether to have a passionfruit slice or a piece of triple chocolate,' she announced when she sat down. 'So I went for both. You'll have to help me eat them.'

'I don't think I can,' Giselle replied, eyeing them. Their gooey sugariness made her feel quite queasy, so she sipped her tea and watched her sister devour both slices.

'That was heavenly,' Izzy declared, dabbing crumbs from her mouth. Then she was on her feet and urging Giselle to go to the gift shop with her.

As soon as she spotted Giselle, Jinny said, 'I was hoping to catch you before you heard it from anyone else.' Her face was sombre.

'I know. Avril told me that Claire is here with an estate agent.'

'That's not all.' Sympathy filled her friend's eyes, and Giselle wasn't sure she wanted to hear what Jinny was about to tell her. 'They were in the shop earlier. I heard them talking.'

'About what?' Giselle was getting a bad feeling about this.

Jinny took a deep breath. 'Claire was looking at your pictures and I heard her say that she already had one of them, the big one of the loch. She said that Rocco likes it, but it's not really her taste, though she was sure she could find somewhere to hang it where she wouldn't have to look at it all the time, and could this guy help her and Rocco find their forever home when the castle is sold.'

Giselle was horrified. 'What?! That's impossible. You've got it wrong.'

'She mentioned the M word,' Jinny added miserably.

'*Marriage?*' The world spun, and Giselle wanted to vomit.

He'd lied to her! And to think she'd trusted him, believed him when he'd told her that Claire was just a colleague.

Anger burnt, bright and hot. How could she have been so stupid? He'd been playing with her, had taken the opportunity to have a bit of fun. He'd betrayed her and Claire both.

Giselle felt sick. She wasn't sure who she despised the most: herself for being so gullible, or Rocco for being such a shit.

It was lucky for him that he hadn't accompanied his girlfriend because Giselle would have loved nothing better than to tear his head from his two-timing shoulders.

Then her anger vanished as swiftly as it had arrived, leaving her broken and inconsolable.

Izzy ushered her out of the gift shop and into the studio, then sat her down and made her a cup of coffee. 'Do you want me to find something stronger?'

'Coffee is fine.' Giselle sipped it, grimacing at the taste.

'Would you like to go home?'

She shook her head. 'I'll only mope around, and I've done enough of that lately. Actually, I'll go see if the cafe has some herbal tea.' She got to her feet. 'While I'm gone, you can get started on a picture, if you like.'

'Zelle…?'

'I need to keep busy. I'll be fine, honestly,' she insisted, but both of them knew she was lying.

—

Rocco tucked his car around the rear of the castle, where Cal's Land Rover and the golf buggy that Mhairi used to use when she wanted to tour her estate were parked. Getting out and stretching, he debated whether to let the estate manager know he was here, but decided not to bother him just yet. Before he did anything, he wanted to see Giselle.

As he walked towards the studios, he felt even more nervous. Once again, he asked himself whether he was doing the right thing, but he was here now, so...

On Bambi legs, his heart going like the clappers, Rocco hesitated outside the door.

She was there! He could see her hunched over the workbench, and he took a long, deep breath, blowing out his cheeks as he exhaled.

Then he opened the door, went inside and—

The woman wasn't Giselle!

She looked up with a smile, her expression open and welcoming, then her eyes hardened abruptly and her full lips tightened.

'Um, I was looking for Giselle?' he said, glancing around the studio as though he expected her to be hiding somewhere.

'You're Rocco.'

'I am.' His reply was guarded as he tried to work out who she was and why—

Then it came to him! This must be Giselle's sister! He should have realised immediately, as the similarities were obvious.

Izzy didn't look at all pleased to see him.

'Is she here?' he asked.

'Why?'

Taken aback, he didn't have an answer. Why was she being so aggressive? What on earth had he done, or not done, to deserve it?

And when she spat, 'Haven't you done enough damage without sniffing around her again?' he was at a total loss.

She cocked her head, studying him as though he were some kind of nasty insect.

Thoroughly perplexed now, he said, 'I don't know what you mean.'

'I don't appreciate anyone playing with my sister's affections. And under your girlfriend's nose, too. You broke my sister's heart, you scumbag. Shame on you.'

'I have no idea what you're talking about,' he protested. 'What girlfriend?'

'Claire.' Giselle's voice came from behind him, and he whirled around, his heart leaping.

'Giselle,' he breathed. His chest tightened at the sight of her and his pulse stumbled.

Her expression was stony. 'What do you want?'

Hell, this was going badly, but he didn't know why. He thought he'd cleared up the nonsense about Claire being his girlfriend. And what had Izzy just said? Something about breaking her sister's heart?

'To tell you I'm not selling the castle,' he said, playing it safe until he could work out what was going on.

'That's why your girlfriend and an estate agent are here, is it? To *not* sell it? Pull the other one,' she scoffed.

'Back up a second! Not only do you still think Claire is my girlfriend despite me categorically telling you she isn't, but you think she's here, in *Duncoorie*?'

'Right on both counts.'

Rocco was so tense his jaw ached. On the long drive to Skye, he'd run Giselle's every possible reaction through his mind, but not one of them had featured her being angry. Or accusing. And certainly not delusional. She must have got the wrong end of the stick. Maybe Claire had informed Cal that someone official would be along shortly to value the place for probate. He wasn't entirely sure what probate entailed, and maybe he should have taken Claire up on her offer to discuss her progress so far (although not over dinner), but all he'd wanted was to go home, pick through Mhairi's boxes and lick his wounds.

He said, 'Claire is in London; I'm assuming she's organising an official valuation, but that'll be purely for probate.'

'Wrong on both counts,' Giselle snapped. 'Claire *is* here, and she's got an estate agent with her. He's already got a buyer in mind.'

'What? That can't be right.'

'Which bit?'

'All of it.'

'Your girlfriend is definitely here,' Giselle insisted.

'Once and for all, she's not my girlfriend, and if she is here, I wasn't aware she was coming.' *Bloody hell, this is all I need*, he thought.

'Why did Claire tell your estate agent that you're getting married?'

'She did *what*?' Taken aback, he said, 'You must be mistaken. We are *not* getting married.'

'And apparently you're waiting for the castle to be sold so you can buy a house together. Oh, and she doesn't like the sea glass picture you bought to hang in your new house, so you might have to rethink where you're going to put it! I can suggest a few places.'

'We are categorically *not* buying a house together,' he growled through clenched teeth. 'And neither am I selling the castle. I want to keep it. I'm going to live *here*, not London, and do you know why?' He was shouting now, boiling with rage. Claire's machinations astounded him. 'Because I love you, Giselle. *You* – not Claire. I know you don't feel the same way about me, but I've said it – *I love you*. Now if you'll excuse me, I've got an estate agent to turf off my property.'

Furious, Rocco pushed past the woman he loved and stormed towards the castle, and when he entered the castle's impressive hall, the receptionist's jaw dropped open.

'Avril, do you know where Claire Wallace is?' he snapped.

'Er, Rocco, Mr Moore, um, hello. We didn't expect— I believe she's in the parlour,' the woman stuttered.

'Thank you,' he called over his shoulder as he strode off.

He didn't bother knocking on the parlour door, and when he pushed it open, both Claire and the man with her jumped. They were seated at the polished wood desk, a tablet propped up in front of them, a laptop at Claire's elbow.

'Rocco? Why—? What—?' Claire recovered quickly. 'You should have told me you were coming; we could have travelled up together.'

'Sorry, could you excuse us, please?' he said to the estate agent. 'I'd like a word with Claire in private.'

The man glanced at Claire, as though seeking permission to leave.

Claire said, 'Rocco, this is Kurt Fuller from Jermyns. Kurt, this is Rocco Moore, the castle's owner. I don't believe you two have met. Kurt will handle the sale personally. In fact, we were just discussing that very thing, so it might be more beneficial if he stayed.'

'In private, please,' Rocco insisted.

'Very well. Kurt, would you mind?'

The man got to his feet with obvious reluctance and picked up the tablet. 'I'll be in the lounge,' he said, casting Rocco a doubtful look. 'Pleased to meet you, Mr Moore.'

Rocco tightened his lips and gave the man a brief nod.

As soon as the door snicked softly shut, Claire rounded on him. 'That was incredibly rude.'

'I'll apologise later, and recompense him for his time.'

'No need. It'll come out of the commission on the sale.'

'There won't be any sale.'

Claire's chin came up. 'Excuse me?'

'I'm not selling the castle.'

'You have to.'

'No, I don't. I'm going to live here and run the castle and the craft centre as a going concern.'

'But what about the company? And Beverly?'

'That's between my mother and I.' He should never have involved Claire. The castle and his personal finances were none of her concern. 'Why are you giving people the impression we're together?'

She blinked. 'I didn't realise I had.'

'People seem to think we're getting married.'

'By people, do you mean that blonde-haired woman you've been seeing? Is *she* the reason you don't want to sell?'

'Who I date is no concern of yours.' How did she know about Giselle, he wondered, then guessed his mother must have told her. 'Did Beverly put you up to it?'

'She only wants what's best for you.'

His mother *had* put her up to it! The pair of them were in cahoots. 'What's best for me is that she stays out of my private life.'

Claire studied him, her brown eyes narrowed. 'I've done some rough calculations on the value of the estate,' she said calmly, moving the laptop closer and turning the screen to face him. 'Do you want to know how much it's worth, approximately?'

'I don't care. I'm not selling,' he declared, but he looked anyway.

The figure on the screen astounded him. He'd thought it was worth a fair bit, but not that much. Dear God...

Rocco collapsed into a chair as the enormity struck him. 'Are you sure?' he croaked.

'As I said, it's a rough calculation, but it'll be there or thereabouts.'

He felt sick. There was no way he could keep the castle. *No way.* Even with the sale of his house and the liquidation of every stock and share he owned, he couldn't afford to keep it.

The forty per cent inheritance tax would ensure that.

Chapter 26

Giselle was in shock. Her instinct had been to go after Rocco, but she held back, wondering whether she'd misheard him. 'Did he say what I thought he said?' she asked Izzy in disbelief.

'I believe he did.' Izzy was staring at her, agog.

'He said he loves me. You definitely heard him, right? I'm not imagining it?'

'You're not imagining it,' Izzy confirmed.

'And he's not selling the castle. Did you hear that bit, too?'

'I heard.'

On shaking legs, Giselle staggered over to the plastic chair and plopped onto it. 'He said he loves me.' Her voice was flat.

Izzy's expression was wary. 'What's going on?'

'I don't know.' Her hands were shaking, and she thrust them under her thighs and sat on them.

'Don't you think you'd better find out?'

'I'm scared,' Giselle confessed. 'What if he didn't mean it?'

'Do you honestly think he'd say something like that if he didn't mean it?'

Giselle didn't know what to think, but a spark of hope had ignited in her chest and was fast taking hold. 'Oh, my God,' she muttered, and a smile spread across her face as the reality sank in. 'I can't believe it! He's really here.'

'He is!' Izzy was giggling. 'This is the best news ever!'

'What do I do now?'

'Go after him. Tell him how you feel.'

Her insides fizzing with joy, Giselle leapt to her feet. 'I can't go like this! I look a mess.' She tugged at the band holding the end of the braid she'd so carelessly plaited this morning and shook her hair free. 'Have you got a brush? And some make-up? I need make-up!'

'You don't need make-up. You're perfect as you are. Although maybe you could do with brushing your hair out,' Izzy laughed.

Hastily, Giselle ran the proffered brush through her tangled hair. Having been plaited for so long, it would never lie straight without her washing it, but at least she didn't look like Medusa. It would have to do.

'Wish me luck,' she said.

'You won't need it. And, Zelle?'

'What?'

'I won't bother waiting up, but message me if you're planning on staying out all night.' Izzy's laughter followed Giselle out of the door.

Halfway to the castle's entrance, Giselle faltered. Should she be doing this? Wouldn't it be better to wait for him to come to her? Or was that being cowardly? Rocco had been brave enough to return to Duncoorie and blurt out that he loved her in front of a total stranger who, let's face it, had been less than welcoming, so he deserved to know she felt the same way about him.

She still couldn't believe it…

Avril spotted her immediately and hurried over. Grabbing her arm, she dragged her to the side and hissed, 'Rocco's here!'

'I know. I've just spoken to him.'
'Are you OK?'
'I'm absolutely bloody marvellous.'
'Why? What's happened?'
'Where is he now?'
'In the parlour with her – *Claire*. The estate agent is in the lounge. They were in the parlour together, but then Rocco arrived and the next minute the bloke comes out with a face like thunder and sets up camp in the lounge. What's going on?'

'I'll tell you later,' she said, dashing off. If Rocco wasn't putting the castle on the market, he should be the one to tell everyone the good news. Giselle didn't want to steal his thunder. And as for the love thing…? She hadn't had a chance to take it in herself yet, and there was a part of her that continued to think she was mistaken.

Scampering through the series of interconnecting rooms which led to the parlour, her heart thudding in her ears, Giselle had just reached it when the double doors opened and out strode Claire. She had a supercilious smile on her face, which stuttered like a faulty light bulb when she spied Giselle. However, it swiftly returned, brighter than ever.

'I'm sorry,' Claire said, closing the door firmly behind her. 'Rocco is busy right now. Do you have an appointment?' Her fingers remained curled around the handle.

'No, but—'

'In that case, could I ask you to make one? I can give you his PA's number. Or, better still, speak to Cal; he's the estate manager after all, so he's the one who should be dealing with any queries or issues relating to the craft centre. Rocco is far too busy.'

'I'm not, it's—' Giselle stumbled over the words '—personal.'

Claire's gaze was hard and piercing. 'I bet it is. Unfortunately— *Oh!*'

The handle was wrenched out of Claire's grasp, and she staggered backwards, her high heels unbalancing her as the door flew open.

Rocco halted, his expression grim. 'Giselle?'

Giselle looked from him to Claire, and she backed away.

Rocco put out a hand. 'Don't go. *Please*. Claire, go join Kurt Whatshisname in the lounge.'

Claire's lips tightened. 'Do you want us to carry on, or should we wait for you, since you're here? It doesn't matter either way, but I thought you might like to be involved, considering you're the vendor.'

'I... No, go ahead.' Rocco looked drawn, his eyes clouded with an emotion Giselle wasn't able to read.

Claire gave her a sideways glance. 'If we work fast, we could have the castle on the market by the end of the week. Is that acceptable? Or do you need more time to think about the asking price?'

Mutely, Rocco shook his head. He wasn't looking at Claire, though; he was gazing at Giselle. Worry coiled in her stomach, making her uneasy. This wasn't the same man who'd stormed out of the studio just now. This man appeared to have the weight of the world on his shoulders.

Claire hesitated, then shrugged and sashayed off.

Rocco slumped, and the worry in Giselle's tummy transformed into dread. 'What's wrong?'

With a stricken expression, he ushered her into the parlour, then leant against the door and rubbed a hand across his face. 'It seems I have to sell the castle after all.'

'But I thought—?' Giselle stopped, confused.

'Inheritance tax,' he stated shortly. 'I can't pay forty per cent, not without selling it.'

'Hadn't you…?' She trailed off.

'Factored it in? Yes, and I had a plan in place, but I underestimated how much the estate is worth.' He laughed, a bitter sound. 'And to think I'm supposed to be an expert in asset management when I can't even manage my own assets. Bloody hell.' He gazed at the ceiling and raked his fingers through his hair.

Giselle reached for him, hesitated, then let her hand fall to her side. She loved him and she'd been as intimate as one person can be with another, yet she felt powerless to comfort him.

He said, 'I had it all worked out. I was going to live here and carry on running the castle and the craft centre. I even had a couple of ideas to generate more income.' He bit his lip and screwed up his face. 'I'm sorry, Giselle.'

So was she, but although the news wasn't good, it wasn't the end of the world. She'd already accepted that the craft centre would probably be no more, so she wasn't as upset as she might have been. Especially since…

'I love you, too,' she said.

Rocco froze. She watched him carefully, waiting for a reaction.

It was a long time coming and she was starting to shrivel inside, when he asked, 'Do you mean that?'

'Yes.'

'You're not just saying it?'

'To make you feel better? No.'

'I didn't think— I didn't dare—' He exhaled loudly. 'You *love* me?'

A smile spread across her face. 'Yes.'

'I don't know what to say.'

'Is there any need to say anything when you can kiss me instead?'

His mouth was hot and urgent, his arms holding her so tightly she feared he'd crush her, but to Giselle, being in his embrace felt like being home, and she kissed him for several delicious minutes.

'What happens now?' she asked, when she finally dragged her lips away from his. She laid a cheek on his chest and listened to the thud of his heart, his arms still tight around her.

'I honestly don't know.'

'You'll have to go back, won't you?'

'I'm afraid so.' She could hear the pain in his voice. 'I want to stay on Skye, but without a job…'

'Could you work remotely?'

'Not a chance.' He groaned and buried his face in her hair. 'I don't want to lose you, Giselle,' he said, his breath warm on her temple, and she hugged him fiercely.

'You won't.'

'I can't stay here, without a job. I—' He broke off, the rest of the sentence unspoken.

Giselle didn't need to hear it. She already knew what she had to do.

—

Giselle glanced behind to make sure they were alone, then she drew Rocco to a halt. They were strolling hand in hand along the path leading to the village and were heading for The Codfather and a fish supper. It had been Giselle's suggestion when Rocco had let slip that he hadn't eaten since breakfast.

'You've got to keep your strength up for later,' she'd told him.

'What's going to happen later?'

'You're going to take me to bed and ravish me.'

'I am, am I? What if I'm the one who wants to be ravished?' he'd teased.

'I'm sure we can come to some arrangement, but you need food, and I bet you don't want to eat in the dining room.'

He shuddered. 'With Claire and Kurt? No thanks! And I wouldn't want to subject you to that, either.'

'Who says I'd be joining you for dinner?'

'You'll have no choice, since I'm not letting you out of my sight ever again.'

'Not even when you're asleep?'

'You know what I mean. Come to London with me tomorrow,' he pleaded.

She kissed him to stop him talking, but that could only work for so long because she had to come up for air. 'I can't; my sister, remember? Plus, I've got obligations here.'

'I absolve you of them.'

'I want to sell as much as possible while I still can, and summer is when the craft centre is at its busiest.'

His face fell. 'Does that mean you intend to stay in Duncoorie until the castle is sold? That could take months. And what if whoever buys it decides to keep the craft centre open? Will you stay, or come live with me?' He looked so worried that her heart went out to him.

'I'll follow you to the ends of the earth,' she vowed. 'But not tomorrow.'

'When?'

They started walking again, Giselle ignoring the scenery for once. All her attention was on Rocco. 'Soon,' she promised. 'I can't just up sticks and leave. There's such a lot to sort out: all my stock, what I'm going to do about the bothy...'

'We could use it as a holiday home,' Rocco suggested.

'Hmm, I think I'd be better off selling it. I can't afford to keep it going and not live in it.'

Rocco halted, turning to face her.

'At this rate, we won't get to The Codfather before it closes,' she warned.

'You won't have to worry about money.' Rocco took her in his arms.

Giselle was shaking her head. 'I'm paying my way; otherwise, I'm staying *here*,' she replied firmly.

'You're stubborn, do you know that?' He kissed the tip of her nose. Then her mouth.

'Talking of the bothy, do you have to go back this evening?' he asked as they set off again.

Giselle smiled. She'd messaged Izzy earlier to let her know what was happening. 'My sister will be fine on her own for one night.'

'I'd like to meet her properly. Not when she's being all fierce and protective.'

'You will, I promise. Not tonight, though. Tonight is all about me and you.'

'I don't want to leave,' he said, and she remembered he'd said the same thing the last time. If only she'd realised that he'd meant he hadn't wanted to leave *her*. This time would be different: he loved her, and they wouldn't be apart for long. The thought of living in London, even in a posh area like Holland Park, didn't fill her with joy, even if she would be living in a house five times the size of her little bothy. She'd miss the peace, the wide-open spaces, the loch, the hills... everything about Duncoorie.

She'd imagined that she would live here for the rest of her life, get married here, bring up children here. But life, and love, had other ideas. It was going to be an enormous wrench for her to leave Skye.

As though he could read her mind, Rocco said, 'If you kept the bothy, we could visit any time you wanted.'

The problem was, she'd want to stay. The thought of moving to London filled her with dread. If there was any way she and Rocco could remain on the island, she'd take it…

—

'If I'd known you weren't going to join me in a fish supper, I'd have asked Cook to rustle up some toast,' Rocco grumbled as he licked his greasy, salty fingers.

'I ate a couple of chips,' Giselle protested. 'You needed a decent meal; I've already had one. Izzy and I went out to lunch.'

'That was ages ago.'

'I'm not hungry.'

'If you feel nibbly later, we can raid the castle's kitchen,' he suggested. He would have preferred to spend the night at the bothy, but Izzy was there. At least he'd moved Claire out of his suite and arranged for her to have one of the guest bedrooms, so he and Giselle would be nicely out of the way in the turret.

Giselle said, 'Mhairi used to do that. I asked her once why she hadn't had a little kitchenette installed in her sitting room and she said, "Where's the fun in that?" She used to love sneaking downstairs and pinching bits and pieces from the kitchen. It used to drive Cook mad when she was in charge of it.'

'I thought she still was,' Rocco said.

He balled up the remains of his supper, popped the wrapper in a nearby bin, and took her hand in his for the walk back to the castle, metaphorically pinching himself. He still couldn't believe she loved him. He'd been prepared for a long, draw-out battle of trying to win her over, and he'd even been prepared for out-and-out rejection. Not in a million years had he guessed that she felt the same way. Although he knew she liked him (*obviously*), he hadn't dared hope her feelings went any deeper.

Saying goodbye tomorrow was going to be hell, and he was sorely tempted to stay another day. Which would morph into another, and another… Anyhow, he had lots to be going on with, to make sure his house was ready for Giselle's arrival. There was a bedroom that needed converting into a makeshift workroom for a start.

Rocco wondered how Beverly would react to the news that Giselle would be moving in with him, and decided he didn't care. He knew she wanted him to recreate her and Dad's situation, where he and whatever woman he married would be partners in the business as well as in life, and he fully appreciated that with respect to the company, Claire would be an ideal choice. However, while he admired Claire in a business sense, he didn't fancy her. And he certainly didn't have any feelings for her.

His mother would just have to suck it up.

Sneaking into the hotel via a rear entrance, Rocco and Giselle crept up the back stairs to the turret, where he wasted no time in showing her just how much he loved her.

Tomorrow could wait. This night and the woman in his arms were all that mattered.

Chapter 27

Giselle kept the smile on her face and waved until Rocco's car was out of sight. Then her smile faded, and her arm dropped to her side. She was exhausted; whether that was from lack of sleep or lack of food, she couldn't say.

She'd been too upset to do more than pick at the breakfast Cook had sent up, which was silly really, since she'd be seeing Rocco again before too long. This wasn't the same as the last time he'd left, when she thought the goodbye was final, but she felt emotional, nevertheless.

Needing to change into fresh clothes and not wanting to face the trek to the bothy, Giselle decided to ask Izzy to come fetch her, before realising she'd left her bag and her phone in Rocco's room.

Wearily, she trudged inside and up the stairs.

Cook was in the sitting room, clearing away the remains of their breakfast.

'Forgot my bag,' she explained, reaching for it.

Cook's face creased into a smile. 'No worries, hen. Now, which of you didn't eat your breakfast?' She gestured to the plates, and when Giselle caught sight of a half-eaten congealed egg, she blanched.

Oh dear, she was going to be sick!

Scurrying to the bathroom, she made it just in time to lose what little she'd eaten.

Shaken, she emerged to find Cook waiting for her, a concerned look on her face.

'Och, lovie, are you all right? Come sit down. You look ever so pale. Can I get you anything? A nice cup of tea, maybe?'

Giselle noticed that the breakfast things were no longer in evidence, and she was grateful to Cook for getting rid of them, as even the thought of them made her want to heave.

'Tea would be nice, thank you. I don't know what's wrong with me. I'm not usually such a wimp.'

'Pregnancy can do that to a lassie. You don't take sugar, do you?'

Pregnant? Giselle gasped and clamped a hand to her mouth, her eyes wide with shock. She *couldn't* be. They'd taken precautions. That first time had been a bit lax, when they'd got carried away, but even then, Rocco had realised in time and—

Pregnant? No, *no way*.

'Here you go, hen. Drink that, then see how you feel. I could fetch you some dry toast to settle your tummy, or some crackers?'

Cook held a cup out to her. Giselle took it, stammering her thanks. She wasn't pregnant. She *wasn't*. Overwrought, that's what she was. She hadn't been right since she'd discovered Mhairi in the parlour. And after that, there'd been the worry about the craft centre, and the trauma of saying farewell to the man she loved, followed by her subsequent broken heart. And hot on the heels of that was Rocco's reappearance and his confession that he loved her. And if that wee lot wasn't enough, she now had the prospect of moving seven hundred miles away and starting a new life in a strange place. No wonder she was out of sorts!

Anyway, she couldn't be pregnant because her period was due any day now. She had all the usual signs and symptoms: sore boobs, tired, moody…

Giselle froze. Those signs and symptoms were the same as the early stages of pregnancy, and she realised with growing dismay that her period should have started two weeks ago.

Oh God, she *was* pregnant.

Aw, shite.

'You need to do a test,' Izzy told her. They were sitting outside the bothy enjoying the morning sun. Rather, Izzy was enjoying it; Giselle couldn't give a fig what the weather was doing.

She'd just finished telling her sister everything that had happened yesterday, from the sale of the castle being back on because of the inheritance tax situation, to her moving to London to live with Rocco. And finally, she'd confided to Izzy that she was pregnant.

'You can't be sure until you've done one,' Izzy insisted.

'I'm sure. My period is late and I've got all the signs.'

'How late is late?'

'Two weeks.'

Her sister shuffled her chair closer and put an arm around her.

Giselle leant into her awkwardly, her chin wobbling.

'It's not the end of the world,' Izzy said.

It was, though. Her twin didn't understand. There was no way Giselle was going to move to London now. She didn't want to bring a child up *there*.

'Rocco loves you and you love him,' Izzy continued. 'OK, maybe the timing isn't ideal, but you'll be fine. And if you need me to stay or come back and help you with the move, I will.'

'I'm not moving. Not now.'

Izzy gaped at her. 'You're not? But why?'

'I want my baby to grow up here, surrounded by nature, not in a concrete jungle.'

Her sister burst out laughing. 'I don't think where Rocco lives is a concrete jungle. I believe it's quite posh. It's not called Holland *Park* for nothing.'

'It isn't Skye.'

'Duh! Obviously. But as parts of London go, it's one of the nicer ones.'

'What about wide-open spaces, fresh air…'

'I'm sure there are parks – lots of them.'

Giselle didn't want parks. She wanted Skye for her baby. Her and *Rocco's* baby. *How will he feel when he finds out he's going to be a father?* she wondered. She honestly didn't know.

'Where can we get a pregnancy test from?' Izzy asked. 'Is there anywhere in Duncoorie?'

'We'll go to Portree,' Giselle said firmly. Even if there was somewhere in the village that sold them, she wouldn't buy one; not unless she wanted it spread all around Duncoorie by the end of the day. She'd had to swear Cook to secrecy as it was. Giselle also wanted to come to terms with it herself first before sharing the news. And Rocco should be told before anyone, including her parents.

The journey into the town was a sombre one. Giselle still couldn't believe it, and Izzy seemed lost in her own thoughts.

'Do you want me to get it?' her sister offered as they pulled into a parking space outside the supermarket.

'Do you mind?' Giselle thought she might cry if she had to stand in front of a shelf of tests and pick one.

'Of course I don't. I won't be long.' Izzy rubbed her arm. 'It'll be OK, Zelle.'

Izzy could say it as often as she liked, but Giselle wasn't convinced. She hated to admit it, but she was scared. Terrified, in fact. This latest shock was one too many, and she felt totally overwhelmed. In a few short weeks she'd gone from being completely in control of her life to riding a roller coaster of emotions, uncertainty and indecision. And when Izzy got back in the car, it all became too much, and Giselle started to cry.

'I don't know what to do,' she wailed, sniffing into a tissue that Izzy had retrieved from her bag. 'I love Rocco with all my heart, but I don't want to bring up a child anywhere but *here*.'

'Let's get you home and do the test first, shall we?' Izzy soothed. 'You might be worrying over nothing. Periods can be late for all kinds of reasons, like if you're unwell, or stressed, or—'

'Pregnant,' Giselle broke in.

Izzy pressed her lips together and didn't say anything further until they reached the bothy. Taking the test out of the bag, she passed it to Giselle, who took it from her grimly.

Her stomach was in knots and her hands shook as she retreated to the bathroom.

The instructions were clear. Pregnant or Not Pregnant. No faint lines to worry about, no room for misunderstanding. Simply two bald, no-nonsense statements.

Not wanting to hover in the bathroom waiting for the words to appear, Giselle left the test in there and went to sit on the sofa for the requisite length of time.

'Will you go and look for me?' Giselle asked, with two minutes left to go. She was brave, but not that brave.

Izzy bit her lip and nodded. She got to her feet.

'It won't be ready yet,' Giselle pointed out.

'I'll go check anyway. You never know...'

Twisting her hands in her lap, Giselle waited.

And waited.

Izzy had been in there for ages. What was taking so long?

Finally, her sister emerged, a stunned expression on her face. She was holding the little plastic stick.

'Pregnant?' Giselle asked, her voice hitching.

Izzy nodded.

'Bloody hell! I *knew* it. I *told* you I was pregnant, didn't I?'

Izzy was staring at her, her eyes wide, her face pale. 'Not you, Zelle. Me. *I'm* the one who's having a baby.'

Giselle had tears in her eyes as she waved her sister off. Izzy was returning to Milan and her plumber fiancé this afternoon, and she had a plane to catch. As well as a wedding to plan!

Adrift and alone, and not in the right frame of mind to do anything creative, Giselle walked down the hill to the loch, and when she reached the narrow crescent of beach, she removed her sandals and stepped onto the sand, wiggling her toes.

Turning her face to the sky, she closed her eyes. Pink and orange filled her vision, the sun's rays bathing her skin, and she breathed deeply, drawing the clean salty air into her lungs, holding it there for a moment, then letting it out slowly.

She felt oddly calm, hollowed out, numb, almost. Her brain had seized up, closed down, and flat lined. *Not* thinking was good. For a while, at least. She'd come to the loch for a reboot, to switch off until she'd calmed enough to think clearly.

The grains of sand shifted as she walked across the beach, her feet sinking into them. Where the waves lapped the shore, wading birds paddled, poking their long thin bills into the sand, looking for food. A gull called overhead, answered by another, and in the distance, she could see a cormorant perched on a rock, black wings outstretched as it dried its feathers in the sun. Beyond the jetty, a seal bobbed in the water, grey and sleek, watching her with liquid puppy-dog eyes.

When she'd walked as far as she could, Giselle perched on a rock, drew her knees up to her chest and wrapped her arms around her legs. She had some serious thinking to do, and where better to do it? But not yet. For a while, she simply needed to be.

Giselle didn't know how long she sat there, letting her mind drift like a strand of seaweed on the current, but when she came back to herself, she knew what she had to do.

There was no baby. Not for her. Not yet. But hopefully one day there would be, and she wanted to raise that baby with Rocco, on Skye.

The fear she might be pregnant had convinced her that she didn't want to live anywhere else, and now her thoughts had become focused, lancet sharp, because there was something she'd read, something in the back of her mind… It would come to her…

If Rocco was content to live in London and carry on working in the firm his father had built, Giselle vowed to live there with him, because she wouldn't want to live anywhere *without* him. Not even Skye. But if he had been serious about wanting to move to Duncoorie, she was determined to find a way for him to stay here and help him keep his castle.

Inheritance tax wasn't something she had any experience of. However, she did have a tiny bit of knowledge of historical buildings, and Avril's dad worked for Historic Environment Scotland.

Then it came to her.

She remembered what she'd read…

—

Rocco was utterly exhausted already, and he was only four hours into the thirteen-hour journey back. He hadn't wanted to leave Giselle this morning, but the longer he stayed, the harder it would be to go, and since his plan of living at the castle and continuing to run it the way Mhairi had was now scuppered, he couldn't afford any more time off.

His mother was right: he was needed in London. The last time he'd taken an unplanned absence things had started to slide, and both Beverly and Claire had been forced to step up to the mark. However, his anger continued to simmer, and it would take him a while to forgive his mother. He didn't appreciate her meddling. It could have cost him Giselle, since both Beverly and Claire had done their utmost to warn her off.

This last hour or so he'd been fighting fatigue, and he couldn't think straight. As well as the physical weariness, he was also mentally worn out. What a roller coaster of emotions these past two days had been.

He was still having difficulty processing everything that had happened.

He'd left London in the early hours of yesterday morning hell-bent on making a go of his castle and winning the heart of the woman he loved, then he'd discovered he'd have to sell the castle anyway, and then he'd found out that he'd had no need to fight for Giselle's love because she'd loved him all along.

Seeing a sign for the next services, Rocco pulled off the motorway. He'd take a break, stretch his legs and get as much caffeine into his system as possible, which would hopefully keep him going for a few more miles.

Unclipping his seatbelt, he reached for his phone.

He'd better call Beverly. No doubt Claire would have informed her of his arrival at the castle yesterday and filled her in on what had taken place. His mother was probably sitting at her desk this very minute, fuming. Plotting. Manipulating... But she'd also be feeling pleased that his plans to live on Skye had been scuppered.

He wondered whether she'd continue to be pleased when he informed her that far from ensuring that he and Giselle would never get together, Giselle was going to come and live with him in London.

When his mother answered the phone on the second ring, he didn't manage to say a single word before she demanded, 'When were you going to tell me she's pregnant?'

'Who's pregnant?' Claire? Nora? Nah, not Nora – his PA was at least fifty.

'Giselle, obviously. Claire overheard her talking to your cook. You'd better sort this out, Rocco,' she hissed.

It wasn't obvious to *him*. He said, 'Don't you think she would have told me if she were?'

'Not necessarily. She can't be that far along. Unless it's not yours. *That's it!*' she crowed. 'The girl is taking you for a ride!'

Rocco lost his temper. 'Enough! I get that you want me to settle down with someone who can help me run the business the way you helped Dad, but you can't recreate what you and Dad had through me. And you've really got to back off about Giselle. I love her, pure and simple, and if you keep trying to split us up, me and you are done. She's coming to London and moving in with me, so you'd better get used to it.' He was rigid with fury, his jaw tense, his palms damp with sweat. 'Actually, do you know what?' he said. 'We're done anyway. I quit. I'm going back to Duncoorie.'

He'd go ahead and sell his house as planned; he'd sell his stocks and shares and cash in his investments. Along with the sale of the castle, he'd have enough to live on for a while, even after paying the sodding inheritance tax. He'd get a job in a bar, on a boat, driving a taxi... It didn't matter what he did, as long as he and Giselle were together.

He'd given the last ten years to his father's business, and the last eight to helping his mother run it, but his heart was no longer in it. His heart was in Skye, with the woman he loved.

'I'm coming back,' was all Rocco had said when he'd phoned, and the words played in Giselle's head, over and over, as she waited impatiently for his return.

And now here he was, the car bumping up the pot-holed lane leading to the bothy, and her heart was so full of love she thought it might burst.

She flew towards him as he climbed out, and he caught her in his arms, kissing her deeply as they clung together, and the rest of the world ceased to exist for several wonderful minutes.

'Why are you back? What's happened?' she asked when they came up for air. He looked tired and tense, his eyes shadowed. 'Let's go inside and you can sit down before you fall down.'

'Are you pregnant?' he asked as soon as he stepped through the door. He sank onto the sofa.

Giselle perched next to him, astounded. Why did he think that? Cook wouldn't have said anything, and apart from Izzy, she was the only person who—

Actually...

'Did Claire tell you?' she demanded. She'd encountered Claire on the stairs as she'd hurried out of Rocco's room this morning, dazed and shocked by Cook's comment. The woman must have overheard.

'She told Beverly, and Beverly asked me. Is it true?'

'No, it's *Izzy* who's pregnant.' Giselle hesitated. So that's why he'd come racing back, because he thought she was carrying his child. And he didn't look happy about it, despite kissing her as though he would never let her go. 'Would you be horrified if I were?' she asked.

He shook his head. 'I'd be thrilled.'

Giselle chewed her lip before deciding to tell him how she felt. She didn't want any secrets in their relationship.

'I did think I might be pregnant. I had many of the signs,' she explained. 'Which was strange, since Izzy didn't. She didn't even suspect she was, but when I did a test and it was negative, she did one, and lo and behold...' Giselle smiled wryly. 'Trust her to send all her morning sickness my way.'

'Where is she?'

'On her way home. She has something to tell her fiancé. And I've got something to tell you. But first, I want to say that I wasn't thrilled when I thought I might be having a baby. I was horrified, actually. Not at the prospect of being a mother, or having a baby with *you*,' she added hurriedly, seeing the dismay on his face. 'It's just that I don't want to bring up a child in London, even if Holland Park is posh. I want my baby to be born here, on Skye, to have the childhood I had. I still want that for any children I might have – *we* might have. I don't want to live in London, Rocco. I want to stay here.'

'Are you saying you won't come and live with me?'

'I'm not saying that at all. I want to be wherever you are, and if that's London, then so be it.' She shuffled closer. 'But if – when – we have children, I really want to raise them on Skye.'

Rocco was grinning. 'I've left London for good,' he said. 'I don't need a high-powered job or a castle to be happy – I need *you*. I love you with everything I have and everything I am, and if I have to live in a shed, I'll be happy as long as you're by my side.'

'I love you more than you'll ever know,' she replied softly, her heart swelling so much she thought she might cry. And when he kissed her again, she knew her heart belonged to Rocco and her soul lived on Skye, and dreams really do come true.

Epilogue

Eight months later

The castle's great hall was packed. Rocco hadn't wanted to mark the occasion with a ceremony but Giselle had insisted, and as she stood at the front of the gathering, a glass of whisky in her hand, she was glad she had.

This was a historic moment for the castle, another chapter in its long and varied history. She would have loved for her sister and her new husband, Edoardo, to be here, but with the very recent arrival of baby Alessandro, they were otherwise occupied. Her parents were here, though, and she shot them a radiant smile.

Her dad raised his glass and winked at her. He and Rocco had hit it off immediately, and Giselle's mum thought he was lovely. This was only going to be a flying visit, however, because tomorrow they were off to Milan to meet their tiny grandson. Giselle and Rocco had planned their own trip to see him in a couple of weeks' time.

Beverly was also here, and hers was a flying visit too, which Giselle was thankful for. Rocco and his mother had made their peace with each other, but Giselle didn't think she and Beverly would ever be best friends. Still, the woman was here to support Rocco, and that was the important thing.

As for the rest of the people assembled today, everyone was thrilled that the castle would remain in Rocco's capable hands, thanks to Historic Environment Scotland. The documents (and there had been many of them, reams and reams) had all been signed, apart from one final set of signatures. And that's what was happening today.

Giselle's hand crept up to her throat, where the red sea glass heart hung on a silver chain. Rocco had arranged for it to be made into a necklace for her, and she wore it often.

Her gaze was on Rocco now. Looking incredibly handsome in his dark navy suit and the crispest of white shirts, he was standing behind an antique table. His hair was longer, his face considerably more tanned than it had been when he'd first come to Duncoorie. Despite the suit, he was more like the man she'd met in Venice, than the corporate version she'd locked eyes with in the graveyard on the day of Mhairi's funeral.

She wished Mhairi was here to see this. The old lady would have been delighted that her beloved castle had survived its latest battle.

Cal, who was overseeing today's proceedings, called for silence, standing in front of the table in his kilt, hose and sgian-dubh, only the hilt of the dagger visible since the blade was tucked into the hose on his right leg.

'Ladies and gentlemen,' he began. 'Thank you for being here to witness this historic day for Coorie Castle, although I suspect most of you are here only for the whisky.' He picked up one of the tumblers of amber liquid on the table and held it aloft before replacing it. 'Your presence is still appreciated, as long as you don't have too many drams. And don't you dare drink yours yet, Mackenzie Burns – it's for the toast.'

Laughter followed when Mack shouted, 'Get on with it, man. I'm parched!'

Cal's smile was wide as he turned to the four people standing behind the table. 'Rocco, would you please sign on the dotted line?'

Giselle's heart was full of love and pride as she watched Rocco pick up Mhairi's fountain pen and sign his name with a flourish.

Cal said, 'And now you, Mr Booth.'

Rocco passed the pen to the gentleman from Historic Environment Scotland, who duly signed.

'Last, but definitely not least,' Cal said, 'I ask the legal representatives for both parties to sign as witnesses.'

A besuited man and a woman wearing a smart dress and jacket moved into position to sign the document that would enable Rocco to keep Coorie Castle.

Then Cal ceremoniously handed the sheet of paper to Mr Booth and faced the room once more. 'I'm thrilled to announce that Coorie Castle has now been declared a site of Outstanding Historical and Architectural Interest.'

Applause, cheers and whistles drowned out his next words and he waved his arms in a pipe-down motion until calm was restored.

'I was going to say,' he ploughed on, 'that the estate itself has also been designated by Historic Environment Scotland to be of Outstanding Natural Beauty and Scientific Interest.' He grinned. '*Now* you can be rowdy.'

Giselle had tears in her eyes as she clapped, her hands stinging when the applause went on and on.

'Speech!' someone yelled, which quickly turned into a chant as people shouted, 'Rocco! Rocco! Rocco!'

Rocco was beaming, his face flushed, as Cal yelled for everyone to 'Hauld yer wheest and let yon chappie speak!'

The ruckus abated and Rocco cleared his throat and began. 'So many people have been involved in this process and every one of them has my heartfelt thanks. However, there is one person in particular who— Oh, sod it. Giselle, come here.' He held out a hand.

Giselle, blushing furiously, walked towards him and took it. His hand was firm and warm as he gave her a reassuring squeeze.

'Without this wonderful woman,' he continued, 'we wouldn't be standing here today. It was Giselle who discovered the castle might be exempt from the inheritance tax that was forcing me to sell, as long as certain criteria and conditions were met. And they have been!'

He turned to the man from Historic Environment Scotland and said, 'I've made a solemn undertaking to care for Coorie Castle and preserve it for future generations to enjoy. And with that in mind, I think this generation might appreciate getting stuck into the single malt. A toast.' He raised his glass. 'To Coorie Castle.'

'To Coorie Castle!' The words rang out, filling the room, and as Giselle took the tiniest of sips of the mellow single malt, tears spilt over to trickle down her face.

Rocco was the next custodian of Coorie Castle, but not the last.

Giselle's hand moved protectively to her stomach, and she smiled softly to herself. There would be time enough to share her news with Rocco.

Today was for celebrating the castle. Tomorrow was for the rest of their lives.

Acknowledgements

As Rocco says in the book, 'So many people have been involved in this process and every one of them has my heartfelt thanks.'

You've probably read numerous times that bringing a book into the world is an act of collaboration: from the author's inception of an idea to the printers who make the physical book a reality. This sentiment isn't any less true for the repetition – which is why I need to start thanking people, beginning with my family. Without their support and encouragement, writing would be that much harder. A special thanks go to Poppy; her cuddles, puppy-dog eyes and waggy tail keeps me grounded, even when my characters run away with me.

On the witing side of things, Emily Bedford, my brilliant editor at Canelo, deserves the biggest thanks for her insight and her help in making the story the best it can be. A further polish was given by Alicia Pountney, Matthew Robertson and Becca Allen, and the icing on the cake is the glorious cover designed by Head Design. Isn't it lovely!

And as always, thank you for reading it, my lovely – you make writing worthwhile.

Love,
Lilac x